MANNING WOLFE

ALIVE BY PROXY

PROXY LEGAL THRILLER SERIES | BOOK 3

Starpath Books, LLC
Austin, TX
www.starpathbooks.com

Paperback: ISBN: 978-1-944225-61-2
Ebook: ISBN: 978-1-944225-62-9

Manufactured in the United States of America
10 9 8 7 6 5 4 3 2 1

1

———

Lightning slashed the Houston sky, illuminating the street for a fraction of a second before plunging it back into darkness. Rain hammered the pavement, pooling in gutters and rising fast. The bayous were already swollen, their muddy currents surging over the banks, consuming roads, homes, yards, everything in their path.

Daniel Price stood at his townhouse window, watching the water creep up his driveway. The power had gone out over an hour ago, leaving him in the dim glow of a flickering candle and ready with a flashlight that he kept turned off to preserve the battery life. He exhaled, rubbed a hand over his face, took a long pull on his bourbon, and contemplated the downpour. Houston always flooded with this much rain.

A sharp knock at the door made him turn and put the glass on the counter next to his phone that was plugged into a lifeless charger. The phone's screen was dark, battery long dead.

He looked at his watch, then walked toward the door, flashlight in hand. He had not seen anyone come up the walkway.

The sound barely carried over the pounding downpour. He wasn't expecting anyone, especially at this hour and in this weather. He hesitated. Another knock. Louder this time. Urgent.

Probably a stranded driver. Maybe a neighbor. With a sigh, he unlatched the door and pulled it partially open.

A figure in a dark blue, rain-soaked poncho stood on the threshold, water sluicing off the garment in sheets. The hood was pulled low, shadowing the face, at first obscuring any defining features, then revealing the person's identity to him.

"Jesus, you're soaked," Price lowered the flashlight. "Get in here."

"Hey, Danny."

Price smiled and pulled the door open farther. "What are you doing here?" He stepped aside so the visitor could enter.

"I surely didn't expect to be seeing you again so soon."

"I'll bet."

"Take that off and get dry."

A blade flashed in the candlelight in the hand of the intruder, then a sharp, driving pain bloomed in Price's stomach. Surprise gave the visitor the advantage, but Daniel swung at the intruder with the flashlight striking the assailant's shoulder.

The slasher was stunned, then came forward with a vengeance, ripping a second, deeper wound, then a third into Price's torso and ribs. He gasped, staggering back, dropping the flashlight, his hands clutching the wound, warm blood spilling over his fingers. Another strike, this one to the shoulder. Price collapsed to his knees, then fell backward onto the floor with a thud.

The perpetrator knelt beside the victim, the blade gleaming wet with blood. A gloved thumb brushed against the victim's cheek, almost tender. The killer leaned in close, breathing warm air against Daniel's ear. A whisper too soft to be heard. Daniel gasped again, the rain drowning out his final, rasping breath.

The figure lingered for a moment, watching the lifeless body, then stood over him, breathing hard, adrenaline turning the hands electric. The room pulsed with a strange silence, the kind that follows unspeakable violence, when even the city outside seems to hold its breath.

The killer reached up, brushing damp hair. The black gloves were sticky with gore, clinging like a second skin. There had been no hesitation. No regret.

With the same eerie calm, the killer became active, grabbing the flashlight and stepping over Price's body. The eerie figure began moving through the townhouse with an unsettling familiarity, gloved fingers brushing over furniture, pausing to glance at a framed photograph on the mantel. It showed Price with two women, laughing, happy. The killer's head tilted, as if considering something.

Outside, the storm raged on, the water rising inch by inch. The power was still out, the streetlights dead. No witnesses. No help coming.

The killer turned back, passed the body and returned the weapon to its hiding place beneath the poncho. With a final look around, the killer moved to the door, then silently slipped out into the night, vanishing into the downpour, as the city swallowed the murderer whole.

***

Detective Clive Broussard parked his City of Houston unmarked Ford on the street outside the townhouse. The street lights on Bellaire Boulevard flickered in the puddles of the early morning rain; their garish colors smeared across the slick asphalt like spilled paint. The storm had passed, but the gutters still gurgled, carrying away the grime of the city. Houston never really slept, but in this hour, the streets whispered rather than roared.

Broussard entered Price's house and was greeted by a half dozen cops who were already assessing the scene. The air smelled of damp clothing and sweat. A ceiling fan rotated lazily, its shadow slicing across the walls in slow, deliberate arcs. Beneath it, the body sprawled across the floor, limbs at unnatural angles, mouth frozen in a painful grimace. Blood pooled thick beneath him, more than seemed possible, having spread toward the sofa and onto a Persian rug, soaking into the expensive fibers, darkening them almost to black. A lamp was on in the corner, the electricity back on. It cast half the room in sharp relief, the other in shadow. The light caught a reflection in the blood.

"Bonjour," Broussard nodded at the medical examiner who was taking the temperature of the body. Addressing no one in particular, he asked in his heavy French Cajun accent, "What do we know about the victim?"

Broussard crossed between the crime scene numbers, careful where he put his shoes. The victim lay on his back, one leg bent at a jagged angle, eyes half open like he'd been interrupted mid-thought.

A young police rookie, Sam Gere, looked at a notepad in his hands and flipped a few pages. "Daniel Price. White male. Late fifties. Nice watch. Designer clothes in the closet."

Broussard straightened and looked back at the officer. *Money has touched this dead man's life.*

"All right. What else?"

"Lives here alone. Single. No roommates, no pets. Townhouse is in his name. It's paid off, according to the neighbor."

"What he do?"

"Sports agent."

Broussard's eyebrows lifted a fraction. "That right?"

"Yes, sir. Represents athletes around Houston. Mostly football players."

"Wildcatters?" Broussard asked.

The officer hesitated. "Yes, Wildcatters. Plus, some personal management work for guys trying to get back in the league."

"Uh-huh," Broussard gave him a look. "The ones with problems."

The officer nodded. "Yes, sir."

Broussard looked back down at Daniel Price. Clean haircut. Trimmed beard. Fingernails manicured. No wedding ring. No tan line indicating he'd worn a wedding ring at all.

"Any priors?"

"No, sir. Clean record. No arrests. Couple of civil filings. Contract disputes. Nothing violent."

"Anybody notified?"

"Not yet. We were waiting on you."

"Good, 'cause this won't be a rush job."

Broussard crouched near the body, careful not to touch. The medical examiner was still working, murmuring to herself, tracing bruises that didn't quite line up with the furniture.

Broussard addressed her without looking up. "Cause of death?"

"Several slicing wounds to the abdomen. At least five. A few very deep. I'll give you a count when I do the autopsy."

Broussard glanced around the room. A chair out of place. A lamp knocked over. But nothing torn apart. No drawers yanked open. No obvious ransacking.

"This doesn't look like a burglary," Broussard said.

Office Gere nodded. "No, sir."

"Any sign of forced entry?"

"Front door was unlocked when we arrived. No damage. Back door intact."

Broussard exhaled.

"Unlocked door. Single man. Late at night. Storm outside. No electricity."

He stood and rolled his shoulders, joints popping.

"Who was he expecting?"

Gere shrugged. "Unknown. One neighbor said she heard nothing because of the storm. Earlier there was some type of dispute outside."

"How long ago?"

"Neighbor says it was early in the evening. Before the storm hit."

The ME looked up. "Doesn't help with the time of death. That was much later."

Broussard walked toward the kitchen. A glass with something brown in it sat on the counter. Half full. A phone charger snaked out of the wall socket, but no phone was plugged into it.

"Phone?"

"Missing. Victim's phone wasn't on the charger, but no juice would have been going to it with the electricity out."

Broussard grunted. He lifted the glass and sniffed the liquid. "Bourbon. Anybody else drinkin' last night?"

"No second drink or glass located so far."

Broussard turned back to the officer.

"Daniel Price. Sports agent. Single. No priors. Represents men with big bodies, big money, and bigger problems."

"Yes, sir."

"Any women in his life?"

"Not that we've found so far. Neighbor said she's seen both men and women come and go. No names."

Broussard touched the mantel with a gloved finger. "And

now he's dead in his living room. Which means either he trusted the wrong person, or someone had a key."

Officer Gere swallowed.

Broussard softened his voice just a notch. "Who found the body?"

Gere looked at his notepad. "A neighbor, in the house next door, named Sheryl Benton. She came over this morning to see if the power was back on, as hers was not. The door was unlocked and she opened it when he didn't answer."

Broussard considered further. "Did she enter the premises?"

"Barely. She stood at the doorjamb. Says she saw the body and ran immediately back home. She called 911 and waited at her place."

Broussard grunted and looked down. The victim's shirt was torn open by the slashing, a roadmap of violence. The detective walked over to the dropped flashlight and hunkered down for a close look. He didn't touch it, even though he was wearing disposable gloves. The yellow evidence marker number "5" was perched on the floor beside it. "Fingerprints might be too much to hope for."

"We'll check." Gere seemed to be speaking for the group although he was the youngest of the lot. His height might have been the reason, as he towered at least four inches over the next in line.

A sudden honk from outside jolted the moment. A couple in the street began yelling, arguing about parking, then a car door slammed and tires peeled away. Just another day in Houston.

Broussard motioned to Gere. "Come with me. I want to talk to the witness next door."

Detective Broussard tapped his pen against the small notepad in his hand, studying the woman across from him. Sheryl Benton sat stiffly on her floral-upholstered sofa, hands folded in her lap. Her short gray hair was neatly styled, and she wore a cardigan despite the warm morning air. Her blue eyes darted to the window every few seconds as if watching for something or someone.

"Mrs. Benton, I know this has been a shock," Broussard said in a calm, measured voice. "But I need to go over what happened one more time. Just to make sure we have everything right."

She swallowed hard and nodded. "I understand, Detective. I want to help."

"Good. Now, you told Officer Gere that before you found the body you noticed something strange when you went outside?"

"Yes." Her voice trembling slightly. "I went over to check with Daniel to see if his power had been restored. I thought I saw a light in his window. My power was still out. I saw that Daniel's door was closed, so I knocked. When he didn't answer, I opened the door and called out to him."

"Were you friends?"

"Neighborly. We weren't close, but we'd chat sometimes when we ran into each other. I knew his routines. He wasn't the type to leave his door unlocked."

Broussard nodded and jotted down a note. "So, you pushed the door open to check?"

"I knocked first. He didn't answer, so I called his name. No answer. That's when I tried the knob and pushed the door open and yelled for him. When he still didn't answer, I pushed it open a little more. Just enough to see inside." Her lips pressed together, and she shook her head as if trying to rid herself of the memory.

"Take your time," Broussard's voice was gentle but firm.

She took a steadying breath. "I saw him lying there. On the floor. Face up. There was so much blood all around him. And a big flashlight on the floor, like someone dropped it. It was still on. A candle was flickering on the table, melted almost to the end."

"That might have caused the light you thought you saw in the window."

"It cast these strange shadows." She looked horrified.

"Take your time."

Her voice wavered, and she wrapped her arms around herself. "I didn't go all the way in. I just turned around and ran back here and called 911."

"You're sure you didn't step inside at all? Not even a little?"

Her gaze snapped to his, indignant. "No! I would never! I knew right away he was dead. I stood at the doorjamb. Didn't need to get closer to see that."

Broussard held up a placating hand. "I believe you, Mrs. Benton. Just have to be thorough."

She exhaled, her shoulders sagged. "Of course."

"Did you hear anything unusual last night? A struggle, raised voices? Anything out of the ordinary?"

She shook her head. "Just in the early evening as I told the officer. Nothing later, but the storm was raging by then. Drowned out most noises. If something happened in the middle of the night, I wouldn't have heard it. And to be honest, Daniel wasn't the noisy type."

Broussard tapped his pen against the notepad again. "Did Daniel have any visitors recently? Anyone who seemed, shall we say, off?"

"There was a man over earlier in the day, before the storm hit. He wasn't real tall, but very muscular. Maybe one of Daniel's football clients."

"Black? White? Brown? Hair color?"

"I think he was White with black hair. Solid and very fit."

"What was he wearing?"

"Casual clothes, sports outfit, maybe a sweatsuit. I don't remember."

"Did you see his vehicle?"

"No. I don't think so."

"Okay. That's good, Mrs. Benton. Any other visitors lately?"

"Daniel had a woman over sometimes a while back. A younger woman, maybe in her twenties or thirties, but I don't know her name. Tall and thin, White, with brown hair."

"That's helpful," Broussard made a note. "Have you seen her lately?"

"Maybe. I can't be sure it was her, but someone in a white car was parked outside several evenings. Might have been the same car I saw her in. I thought it was a man inside, but it may have been a woman."

"Could you identify the type of car? SUV? Four doors? Sporty?"

"No, just your average four-door sedan. Not a truck or SUV."

"One last question for now. Did you touch the door handle when you pushed it open?"

She blinked. "Yes. I suppose I did. Just for a second."

"Alright. We may need to take your fingerprints for elimination purposes. It's just routine."

She wrung her hands in her lap. "Of course, anything to help."

Broussard gave her a reassuring nod. "You're doing fine, Mrs. Benton. If you remember anything else, even if it seems small, give me a call."

He handed her his card, and she took it with unsteady fingers. "Thank you, Detective. I just can't believe this happened next door. Am I safe? I'm worried."

Broussard stood. "I'm sorry. But we're going to find out who did this. I don't think you need to worry. It doesn't look like a robbery."

As he stepped toward the door, he saw her glance at the window again. He made a mental note of that. People watched windows for a reason.

2

———————

On the 610 Loop, Quinton Bell hustled into his office and dropped down behind his large wooden desk. He'd finished a hearing in the downtown courthouse and had hurried to get back to his office before rush hour hit. The Law Office of Quinton Lamar Bell had only been open for about a year, and he was already turning away clients. He'd moved to The Galleria area, near Westheimer and Post Oak, to open a solo practice. Quinton was what they called a loop lawyer, one who offices around and outside the 610 Loop. It circled Houston from interstate to highway and back again, surrounding the downtown offices rising out of the ground like Stonehenge in the middle of the ring.

The reason that clients were not hard to come by was because Quinton had created a reputation on several high-profile cases, including a murder involving the defense of his friend and lover, Joanne Wyatt. That seemed a lifetime ago, and Quinton had become a loop lawyer in part to get a fresh start. It was also to protect his former firm from his past life in New York City, involving his pseudocide off the Staten Island Ferry.

13

He straddled the difficult line between having enough exposure to pull in good clients and not so much that someone from New York might recognize him.

Quinton Lamar Bell was not his real name. It was Byron Douglas, but only he knew that, or so he thought. It seemed there may be a few other persons privy to that information, identities and locations unknown. Those were potentially dangerous people. When Quinton had opened his new office, he thought he was the only one on earth who knew he had faked his own death in New York and come to Houston to hide in plain sight. He looked different with a little plastic surgery, and had assumed not only the face, name, and demeanor, but the entire life of his childhood friend, Quinton Bell. He did so, not because he hated his prior life but because it was too dangerous to live it anymore. Besides, Q, as he'd dubbed his friend and benefactor, no longer needed his name or his face as he had been cremated and sprinkled in the Gulf of Mexico as Byron Douglas. So, in essence, Quinton had been killed twice, and he wasn't even dead.

This new Quinton had worked for a downtown Houston firm, in order to establish himself as Quinton Bell. It was at the insistence of his faux father, Judge Sirus Bell, who was also now deceased. He'd been supported a great deal by the three women partners in his prior office and would not forget their kindness. It was one of the reasons for the separation and move, to protect them, and to get out of their hair. They were unknowing participants in his estranged identity, thinking he was actually Quinton Bell.

He could never go back to New York or to his old name. He'd broken the law, lied, cheated, stolen, and illegally taken Quinton Bell's legacy as his own. Now, he went through each day alive by proxy and hiding in plain sight. He was constantly terrified that one of the few who knew his real name would surface, but he actually felt a type of fusion between his former self and new persona, speaking the acquired language as if he'd been born to it. Still, he'd walked on eggshells for months, eventually settling in, to what he thought was a fairly safe place.

That is, until a strange thing happened. Someone had left a small replica of the Staten Island Ferry in his new home while it was being remodeled. No demands, no further contact, and no requests of any nature. It was like waiting for the proverbial 'other shoe' to drop. Was he going to be blackmailed? The trespasser wanted something, but what? Would Quinton one day be arrested without further notice? Law enforcement wouldn't send a warning. Who had bestowed the unwanted gift, and what did they have planned for him?

Anna, Quinton's office manager who was fast becoming indispensable to him, came into the office with a stack of files. She placed them in his in-basket. "Rough day? Want a cup of coffee?"

"No, thanks. I'm going to wrap up here and get to the gym for a swim on my way home. You go ahead when you're ready."

Anna had come to Quinton by way of an ad in the *Texas Bar Journal*. He'd stolen her from a big law firm downtown and paid her top dollar and a bucket of benefits to entice her into the office of a loop lawyer. One of the reasons he'd hired her was that he had no attraction to her at all. The drama of sexual tension had no place in his office, and her conservative knit suits and sensible shoes set up a professional aura that worked for both of them.

Anna moved toward his door. "Have a good swim. See you tomorrow."

"Night." Quinton began sorting the files on his desk into stacks by date priority.

A few minutes later, Quinton heard Anna closing some drawers in the outer office and loading her bag to leave for the day. The phone rang and he heard her answer, "Law Office of Quinton Bell."

A pause, then, "I'll accept the charges."

"Cassidy West on the line." Anna communicated through the intercom on Quinton's desk. "Seems she's calling from jail."

Quinton clicked the intercom speaker. "From the jailhouse, or she's in jail?"

"She didn't say."

Quinton puzzled. He'd recently met Cassidy when she'd represented a lowlife named Lyme, who tried to claim an alleged common law marriage entitled him to the estate of one of Quinton's more vulnerable clients. Although her client was a sleazebag, he'd taken to Cassidy immediately. She was a few years out of law school and trying to establish a solo practice by hanging out a shingle and taking whatever came in the door.

Since they'd mutually solved the case of the sleazebag, he'd kicked a few cases her way that were too small for him to handle. Just a couple of DUIs and a home foreclosure. He hoped she'd eventually send him a case or two as well. Maybe something bigger and over her head. Today might be the day.

Quinton clicked on line one. "Hey, Cassidy. You trapped in the jailhouse?"

"You could say that. They took my cell phone. Had to call collect from a landline." Her soft voice sounded stressed.

"Why? What's up?"

"My friend and client is being questioned by Clive Broussard for the murder of Daniel Price."

Quinton had been in plenty of jails before. They all smelled the same, a mixture of stress sweat and something stale, like old fear baked into the walls. He adjusted his tie as the guard led him down the corridor toward the interview rooms.

"Suspect is already inside with the lady lawyer," the guard grunted, unlocking the door.

Quinton paused just inside the attorney interview room, letting the door close behind him before he spoke.

His eyes went first to Cassidy. Her blonde hair was pulled into a loose, careless bun, strands already slipping free. "I told Broussard we wanted time to talk to our client before he questioned him further."

Our client? Quinton thought.

The man beside her stood and extended his hand.

"Quinton, meet Marcus Hale."

Hale didn't look like the picture most people carried in their heads of a Houston Wildcatters linebacker. Up close, the differences settled in. His features carried a quiet trace of his Asian heritage. The clean lines of his cheekbones, the slight almond shape to his eyes, dark and steady beneath a straight brow. He had a lotus blossom tattoo on his right bicep. His skin held a warm, even tone that caught the light without glare, and his black hair, cut short for the season, lay thick and straight against his scalp.

None of it softened him. If anything, the contrast made his size and presence more striking, like something honed rather than built, controlled rather than unleashed. Quinton guessed he was about six feet, but every inch muscle. Broad shoulders. Two hundred and twenty at most. A Wildcatter red T-shirt stretched tight across his chest. The sleeves rode up thick forearms that still bore the faint impressions of tape and turf burn.

Quinton shook his hand. "Mr. Hale."

"Thanks for coming. Please, call me Marcus," the man cut

in. His voice was low, controlled, trained to project in stadiums but restrained now. "Cassidy said we need you."

Quinton raised an eyebrow.

Cassidy leaned forward, folding her hands on the table. "Marcus is being held for questioning. Not charged yet."

"Yet," Marcus echoed.

Quinton set his briefcase down but didn't open it. "I heard it on the news, but they didn't mention a suspect. How do you fit into all this?"

Marcus looked at Cassidy, just for a second. She gave him a small nod.

"They say Daniel Price was murdered. They're circling me. Hard."

"Why?"

"Because I knew him. Because I trusted him until I didn't." His jaw tightened. "And because if they look hard enough, they'll find things that look like I threatened him."

Quinton glanced at Cassidy. She filled him in. "He called me last night. Before the news broke. Daniel was his agent. Handled contracts, endorsements. Private stuff."

"Private how?" Quinton asked.

Marcus's eyes dropped to the table. His hands clenched once, then stilled.

"Personal."

Quinton didn't rush him. Silence had a way of loosening things people thought were locked tight.

"They think I killed him because we'd been fighting over my contract. Because I was angry. And because men like me are supposed to be violent when we're cornered."

Quinton studied him. Fear was there, but not the frantic kind. This was a man used to pressure, to hiding pain behind discipline.

"You say you didn't do it."

"I didn't," Marcus said without hesitation.

Cassidy watched Quinton closely. "He didn't come to me for spin. He came because he knows what's at stake, and because he knows I have connections to you."

Quinton exhaled slowly. "Houston PD won't charge you unless they think they can make it stick. If I take this on, it won't be quiet. And it won't be clean."

Hale met his gaze. "Nothing about my life's been clean."

Cassidy held her breath and waited.

Quinton reached down and finally opened his briefcase. "All right. Then we'll need a secure place to talk about the details."

Cassidy didn't relax but she did sit back. They were past introductions now. And whatever had killed Daniel Price was already bleeding into all of them.

"For now, let's try to establish an alibi and cut things off before they get started. Where were you around two in the morning?"

"At home. Alone. Remember it was storming and flooding. I would never go out in that." Hale leaned forward. "I swear, I didn't kill him."

"Why do you think they suspect you?"

"The cops will find my fingerprints in the house, but I'd been there before. Not lately, but many times."

Quinton stilled. "On the murder weapon?"

"Of course not. I wasn't there." Hale took a breath. "They haven't said anything about that. But they say they have a witness who saw me leaving his place."

"Do they have a witness or are they lying about a witness?"

"I don't know, but there's something funny going on here. I don't even know how they decided to arrest me. Who would know me or where I live?"

Quinton leaned back, considering. "Did Price have any enemies that you know of?"

Hale let out a humorless laugh. "Unhappy clients. Old lovers. I don't know. How much time do you have?"

Cassidy's fingers clenched together.

Marcus pleaded to Cassidy with his eyes. "You believe me, right?"

Quinton didn't know what Cassidy thought, but he wasn't in the business of believing. He was in the business of defending. And right now, all he had was a man with no alibi, a possible motive that he'd yet to hear, and his prints around the victim's house after he'd admitted to being there. Quinton had a gut instinct that said something wasn't right with Hale.

"Tell me about your relationship."

"He was my agent. I recently tried to part ways with him."

"How long had you been together?"

"About five years."

"What made it so complicated? People fire their agents all the time."

"He had something on me. Dirt."

Quinton pointed to the wall. "Don't say it in here. It's supposed to be clean, but if it's really sensitive, keep it for later."

"Okay. Later."

"I'm considering taking your case. But if I do, I need to know everything. No surprises. No half-truths."

Hale's gaze was steady. "There's more. I'll tell you every-thing. Just get me out of here."

Quinton nodded, but he wasn't convinced, and he wasn't sure Hale was going anywhere.

3

———————

Sheryl Benton sat in the dimly lit viewing room, her hands folded so tightly in her lap that her knuckles turned white. On the other side of the one-way glass, five hulks stood shoulder to shoulder, their faces blank, their arms hanging at their sides. Two Asian, one Hispanic, two White. All wore the same gray sweatsuit purchased for the lineup. Hale was in the number three slot. The cheap sweatsuit looked wrong on him, like a costume someone had forced him into, and they had. The fluorescent light above them cast harsh shadows over their features.

Officer Gere stood at her side, towering over her, clipboard in hand. "Take your time, Mrs. Benton," His voice was steady but not exactly warm. "If you recognize anyone, just tell us."

Two men in dark suits stood in the shadows behind the witness. Neither spoke.

Sheryl swallowed hard. She'd told herself this would be simple. See the man, point him out, and let the detectives do the rest. But now, looking at the lineup, uncertainty settled in her chest like a heavy stone.

She leaned forward, eyes scanning the men in front of her. They all fit the description. Same height range, similar dark hair color, same general build. But one of them, third from the left, set off a whisper of recognition in the back of her mind.

Sheryl exhaled through her nose. Was it him? She was almost sure she'd seen that face before, but was it at the victim's townhouse? And was it on the day of the murder?

"Third from the left. Maybe."

"Maybe if you stand, you can see better," Gere said.

"I don't know." Sheryl stood. She paused, then admitted, "I mean, he looks familiar, but I can't say for sure he's the one I saw at the townhouse that day."

Behind her, Detective Clive Broussard exhaled, stepping away from the wall where he'd been watching. He turned to Gere, his jaw tight.

"That's not what I was hoping to hear," Broussard muttered.

Gere cast him a glance but kept his focus on Sheryl. "When you say he looks familiar, do you mean you've seen him around the complex? Near the victim's place?"

Sheryl hesitated. "I think so. I mean, I know I've seen him, but I don't know if it was around town or around the townhouses. I wish I could be more help."

Broussard let out a quiet curse under his breath and ran a hand over his hair. "Dammit."

Quinton, who had been standing silently in the corner, finally spoke up. "Detective," he said smoothly, adjusting the cuffs of his tailored suit, "I think Mrs. Benton has made it clear she's unsure. Let's not turn uncertainty into coercion."

Broussard shot him a look. "I'm just trying to get clarity."

"No, you're trying to get her to say what you need for your case," Quinton scowled. "She said she doesn't know. That should be the end of it."

Gere cleared his throat. "We appreciate you coming in, Mrs. Benton. Even if you're not certain, any recognition helps."

Broussard wasn't as patient. He turned to her, his voice just a shade too sharp. "Try to think. Anything, even a small detail?"

Quinton stepped forward. "Detective." His tone was calm, but firm. "This is a lineup, not an interrogation."

Sheryl's shoulders hunched. "I don't know. I wish I did."

The silence stretched. Then, Broussard nodded curtly, once, to Gere, who addressed the witness.

"Alright. That's all we need from you today. Thank you."

Sheryl rose, eager to escape the room, but as she reached the door, she paused. "Detective?"

Broussard looked at her, waiting.

"If I remember anything else, I can call you, right?"

His expression softened just a fraction. "Yeah. You have my card."

Sheryl was escorted from the room by Gere, the door clicking shut behind them.

Quinton turned to Broussard, a knowing smile tugging at the corners of his lips. "That didn't go quite the way you wanted, did it? She could have seen him playing ball on television, in the newspaper, or online."

Broussard scowled at the lineup through the glass. Hale, standing behind the glass in spot number three, hadn't flinched once.

Broussard shook his head. "Don't count your *poulet*, Bell. We'll see where the rest of the evidence takes us. Maybe the truth."

Quinton buttoned his jacket. "That's the only place it should ever go. I'll take my client now." With that, he turned and walked out, leaving Broussard staring through the glass, jaw tight.

4

———————

The view from the twenty-second floor of Quinton's office was pure Houston. Lanes of looping traffic, smog haze lifting just enough to see the distant skyline, and heat radiating off concrete like breath from a beast. Inside, the law office was calm. There was a lot of brushed steel and glass with plenty of wooden furniture to admire. Quinton stood at the window, coffee in hand, watching the traffic crawl like ants on asphalt.

Behind him, Dart Owens, the firm's investigator, sat in one of the two guest chairs across from Quinton's desk. He had been a client over a year ago, a court-appointed case in which he'd been accused of murdering a narcotics dealer in a drug purchase gone awry. Quinton was able, in court, to assert and prove self-defense and get the big not guilty verdict that was hard to come by in a town like Houston. Dart had been forever grateful and started doing a few security and research projects for Quinton from time to time.

Eventually, Dart had gotten his private investigator's license, with Quinton's support and at his request. Dart was the only person in the office Quinton knew well or intended to know beyond employment. Quinton would never share the truth of his secret prior life, and current deceit, not even with Dart. But, in the event that something dangerous did happen, Dart could take care of himself. He was a tank of a man with a huge black head, no hair, and a neck that no tie would ever embrace. Muscles bulged around him making him appear even larger than he was.

Quinton sat, stretched his arms over his head, and leaned back in his chair. "I need you to do some work on the Hale murder file."

Dart cocked his head. "The Wildcatter linebacker?"

"Yes, he was referred by Cassidy West. She knows better than to take this on by herself."

Dart folded his arms across his chest causing his shirt to stretch to a dangerous width. He was actually bigger than Hale. "He's got more gap penetration than anyone on the team. Real explosive first step."

"I've heard he's a beast. I don't have any discovery yet. Hale says he and Price were in the middle of a bad split over some type of contract dispute. They put Hale in front of a lineup. The witness couldn't ID him. They haven't charged him yet, but they're circling. He's lawyered up—that would be me—and keeping quiet."

"You think he did it?" he asked.

"Don't know. Doesn't seem likely."

Dart nodded. "On any given day, and with the right motive, anyone can do just about anything."

Quinton felt guilty about his own deception. "True. I'm waiting on the evidence from the prosecutor's office. In the meantime, I'd like for you to start working the case."

"Can do."

"I want you to dig into Hale's alibi and background. Check out the crime scene first. There's an elderly lady who lives in the townhouse next door, a Mrs. Benton. She may pop up if she's at home when you're there. Maybe chat her up a little. She found the body."

"Was she the witness at the lineup?"

"Yes. She seems sweet and harmless, but also a busybody."

"Got it."

"And, Dart, don't let anyone know we're representing him yet. Not until I say. He seems to have some stories."

"No problem." A smile tugged at the corner of Dart's mouth. Quinton was always secretive. He was getting used to it.

"What about the victim?"

"Yes, get into him next. Find out how many clients he had and what he was doing for them."

"On it."

The hallway outside the lineup room was quiet except for the low hum of fluorescent lights and the occasional crackle from the intercom system.

Quinton stood beside Cassidy at the long observation window. The glass was dark on their side, bright on the other. Detective Clive Broussard leaned against the wall nearby, flipping through a thin folder.

Inside the lineup room six men stood shoulder to shoulder beneath the hard white lights. Marcus Hale stood in position four this time so there could be no question about cross-contamination of the two lineups. Cassidy watched him through the glass. Quinton said nothing.

Broussard closed the folder and straightened.

"Mrs. Benton called me late last night. Said it had been bothering her that she couldn't pick him out of the lineup. She thought maybe she could recognize the voice."

Cassidy glanced toward him. "That's not the same as seeing someone."

"No," Broussard agreed. "But it's something."

Quinton kept his gaze on Hale. The linebacker looked enormous under the lights. Quinton could see the tension in his shoulders.

"Where is she?" Cassidy asked.

"They'll bring her in shortly. We'll kill the viewer so she can't see them. Just hear the voices."

He gestured toward a small speaker mounted near the window.

"Standard procedure. Each man steps forward when his number is called and reads the same line."

Quinton nodded once. "Earwitness."

"Right."

The glass went dark and Sheryl Benton was brought into the room by Officer Gere. She seemed a little less nervous than she'd been during the visual lineup. She clutched a leather purse against her stomach as if it might steady her.

The technician guided her to a chair facing a speaker. Quinton and Cassidy receded to the back wall to watch.

"Mrs. Benton," a technician spoke through the intercom, "you're going to hear several men speak the same phrase. Listen carefully. If you recognize the voice that you heard during the fight next door, let the officers in the room know."

She nodded nervously.

The speaker crackled then the tech started the lineup. "Number one."

The first man read from a card they could not see.

"You don't work for me anymore. Get out of my business."

His voice was thin, nasal.

Mrs. Benton leaned forward, listening carefully. She shook her head.

The officer's voice came again.

"Number two."

The second man stepped forward.

"You don't work for me anymore. Get out of my business."

Deeper voice. Rougher.

Mrs. Benton closed her eyes for a moment, concentrating. "No."

"Number three."

The third man stepped forward and read the same sentence. Slow. Deliberate.

"No."

Cassidy shifted beside Quinton.

The officer spoke again. "Number four."

Marcus Hale's voice carried easily through the speaker. Deep. Controlled. "You don't work for me anymore. Get out of my business."

In the small identification room, Sheryl Benton stiffened. Her eyes opened.

She leaned closer to the speaker. "That's him."

"Mrs. Benton, are you saying that you recognize number four as the voice you heard arguing with Daniel Price that afternoon?"

No hesitation. "Number four."

A long breath from Cassidy as she observed Mrs. Benton.

"Number four. The fourth man. That's the voice I heard that afternoon."

Detective Broussard stepped forward. "You're sure?"

"Yes."

After Mrs. Benton was thanked and escorted from the room, Quinton turned to Broussard.

"Earwitnesses are weak evidence. Courts have said so."

"Sometimes."

"They say relying only on somebody's opinion about a voice carries a real risk of misidentification."

Cassidy added quietly, "Long v. Dutton."

Broussard gave her a small disapproving look as he flipped the switch turning on the screen. Inside the lineup room, Hale stepped back into position with the other men, staring straight ahead.

Quinton watched him through the glass. "Earwitness my ass. Smoke and mirrors." But he had tried enough cases to know that smoke could look solid to a jury if someone kept pointing at it long enough.

Broussard shrugged. "Sometimes you got to add it all up. Circumstantial considers all the evidence."

Quinton spoke without looking at him. "Add it to what? What evidence?"

5

———

The next day, Hale showed up at Quinton's office. He had come without Cassidy at Quinton's request. If his secrets were as damaging as Hale had alluded to, Quinton wanted him to be able to speak freely.

Anna buzzed in from the outer office. "Quinton, Mr. Hale is here."

Quinton stood. "Send him in."

Hale hesitated. He looked at the floor as if it were thin ice he was about to step on.

"You can go on in, Mr. Hale. He's ready for you."

Hale took a step inside Quinton's office. His linebacker shoulders filled most of the doorway. His posture should have boasted confidence, but today his shoulders sagged. He didn't sit right away. He stood inside the office, hands clasped in front of him, eyes flicking to the window, the bookshelves, the framed degrees anywhere but Quinton.

Quinton closed the door himself and gestured to one of the client chairs. "Have a seat."

Hale nodded and lowered himself into a chair across from

the desk. The furniture creaked under his weight. He looked too big for the room, like a man used to open fields and bright lights now boxed in by four demanding walls.

"How are you?" Quinton didn't rush him. He'd learned that silence was sometimes the only safe onramp.

Hale cleared his throat. "I've never been in a lawyer's office alone before."

"That so?"

Hale gave a weak huff of a laugh. "Daniel always did the talking."

The name hung between them. Daniel Price. His agent. Now a corpse.

Quinton folded his hands on the desk. "Yesterday, you told me Price had something on you. Something he used to keep you under contract. You said if it came out, it would destroy you."

Hale's jaw tightened. He nodded once.

"This is the part where you stop protecting. He's gone. Whatever hold he had on you only works if you keep it secret from me."

Hale stared at the carpet. "You don't understand the league."

"I understand leverage, and I understand extortion."

That got Hale's attention. He looked up, eyes bloodshot, rimmed red like sleep hadn't come easy since the murder.

"I'm gay," Hale said.

The words came out fast, like he'd decided hesitation was worse than impact.

Quinton didn't react. He didn't nod. Didn't blink. He simply waited.

Hale let out a shaky breath. "Nobody knows. Not the Wildcatters or the coaches. Not the locker room. Hell, not even my friends."

Quinton said quietly, "Daniel knew."

"Yes." Hale's hands balled into fists on his thighs. "He found out a few years ago."

"How?"

Hale shook his head. "Daniel showed up unannounced at my door one weekend. I had just gotten home and was sitting in the driveway."

"And he saw you?"

"With someone. Someone I was seeing."

He rubbed a hand over his face, dragging it down hard. "He apologized and left. I saw him at the Wildcatters facility later that week. At first, he acted like it was nothing. Cracked jokes in whispers so no one would hear. I asked him to stop and just forget it."

"What did he do?"

"He said he didn't care what I did off the field as long as I kept hitting people on it."

"But he did care?"

"He did and he didn't. When my rookie deal was up and I started talking about switching agents, that's when it changed."

"What did he say?"

Hale's voice dropped. "He said the Wildcatters were a family organization. That sponsors didn't like surprises. That fans liked their heroes clean and uncomplicated. Also, I make a lot of my income off products. You know, deodorant, food bars, things like that. He said no one wanted a gay guy selling their goods."

"Was he serious?"

Hale laughed bitterly. "Yes. He told me he was the only thing standing between me and a headline."

"Aren't there pro football players who are out?"

"A few, but not in Texas, and not without years of quality football to show a good record. I'm still fairly new."

Quinton leaned forward. "Did he show you proof?"

"Yes." Hale closed his eyes. "Photos. Dates. Locations. Stuff he'd dug up after the fact. Like he was proud of it. He must have hired someone to track me."

"He used the information to keep you?"

"To keep me quiet. To keep me signed." Hale's eyes burned. "Every time I pushed back on a contract term, he reminded me what would happen if I walked."

"Did he ask for money? Anything beyond his commission?"

"Not directly. But he squeezed me. Longer terms. More control. Fewer options. He knew I couldn't risk arbitration or public fights. But recently..."

"Recently?"

Hale hesitated.

"It was time to sign the new contract extension and I pushed back."

"What did he do?"

"Said he'd carried me long enough. That if I wanted to keep playing, I needed to remember who owned the narrative."

Quinton let that settle. "When was that conversation?"

"A few weeks before he died."

Silence pressed in.

"You didn't kill him?"

Hale snapped his head up. "No. I swear to you, I didn't."

"I want to believe you," Quinton said evenly. "But if the police find out you're in the closet, they're going to see motive. A man with his career, his identity, his future on the line."

Hale slumped back in the chair, the fight draining out of him. "I just wanted to play football. That's it. I never wanted to be a symbol or a headline. I wanted to hit hard, do my job, and go home."

Quinton stood and moved to the window, giving Hale space.

"Daniel Price didn't just manage you. He controlled you. That matters."

Hale's voice was raw. "If this comes out, I could lose everything."

Quinton turned back. "You lose the lie. There's a difference."

Hale looked at him, really looked at him, like he was weighing whether that difference could save him.

"You're sure no one in the organization knows?"

"No one. If they did, I'd already be gone. The owners of the Wildcatters would never keep a gay player. It's against their religious beliefs."

Quinton nodded once. "Then we're going to keep the focus where it belongs. On Daniel. On what he was doing. And on who else he might have been doing it to."

Hale frowned. "I think there are others that he was squeezing. He slipped a couple of times."

"That makes sense. Men like Daniel Price don't build leverage for just one client. If he was a fixer for his clients, he probably kept files. I'll have my investigator get into it. Delicately, of course."

Hale looked worried. "Okay."

"You're going to need to tell Cassidy. She'll need to know. If you don't want to, I'll do it."

"No, I'll tell her." Hale stood. At the door, he paused, his hand resting on the knob.

"Thank you. For not looking at me differently."

Quinton met his eyes. "This office isn't a locker room."

Hale nodded once and left.

The door clicked shut, and things settled into a familiar quiet. Quinton remained standing, staring through the glass long after Hale disappeared down the hall.

Hale had told him enough to explain motive. Enough to

explain fear. Enough to explain why the police thought they had motive. But not everything. It would be catastrophic if Hale was outed, but it wouldn't be the end. He might not play for the Wildcatters, but other gay NFL players had found homes where they were accepted.

It was something else. Quinton had seen it before. The part of the truth a witness kept buried because even saying it out loud, even to a lawyer, might change everything.

Whatever Hale was still holding back, Quinton was certain of one thing: Daniel Price's hold on him had gone deeper than just being gay.

The next morning, Quinton was going over the day's schedule with Anna, when the television on the credenza against the wall flickered. A graphic slid onto the screen.

BREAKING NEWS: HOUSTON WILDCATTERS' LINE-BACKER ARRESTED IN MURDER OF DANIEL PRICE!

Anna was standing near his desk with a legal pad and pen in her hands facing the television. "Quinton..."

Quinton looked up from a file and turned toward the screen. For a second he didn't move, like his brain refused to accept what his eyes were telling him. The reporter stood on a rain-slicked sidewalk downtown, red and blue lights pulsing behind her. Police cruisers lined the curb. Camera operators jostled for position.

Quinton took a sharp breath. "Turn it up."

Anna reached for the remote on the credenza and raised the volume.

The reporter raised her microphone and looked at the camera. "This is a developing story. Houston Wildcatters' line-backer, Marcus Hale, known as Halestorm, has just been taken into custody in connection with the murder of Daniel Price, whose body was discovered earlier this week in his townhouse."

Onscreen, Hale was guided out of a black SUV, wrists cuffed, head lowered. Cameras flashed. Someone shouted his name. Officer Gere placed his hand on Hale's shoulder and steered him toward the police station like a prize on display.

The reporter continued. "The arrest comes after days of speculation surrounding Price's death. Authorities say they moved quickly due to concerns the suspect might attempt to leave the area."

Quinton's jaw tightened. "Concerns my ass."

The picture shifted again, this time to a podium set up in front of the police station. The seal of the District Attorney's Office filled the screen. The district attorney, Sawyer Durant, stepped forward, composed, tie perfectly centered, sun shining on the microphones.

"At this time, we can confirm that Marcus Hale has been charged with the murder of Daniel Price. This office worked closely with the Houston Police Department to ensure a safe and timely arrest. Given the high-profile nature of the suspect, transparency with the public is essential."

Quinton let out a sharp breath through his nose. It came out like a snort.

"Transparency? That's what they're calling a televised perp walk now?"

Anna glanced at him. "Broussard?"

"Yes. Not a word. Broussard didn't give me a heads up. Not a courtesy call. Nothing."

He paced once in front of his desk, then stopped, anger rolling just under the surface. "I told Broussard we'd bring him in. He knew that."

Anna frowned. "So why do this?"

Quinton jabbed a finger toward the screen. "Because the DA wanted the show and didn't mind standing in front of the cameras to take credit for the arrest."

The television cut back to footage of Hale being taken into the building, the door closing with a final, heavy thud.

Anna frowned. "They're already convicting him."

"They're trying to." He crossed to the credenza and shut the TV off.

"They poisoned the jury pool. They stripped him of any presumption of innocence before he ever saw a judge."

Anna stood with her pen and pad ready.

"Get Broussard on the phone. While I give him a piece of my mind, find out where they're holding Hale. "

Anna went to her desk and dialed. Quinton stood there for a beat, staring at the blank screen like it might blink back on and prove this was all a mistake.

Anna called to him from the outer office. "Broussard on the line."

Quinton stabbed the blinking button on the landline and put the phone to his ear, pacing once before stopping in front of the credenza.

Broussard answered. "Bell."

"What the hell was that?" Quinton's voice already hot. "You knew I would bring him in. You knew he would surrender."

A pause. Not surprise. Calculation.

"This wasn't my call."

"You didn't even give me a heads up. It was a chickenshit move," Quinton snapped. "You don't blindside defense counsel like that. You don't parade a man in cuffs when he's cooperating. If for no other reason, you owe me."

Broussard's tone was flat. "I do owe you, and I would have given you a heads up, but I didn't have a choice."

"You always have a choice."

"No. Not this time. The DA's office insisted. They wanted him arrested in public. Cameras. Statement. The whole damn thing."

Quinton closed his eyes, jaw tightening.

"High-profile suspect. Public pressure. You know how it works."

"Yeah. I do, but it needs to be fair. You just handed them a headstart."

Silence stretched between them.

"I did what I had to do."

Quinton pulled the phone away from his ear and ended the call without another word.

"And now we fight uphill."

He grabbed his jacket.

"They wanted a spectacle. Fine. Now they get the other side."

6

———

The courthouse steps were slick from a morning rain that had passed through just long enough to make everything steam. Cameras were already set when Quinton rounded the corner from the parking lot and climbed the steps toward the glass doors. The limestone façade of the Harris County Courthouse shrouded him like a silent witness.

The press spotted him immediately.

"Quinton Bell."

"Mr. Bell, over here."

"Is your client guilty?"

Microphones thrust forward. A boom dipped into his space.

Quinton stopped near the top of the courthouse steps. He turned slowly, just short of the doors, and faced them. He had learned long ago that silence made reporters nervous. Nervous reporters stopped shouting and started listening.

He set down his briefcase and straightened his jacket.

"My name is Quinton Bell." His voice carried without strain. "I represent Marcus Hale."

A dozen red lights blinked on. Quinton began speaking but was cut off with a question from an eager beaver.

"Mr. Bell," a woman from Channel Thirteen called out, "the district attorney says your client was arrested out of concern he might flee. Can you respond to that?"

Quinton nodded once, as if he had expected the question.

"Yes, I can. It is false."

A murmur rippled through the crowd.

"Mr. Hale was cooperating through counsel. He was not hiding. He was not running. And at no point did law enforcement indicate they were concerned about flight until they decided to make a show of his arrest."

"Are you saying the arrest was staged?" a male voice in the rear asked.

"I am saying it was unnecessary," Quinton said evenly. "And it was prejudicial."

A cub reporter pushed forward. "Your client is a high-profile athlete accused of murder. Doesn't the public have a right to transparency?"

Quinton's eyes flicked to his badge, then back up.

"The public has a right to the truth. And the truth is this: An arrest is not a conviction. A charge is not proof. Marcus Hale is presumed innocent under the law, whether he plays football or stocks shelves."

Another voice cut in. "But the victim, Daniel Price, had a troublesome relationship with your client."

"Which has not been defined in any charging document. And will not be litigated on these steps."

Cameras zoomed in. Quinton didn't blink.

"What I will say is that this case is built on speculation and optics. The same optics you saw on television. Handcuffs. Cameras. Headlines."

He let that hang for a beat.

"Those images were meant to suggest guilt. They do not establish it."

A female reporter asked, "Are you criticizing the district attorney's office?"

Quinton allowed himself a thin smile.

"I am reminding them that justice is supposed to be done in a courtroom, not in front of a camera or in the court of public opinion."

The crowd expanded and pressed closer.

"Is your client entering a plea today?"

"Innocent," Quinton said without hesitation. "And we look forward to demonstrating that in court."

"Do you deny that your client knew the victim?"

Quinton glanced briefly at the courthouse doors behind him, then back to the press.

"This case will be decided by evidence, not by press conferences. By facts, not by fear. And certainly not by a televised perp walk designed to sway opinion before a jury is ever seated."

A few reporters scribbled faster.

"That's all I have to say today."

He stepped inside, the cameras still rolling behind him, voices still calling his name. He didn't look back.

The heavy doors closed with a dull, final sound. Quinton paused, letting the noise fade, letting the anger settle into something colder and more useful.

The DA had drawn first blood.

He had fought back. Now justice was where it belonged. In a system that he trusted and believed in. In a court of law.

When Quinton entered the attorney client room, Cassidy and Hale were already waiting for him. Hale was not handcuffed to the table but appeared to be more stressed than the day of the police lineup. Quinton sat across from Cassidy but looked at Hale.

"How are you holding up?"

"About as well as you'd expect. Food's rotten, lots of noise."

"You need to eat and sleep to keep up your strength. I'm going to need your brain on high-power mode when we start to prepare the case."

"So, there's no chance of them dropping the charges?"

"On what grounds?"

"Lack of evidence?"

"Doubtful. I'm waiting for the delivery from the prosecutor's office, but you know that they would not have gone this far without something incriminating."

"Like what?"

"You had reason to be in the townhouse, so even if your fingerprints are there, that's not enough. You had conflict with him, but there's lots of conflict in the world. Did you ever have a weapon or a blade like the one used to kill Price?"

"How would I know? I've never seen the weapon to compare it."

Quinton looked away. He had laid out the question in such a way that Hale could trip on it if he wasn't being truthful. He'd passed the first test.

In the courtroom, Quinton handled the arraignment like he'd done it for years, which he had.

Hale's case had drawn Judge Robert Blaylock, Quinton's

favorite judge. If there had been even a flicker of concern that Judge Blaylock might be biased in Quinton's favor, the judge would have stepped off the case without hesitation. Fortunately, or unfortunately, Quinton knew the judge too well. Blaylock never tipped the scales for him. In fact, he'd overcorrected more than once, denying motions Quinton knew any other judge might have granted.

The arraignment courtroom buzzed with the low hum of overworked air vents and restless defendants waiting their turn. Fluorescent lights flickered overhead, washing everyone in a pale institutional glow. The gallery benches were crowded. Public defenders juggling stacks of files, family members whispering anxiously, deputies shepherding handcuffed defendants in and out like a steady tide.

Hale stood beside Quinton and Cassidy at the defense table. He wore county-issued scrubs, and his wrists were cuffed in front. He kept glancing toward the courtroom door, as if hoping someone familiar might walk in and rescue him.

George Grant, Judge Blaylock's longtime bailiff, read the case number and called the case. "State of Texas versus Marcus Hale."

Judge Blaylock adjusted his glasses and looked down from the bench. "Mr. Hale is present with counsel?"

"Yes, Your Honor," Quinton stepped slightly forward. "Quinton Bell for the defense."

At the State's table, a young ADA stood. He looked barely old enough to shave his brown face, though his stiff posture suggested he had practiced looking intimidating in the mirror.

"Your Honor, the State appears by Assistant District Attorney Mark Benavides. I'd also note that the prosecutor of record is DA Sawyer Durant. Mr. Durant is currently in trial in the 248th and asked me to stand in for him today."

Blaylock let out a dry snort. "Durant's always in trial. Tell him to come up for air once in a while."

A ripple of soft laughter traveled through the gallery. Benavides straightened his already straight tie.

"Proceed," Blaylock nodded at the ADA, who opened his file.

"Mr. Hale is charged with first-degree felony murder. The State is asking for life without parole."

Blaylock lifted a hand. "Let's get his plea on the record first. Mr. Hale, how do you plead on the murder charge?"

Hale stood beside Quinton. "Not guilty, Your Honor."

Quinton addressed the court. "Your Honor, Mr. Hale has no criminal history, no failures to appear. He's a linebacker for the Houston Wildcatters football team. He has every reason to stay and fight these charges."

Benavides stepped forward quickly. "Your Honor, the State is requesting that the defendant be held without bail."

The words landed like a slap.

Hale gasped.

Cassidy whipped her head toward Quinton. "No bond? Why?"

Quinton touched her wrist. "Let me handle it."

He faced the judge again. "Your Honor, that's extreme. The State's evidence is circumstantial and flimsy. They allege he was near the decedent's townhouse earlier in the day and that the two had an argument. They point to fingerprints, but they are old and not tied to the night in question."

Benavides lifted a page from his file. "The victim, Daniel Price, was discovered slashed to death in his townhome on Bellaire Boulevard. Mr. Hale has a known past connection to him. The surveillance suggests he was in the area within the relevant timeframe. We are compiling additional evidence."

Quinton shook his head. "What additional evidence? The State has nothing placing Mr. Hale at that house on the night in question. Denying bond under these circumstances is punitive and unnecessary."

Benavides countered, "The State believes he poses a danger to the community if released and is a potential flight risk. He has millions of assets at his disposal."

Hale's voice cracked as he whispered, "I'm not going anywhere."

Blaylock looked down at him, then at Quinton, then at the file before him. His posture was stiff, a leftover from his military days. The judge was weighing the optics as much as the facts.

"Mr. Bell, your arguments are noted. However, the seriousness of the allegations and the nature of the injuries give this court significant concern."

Quinton's jaw tightened. "Your Honor, denying bond for a first-time offender, based on circumstantial evidence, is excessive and atypical."

Judge Blaylock removed his glasses, wiped them, then replaced them with deliberate care.

"The request is denied. No bond will be set at this time. This ruling may be revisited at a later hearing when the assigned prosecutor, Mr. Durant, is present."

Hale froze. His breath hitched, panic flickered across his face.

"Next setting in two weeks," Blaylock concluded. "Bailiff, take Mr. Hale."

The court officer stepped in, guiding him back toward the holding area. Hale turned to Quinton, desperation rising.

"You're not leaving me in here, right? Please, Quinton. Cassidy?"

Quinton forced calm into his voice. "I'm working on it. I'll be there as soon as I finish here. We'll challenge this. Hold on until we get there."

But the door slammed shut behind his client before he could finish. No bond meant Hale wasn't just a client. He was a trapped one. And Sawyer Durant, a formidable foe, had just become Quinton's next big problem.

7

The hiss of a table saw cut through the late-afternoon heat as Quinton Bell stepped over a coil of electrical wire and into the foyer of his new Afton Oaks home. It felt like he'd been in a construction zone for years, but it had only been twelve weeks. The place was a work in progress, a fixer upper. Oak floors were half refinished, crown molding stacked in neat bundles, dust thick enough to write a verdict in. He was trying to be patient as his contractor added more and more change orders to the job.

Against the advice of Anna and his realtor, Quinton had departed his former condo in the medical center and moved into the house during construction. He'd had his contractor finish the master bedroom and bath before he moved. They had cordoned it off with a door of plastic to keep his clothes and bedsheets as free from dust as possible.

What Anna and the realtor did not know was that Quinton felt he needed to guard the house. After a break-in and a fire, post purchase, and during the first round of construction, he'd gotten rid of the hired gun who'd caused the damage. Actually, his frenemy, Alcott Wyatt, had gotten rid of him by pushing him in front of a bus. But, that's a story for another day.

With the stalker gone for good, Quinton thought he was finally safe, hiding in plain sight. That was short lived, and the terror of being discovered returned, when he'd found a warning in the form of a replica of the Staten Island Ferry. When he saw it sitting on the hearth, he knew someone was up to no good. For the life of him, he could not figure out who it might be. He'd outwitted Tua Dannon and his goons. There were a couple of people Judge Sirus had paid to replace some fingerprints and a few other minor favors he'd called in, but those people had all been as culpable as the judge and didn't know that the favors were for Quinton. Alcott, Joanne's brother, was handled by mutual detente, and besides, he'd taken his pound of flesh already.

He could not pay a guard around-the-clock to protect his new home, and he was determined to finish the house without further damage to it. Hence, the early move in, dust and all.

The workers cut a last few boards and left for the day. Quinton listened to the house settle around him. But now, the quiet was dangerous.

He pulled a bottle of Saint Arnold beer from the temporary mini-fridge and stepped onto the back patio, overlooking the freshly resurfaced pool, recently filled with water. The dream was starting to take shape. The overgrowth had been cut back, leaving short palms and banana trees as the basis for the land-scaping to come. He allowed himself to dream of a private oasis. He sat in a partially rusted lawn chair and took a deep breath. Then came the flicker.

A shape. A shadow. Movement behind the neighbor's

fence. Not unusual in Houston. But something about it didn't sit right. Quinton stiffened. He stood and went inside the house, locked the patio door, and drew the curtain so that he could peek out. Paranoia was a habit he couldn't shake. The silence in the house felt different now. Not calm. More like empty.

There was no one to call. He could rely on Dart for anything, but he dared not reveal his secret past. Dart had already started to figure out that something wasn't right, but he'd respected Quinton's privacy and did not dig into his personal life.

Quinton was barred from asking for help from Clive Broussard at HPD. It would be far too complicated to make up a story that excluded his own culpability in so much stalking history. He was, as it were, living the life of a man, his childhood friend, whom he could easily be accused of killing. Broussard was too principled to let that go. He would put Quinton's life under a microscope if he involved law enforcement by asking for help. Not to mention Broussard had just publicly arrested his client. They weren't exactly friendly at present.

The shadow was probably nothing. A landscaper next door or his neighbor checking on his yard. Still, Quinton made a mental note to review the security footage from the exterior cameras. Whatever this was, or was not, he needed eyes wide open.

He was always walking on eggshells. The life he'd run from in New York left him with strings he'd tried to cut, but he just couldn't seem to get full closure. Regardless, he'd made his bed, and it required that he be alone in it. Hopefully someone wasn't trying to climb in it with him.

Quinton checked on the backyard off and on but didn't see anything further. When the house had fallen into its familiar creaks and groans, Quinton turned on the lights and opened his laptop.

He navigated to the security feed and queued up footage from the side-yard camera. The resolution was poor, but the timestamp told him everything: 10:07 p.m. He scrubbed through frame by frame, feeling the tension mount in his shoulders.

Cars passed. A man jogged by with a dog. Then stillness.

A figure emerged from the far side of the frame. Stopped walking, then stood perfectly still in the narrow setback between his property and the neighbor's fence. Too far from the camera for a facial shot. The man never looked up, never moved beyond a slight shift of weight. His hands remained deep in his coat pockets.

Quinton leaned closer, squinting at the grainy footage. This wasn't someone lost or loitering. This was someone with purpose. Was he casing the house or was he observing? Watching from a distance like a hunter waiting for an opening.

Quinton's mind flipped through possibilities. Could this be someone new and unrelated to his past? Angry client? How could they know about the ferry? No, this was someone who knew about New York, and Byron Douglas.

He considered reaching out to a contact in law enforcement. Maybe pull some favors, ask for a cruiser to make a pass once in a while. But what would he say? That someone was standing near his fence and then walked away? That he got a ferry replica like some mafia cliché? He could already hear the polite dismissal. He could hear the questions from Broussard if he was looped in.

No, this was still his to handle.

He opened a fresh legal pad and began documenting the incident like evidence:
- Time of appearance: 10:07 p.m.
- Approx. height: 6'0"
- Jacket or hoodie, hands in pockets
- No attempt to breach
- Body language: watchful, prepared, confident
He paused. The last line felt too clean. He added another:
- Intent unclear but calculated.

He closed the laptop and stood. He crossed the living room and carefully peeled back the edge of the curtain, just enough to see the empty street out front. A few parked cars. No head-lights. No silhouettes. Just the late-night lull of a city too big to ever be truly silent.

His phone buzzed. Blocked number. He stared at it as it rang. Once, twice, three times. Then it stopped.

A text message appeared on the screen: *Don't get too comfy.*

He read it twice. His hand didn't shake, but something in his chest tightened, like a fist around his ribs.

He locked the screen and powered the phone off. The air inside the house felt thinner now, like all the oxygen had quietly drained.

Whatever this was, it wasn't just a warning. It was the beginning of something.

8

———————

Quinton and Cassidy sat with Hale in the attorney client room at the jail. The room was as cold and unfriendly as ever, with its metal table and flickering lights. Quinton tried to focus, but the memory of sitting across from Joanne in this same place rose like an unwelcome shadow. He practiced the deep breathing he'd read about when researching PTSD after the incident in the empty courtroom.

Hale sat rigidly in his chair, hands clasped in his lap, his expression a mix of fear and disbelief.

Quinton opened the folder between them. "We have reviewed the evidence proffer from the prosecutor. As you heard in court, District Attorney Sawyer Durant has taken the case. He's a pit bull, and we need to be very careful with him in charge. He said he sent over all he had, but I still don't think we've seen everything."

Hale's voice trembled. "What could they have?"

Quinton lifted the first document. "This is the timeline they built. Daniel attended an agent's meeting that afternoon in a building where you'd been signed in earlier in the day."

"All the major sports related offices are in that building. It's only natural that Price would be there."

Cassidy nodded. "That will help, he had good reason to be there. So did you."

Quinton nodded agreement. "But you never signed out."

Hale frowned. "I left through the side door. The front desk was closed for lunch."

Quinton observed him. "But Durant is saying you stayed in the building and waited for Price."

Cassidy slid a grainy photograph across the table. "This is the footage from across the street. It's blurry. Low quality. But they claim the figure standing in the lobby is you. Watching him. Following him."

Hale stared at the picture, horrified. "That could be anyone."

"True," Quinton said. "But the prosecutor does not care that the image is unclear. He only cares that it can be argued. We'll ask for an evidentiary hearing and try to keep it out."

"Good."

He tapped the next document. "Then there are the prints. They found your fingerprints at Price's townhouse. You told detectives you had not been there for about six months."

Hale nodded quickly. "Yes. That's about the time I started trying to get out of the arrangement."

"And the prints match that version. But there are very few instances with prints over yours." Quinton pointed at the document. "There is nothing fresh from anyone else. No new overlay."

"That doesn't mean anything." Cassidy blinked. "Maybe Price was a slob and didn't clean much, or maybe he didn't have many people over."

Quinton admonished her with a look. "True. But they are still using it to show access. They can assert that you knew the layout of the house. And while making that assertion, they can intimate that you were recently there. They can also show that he might have let you in."

Cassidy agreed. "Yes. There was no forced entry, so Price obviously opened the door to his assailant."

Hale squared his broad shoulders and pressed a hand to his forehead. "This is insane."

"I know," Cassidy said calmly.

Quinton looked at Cassidy. "But they are building a story, not a certainty."

Cassidy sat back in her chair, getting the unsaid message.

Quinton placed a sheet on the table. "This is the last piece. Completely circumstantial. They say the killer took his phone to hide evidence. They recovered the text messages from the cloud for Price's phone. Looks like you were texting with him that day and it was not peaceful."

Hale blinked fast. "But I did not threaten to kill him."

"It's not what you texted, it's what he texted. They say it shows he intended to confront you, and they are combining that assumption with the evidence of the contract dispute."

Hale shook his head. "Nothing unusual there."

Quinton tapped the folder with a heavy finger. "The prosecutor says you were pressuring him. That gives weight to motive. They can say you went by to settle your business and things got out of hand."

Hale's eyes filled with fear. "In his home. In the middle of a rain storm with a weapon? Ridiculous. I did not kill him."

Quinton leaned in, lowering his voice. "We know. But the case they are building is straightforward. You were at the office building that afternoon. You left without signing out. You were possibly waiting for Price. You had been in his townhouse. Your prints are there. The argumentative phone texts between you.

Every piece alone means nothing. Together they look suspicious."

Hale stared down at his hands. "Someone is twisting all of this."

Cassidy tried to reassure Hale. "Yes. And we are going to untwist every piece of it. We need a little time to work on it. That's how circumstantial evidence is defeated."

Quinton gathered the pages into a stack again. "I think they have more that they've not given us. This is far too thin and flimsy to convict on. Can you think of anything else they might have?"

Hale searched his mind with his eyes rolling up. He hesitated, then said, "No. Nothing except what I already told you."

"I don't think that's enough to tip the scales unless there's some physical evidence of threat."

Cassidy looked confused. "What isn't enough?"

"We'll get into all that at the office, we're out of time today."

Cassidy accepted the answer but didn't seem to like it.

Quinton looked at Hale. "Once you get moved to the main jail, I'd like to set up a workday and meet again. We can get you some decent food and a laptop or some legal pads and files. Also, I want to bring in another attorney to second chair the case."

Hale looked at Cassidy who in turn gave Quinton a funny look. "Maureen?"

"Right, you met her at the courthouse a few months back. Mo is excellent at strategy, and the judge is not going to let me try a murder case alone."

"You won't be alone. I'm a lawyer, too, don't forget."

"I haven't. Not for a minute. We will be needing all your skills and hers too."

Hale nodded. "I want the best team I can get."

Cassidy's shoulders dropped.

"Okay. We're running out of time for today. You keep writing it down. Every detail and odd thing from that day. We will build our own story, the correct one."

Outside the door a guard coughed, impatient.

Inside, Quinton, and Cassidy shared a look over the growing pile of contradictions, the case tightening around Hale like a net.

Quinton intended to cut every strand.

9

Quinton said goodbye to a disgruntled Cassidy and was halfway down the courthouse steps, files tucked under one arm. The press had dispersed, not knowing what time Quinton might exit. He looked up and a shape in the glass entryway caught his attention. Tall. Still. Watching.

For a second he thought he recognized the posture, the way the figure kept his head slightly lowered. It pulled something old out of Quinton's memory, something he had spent a long time trying not to think about. But the reflection was distorted, warping the shoulders and stretching the outline. He could not be sure where he had seen that shape before, or if he even had.

The man wore a baseball cap pulled low and a long-sleeved shirt far too warm for the thick Houston heat. Sweat should have been pouring off him, but he stood motionless, as if the temperature did not matter.

Quinton took a few more steps then turned to get a clear look, but no one was there. He scanned the area. The sidewalk was almost empty. A few attorneys crossed the street toward the parking garage. A security guard leaned against a pillar, sipping from a bottle of water. No one resembled the figure he had seen.

Quinton made himself keep walking, though every instinct pressed him to turn back again. The files felt heavier in his grip as he reached the row of cars.

Then he saw it.

A diner napkin, folded once, tucked under the windshield wiper of his SUV. The paper was faintly crinkled, like it had been held too long in someone's hand. Written across it in small block letters were the words:

STILL WATCHING YOU BYRON.

No signature. No explanation. Just those three words and his old name. His real name.

Quinton glanced around the parking lot, but the sunlight lay harmlessly across the asphalt. No movement. No sound except the hum of traffic from the street.

He opened the door and slid into the driver's seat, the door closing with a dull thud that seemed too loud in the quiet space. Every muscle in his body locked tight. He put the files and the napkin on the passenger seat and stared at it as if it might change.

This was not a message. It was not even a warning. It was a taunting.

Near the courthouse, in the shadow of a stone pillar, a man had stood with his hands in his pockets. He'd watched Quinton walk away, his expression unreadable. His eyes cold. His patience seemed carved by loss and resentment.

Quinton started the engine and pulled out slowly. Instead of heading straight to the office, he took the longest route possible, weaving through side streets, watching the mirrors for anything that looked out of place. A white truck lingered behind him for two lights before turning. A dark sedan appeared in his rearview mirror, then vanished behind a bus. Every reflection felt like a trap waiting to close.

He knew the rhythm of being hunted. The quiet that came before the next move. The waiting. The pressure. The fear that settled deep enough to feel like a second heartbeat.

He looked down at the napkin laying in the passenger seat. This note carried all of that. It had weight. It had intent. It had memory behind it. But he did not know whose memory it belonged to.

Quinton spent the evening at home trying to act normal. Emails, dinner, a few billing hours on his other clients' files to distract himself, but his mind kept looping back to the courthouse and that napkin tucked under the wiper.

It wasn't the message so much as the delivery. Anyone could send a threat. Anyone could scribble something menacing and slip it under a door or into a mailbox. But the courthouse parking lot was a statement. It said: *I know where you are when you think you're safe.* It said: *I'm close enough to touch your car and walk away unnoticed.*

That was what bothered him.

By nine o'clock he gave up pretending. The emails blurred. The billing software mocked him with its blinking cursor. He closed the laptop, stood, and walked the length of the house, bare feet whispering against the hardwood floors. Outside, Houston hummed in the distance, traffic and cicadas and the low summer thrum of a city that never quite slept.

He stopped at the kitchen island and stared at the napkin again. He hadn't thrown it away. He told himself it was prudence, not obsession. Evidence shouldn't be destroyed, even when it wasn't evidence yet. Especially when it might become evidence later.

The napkin was cheap. White. The kind you grabbed without thinking at a taco truck or courthouse café. The ink had bled slightly into the fibers, as if the writer had pressed hard, angry or hurried or both.

Quinton folded it once, carefully, and slipped it into an envelope he'd brought home from the office. He set it in the drawer beside his keys and shut it with more force than necessary.

If I'm going to worry about something, it might as well be an issue I can do something about.

He opened a beer he didn't really want and carried it into what would soon be the study. Hale's file waited on the desk, thick and ugly and familiar. Quinton sat, rolled his shoulders once, and opened it.

Marcus Hale didn't look like a murderer on paper. Most defendants didn't. On paper they were jobs and addresses and arrest dates, flattened into black and white. Hale was a Houston Wildcatter, a football player whose body had made other men rich. Clean record. No priors. A public persona polished by agents and press releases.

And then there was Daniel Price.

Quinton flipped to the photographs he'd avoided earlier. Price's house. The living room where everything had been upset with blood. The kitchen and hallway where nothing was out of place.

Quinton didn't linger. He'd seen enough dead bodies in case files to know when to stop. He turned instead to timelines, notes, phone records. He read what the prosecution wanted him to read and what they didn't.

He flipped to the financials that Dart had prepared. Price's accounts were a mess. Layers of LLCs, money sliding sideways in ways that made accountants sigh and prosecutors salivate. There were payments Dart hadn't explained yet. Consulting fees. Retainers from entities that didn't appear to exist beyond a mailing address and a registered agent.

Quinton glanced at the clock. After ten. Too late to call Dart. Too late to call Mo unless it was urgent. This wasn't urgent yet. This was something else. A slow burn, the kind that either fizzled out or exploded when you weren't looking.

He gathered the file into a neater stack and closed it. Tomorrow he'd ask better questions. Tomorrow he'd push harder on Price's paper trail. Tomorrow he'd talk to Hale again, see what cracked when the pressure shifted.

Tonight, he needed to sleep. He was dead tired.

He locked the house the way he always did. Methodical, practiced. Front door. Back door. Alarm set. He paused at the bedroom window and looked out at the dark backyard, half expecting movement where there was none.

Get a grip, he told himself.

He slept poorly anyway.

The dream was disjointed. Courthouse marble floors stretching too long. The sound of footsteps behind him that never closed the distance. A napkin drifting through the air like a white flag, landing at his feet no matter how fast he walked.

He woke before dawn, mind already racing. By eight he was back in the office, coffee in hand, jacket draped over the chair. Anna gave him a look he'd learned to respect.

"You look like hell."

"Morning to you too."

"Did you eat?"

"Define eat."

She slid a protein bar across the desk without comment. Quinton caught it, unwrapped it, and took a bite he didn't taste.

"Any messages?" he asked.

"Nothing exciting. Dart called late yesterday. Said he'd stop by today."

"Good."

Anna hesitated. "Everything okay?"

He considered lying. He always did. Then he shook his head. "Not sure yet."

She nodded, satisfied with that non-answer. Anna understood timing better than most lawyers he knew.

Quinton went into his office and shut the door. He thought of Hale. He knew he couldn't save him. Lawyers didn't save people. They told stories that made room for reasonable doubt. They reframed fear into context, violence into reaction, motive into survival.

But sometimes, rarely, that was enough.

Quinton drained his coffee and opened his laptop.

Whoever had left the napkin wanted him distracted. Wanted him looking over his shoulder. That was a mistake. If someone was watching him, they were about to learn something he already knew.

Quinton Bell did his best work when he was cornered.

10

The next day, Friday, Quinton headed south on I-45 toward Galveston and the Bell house. Traffic thinned as Houston fell away behind him, the skyline dissolving into flat stretches of concrete and sky. He rolled the window down halfway and let the humid air creep in.

Quinton went old school. FM. The radio crackled as he pressed the preset button to a local coastal station. The fishing report was already underway.

"Light chop in the Gulf this morning. Winds out of the southeast at ten to fifteen. Redfish running along the flats. Speckled trout biting early near the jetties. Incoming tide around midmorning. Should be a good day if you can get out before the storms build."

Quinton listened. Something about the cadence of it, the calm certainty, grounded him. Conditions. Tides. Movement. Things that followed rules.

He drove and listened for a while after that, then reached over and switched to music. An old track came on, low and steady, something with a slow build and a heavy bass line that matched the rhythm of the tires on pavement. He didn't change it. Let it play.

The closer he got to the coast, the lighter he felt. Not free, not even close, but lighter. Like something pressing on his chest had eased just enough to let him breathe.

After Judge Bell's death, Quinton, under the name he wore now, had become the sole heir to the Bell estate. He had moved most of the assets into a charitable trust, as if distance could insulate him. But he had kept one thing. Only one.

The Bell house in Galveston.

A Victorian near the beach, tested by salt and storms but the old girl was still standing with quiet dignity. He could not let it go. Too many memories lived there. Summers with Q. Evenings with Judge Bell. The place felt anchored to something real in a life that had become almost entirely constructed.

Keeping it was a risk. Hiding in plain sight was a risk. Everything about his existence was a risk.

If anyone ever pulled the thread and unraveled who he really was, the trust, the donations, none of it would matter. There were people who would not hesitate to argue that his life had come at the expense of another man's.

Murder, if they wanted to push it that far.

Quinton tightened his grip on the wheel and forced the thought aside.

He had enough in front of him. Hale's case. The gaps in the story. The way the evidence felt just slightly off, like a picture hung crooked on a wall. And then there was the ferry model, sitting on his hearth like a question he had not yet learned how to ask.

He needed space. Movement. Water.

By the time he crossed onto the island, the air had changed. Saltier. The sky stretched wider, low clouds hanging in a pale-gray sheet over the Gulf.

He pulled into the drive at the Bell house and cut the engine. For a moment, he just sat there, listening to the ticking of the cooling car and the distant, steady pattern of waves.

Inside, the house smelled of wood and salt. Closed up but not forgotten. He moved through it without turning on many lights, muscle memory guiding him. He went into the bedroom and pulled on shorts and beach shoes. He left his shirt on a chair.

Back outside, the humidity wrapped around him. The breeze carried the sharp, clean smell of the Gulf. He locked the door behind him and headed toward the Seawall.

The water was restless. Gray and uneven, pushing higher than usual, slapping against the rocks in short, impatient bursts. The sky and sea blurred together at the horizon.

He walked along the hard sidewalk, the wind tugging at his hair, the sound of the surf settling in behind everything else. Normally, this was where his mind would begin to clear. Where problems broke apart into manageable pieces.

Not today. The questions followed him.

The blurred figure behind his house in Houston. The text. The napkin. Small things on their own. Together, something larger.

Whoever it was, they were getting closer. Bolder. More deliberate.

Quinton slowed, his gaze drifting out across the water. A cargo ship moved along the horizon, slow and steady, almost motionless at that distance.

For a moment, an image slipped in uninvited. Someone on deck, binoculars raised, watching him. Waiting. He let out a quiet breath.

Silly.

But he didn't entirely disbelieve it.

He turned and kept walking. Moisture gathered beneath his shoes, the faint squeak marking each step against the concrete.

Hale's case pressed in next. The fear in his voice. The insistence. The way he had looked at Quinton like the outcome already depended on him. Hale said he was innocent.

Quinton had told him he would help. But promises had weight.

He stopped and glanced back toward the line of beach houses. Structures that had survived more storms than they should have.

Another thought slid in. If the person watching him tried hard enough, he might be forced to run again. He couldn't bear to think about it. He pushed the thoughts from his mind and turned back toward the Gulf.

The waves rolled in, one after another, steady, relentless, unconcerned with anything onshore.

Whatever was coming, it was already in motion. And it wasn't going to stop.

***

By the time Quinton turned back toward the house, the wind had picked up and the sky had darkened another shade. The Gulf had that look to it. Restless, building toward something.

He climbed the steps from the sand to the Seawall and crossed the street without breaking stride.

The Bell house sat the way he'd left it. Quiet.

Still, something slowed him. Not a sound. Not movement. A feeling.

Quinton paused at the edge of the walkway and let his eyes move across the property. Porch. Windows. Eaves. The strip of yard. All intact.

He stepped closer.

The ornate front gate stood slightly open. He was certain he had latched it. Not wide. Just enough that the wind could have worked it loose.

Quinton pushed it open the rest of the way and walked up the path, his pace unchanged. The porch boards creaked under his weight as he stepped up. He glanced at the front door. Tried it. Still locked.

He went around the side to the garage door, the way he had left, and went in there as was his habit. He reached into his pocket for the key, then stopped. The doormat. It had been straight when he left. Centered with the door. Now it sat at a slight angle, one corner turned up as if it had been stepped on and not put back.

Quinton stood there for a moment, the key resting against his palm. Could have been the wind. Except the entry was sheltered.

He bent, flattened the mat with his hand, then straightened again.

That was when he saw it. Sitting on the top step. He hadn't noticed it when he walked up.

It was a ferry with wording on the side. The Robert H. Dedman. One that operated out of Galveston's East Beach over to Port Bolívar.

His jaw tightened.

He stepped back off the porch, slow, deliberate, giving himself a wider angle. The street was empty. The neighboring houses quiet. Curtains drawn.

He returned his attention to the step. Quinton picked up the model. It was dry. He turned it slightly in his hand.

For a moment, the distance between the two places collapsed. Houston. Galveston. New York. Staten Island. All of it pulled tight into a single line.

Quinton exhaled slowly and looked back toward the street.

Empty. No car idling, or figure walking away. No one watching. Or no one he could see.

He carried the model up onto the porch. He tried the door. Still locked. He stood there, the wind pushing at his back, the weight of the small boat solid in his hand.

Whoever had left it hadn't needed much time. Just enough. Enough to walk up his steps. Enough to stand where he was standing now. Enough to let him know.

They could reach him anywhere.

11

Quinton chose the place for dinner on purpose. Roost Bistro in Montrose, between downtown Houston and the 610 Loop, provided a neighborhood hangout feel. It was close to both of their offices, but far enough to feel like a break. Linen napkins. Decent wine. The kind of spot where conversations stayed low.

Mo was already there when he arrived, glasses on, menu folded neatly beside her water. She had the same posture she'd always had. Upright without being stiff, alert without looking like she was on guard.

Maureen Powers of Jamail, Powers & Kent was a no-nonsense woman of substance. She specialized in litigation in the area of energy law. As a University of Texas Law School grad, she was a few years ahead of Quinton, where he also attended. Fortunately, they had never crossed paths while he was Byron Douglas. Q had gone to law school in Florida, so they were spared the college reminiscing discussion.

Mo was connected, and her reputation was stellar. She was good. Everyone knew that. Polished without being slick. Calm in a way that came from having seen worse. Few knew she spent the weekends riding a horse and barrel racing on the rodeo circuit in her spare time with her partner, Abigail.

Quinton slid into his chair and signaled the waiter for a wine list.

"You look like you're about to ask me for something," Mo said as he settled in across from her.

Quinton smiled. "Good to see you too." Quinton had tried several cases with Mo and found her an invaluable partner as his second chair, but he knew she wouldn't take just any old case. She had to be interested and invested to pull away from her busy practice to add something else. Quinton hoped this would be that something else.

"I mean it. You don't pick this place unless it's either bad news or a favor."

"Or both."

Mo exaggerated a sigh.

They ordered. Hunan Glazed Salmon for her, Pepper Pot Texas Quail for him, and they shared The Famous Fried Cauliflower. Quinton added a bottle of the 2023 Albino Rocca Langhe Chardonnay from Piedmont, Italy. Mo nodded her approval.

Quinton waited until the server disappeared before he leaned back and exhaled.

"I've got a problem."

Mo lifted her water glass. "You always do. Is this a small problem or a ruin-your-life large sized problem?"

"Medium. But trending upward."

She tilted her head, listening now.

"Hale. Marcus Hale."

"The Wildcatters' linebacker?" she said immediately.

They paused for a moment as the waiter returned, opened the wine, and after Quinton's approval, poured them both a glass. After placing the wine in an ice bucket by the table, he retreated to the kitchen.

"I saw the arrest."

"Of course you did. Who didn't?"

"Public arrest. That was intentional."

"It was. And now they've got him tied to his dead agent, phone texts that don't quite make sense, and a motive that looks ugly if you know where to look."

Mo's expression sharpened. "And you looked?"

"I'm looking. This won't be a one-person job."

He walked her through it. Not theatrically, just the way he always did, like stacking bricks. One at a time.

He described Daniel Price and the relationship that had curdled long before it ended. Hale's secret, dangerous in the wrong hands. The State's theory, clean and simple, built to play well on the evening news.

"How'd you get the case?"

"Cassidy West. She's a baby lawyer with a lot of spunk and potential."

"Is she helping?"

"Yes, and will stay on the case. She's smart. Capable. Hungry. She's done good work so far on other matters."

"But?" Mo asked.

"But this case is going to turn on nuance. Experience. Strategy. Jury psychology. Cross-examining experts who know how to sound certain while saying very little."

Mo leaned back. "You're asking me to be second chair."

"I am."

She didn't answer right away.

Instead, she studied him the way she used to at the downtown firm, back when they shared conference rooms and designer coffee and impossible deadlines. Back when they learned each other's rhythms.

"What about Cassidy? You bring me in, she's going to feel like she's being replaced."

"That's my worry. Not yours. She wants to win. She and Hale are friends."

Mo folded her hands. "You remember what it felt like to be young and finally trusted with something big."

"I do. I also remember what it felt like to be drowning because nobody had my back."

The food arrived. Both ate as if it were their last meal. When satiated, Quinton took a swig of wine and said, "This case could break Hale. He needs more than one voice in the room. And I need someone who knows me well enough to tell me when I'm wrong."

Mo smiled faintly. "That narrows the list. Not a job for a baby lawyer."

"Exactly. I'm asking you because you won't let me bulldoze. And because you've seen juries turn when everyone else thought the story was locked."

She took a sip of her wine.

"You'll have to talk to her. Not after. Before."

"I have. No surprises. We can both mentor her."

She looked out the window for a long moment, traffic inching past in the Houston heat.

"You always find the hard ones."

"Someone has to."

Mo sighed, then nodded once. "Let me check with the office for conflicts, but otherwise, I'm in."

Relief loosened something in his chest he hadn't realized was tight.

"Thank you."

She smiled. "When do we start?"

Quinton smiled. "Yesterday."

The attorney workroom at the jail hadn't changed in decades. Gray walls scuffed by years of bad news. The air carried the faint smell of old paper, like the room itself had absorbed every conversation it had ever witnessed.

Hale was already waiting when the attorneys were brought in. His orange jumpsuit tight on his linebacker frame, hands folded in front of him.

Quinton nodded once. "Marcus."

Hale's eyes flicked to the woman beside him, a question already forming.

"This is Maureen Powers. We call her Mo. She's joining the defense team."

Mo stepped forward and offered her hand without hesitation. "Good to meet you, Mr. Hale."

Hale shook it carefully, like he was afraid of doing something wrong. "Please. Call me Marcus."

Cassidy stood beside Quinton, hands clasped tight, watching the exchange a little too closely.

Mo took a seat, setting her legal pad on the table. "I won't waste your time. I've worked with Quinton a long time. My job is to help tell your story clearly and make sure the jury understands it."

Hale nodded. "I appreciate that."

Mo glanced between him and Cassidy, then back to Hale. Her tone shifted. It was gentler, conversational. "Quinton has filled me in on the facts of the case. I just have a few questions."

"Fire away."

"Let's start at the beginning. How did you arrive in Houston?"

"A scout was in Hawaii for another player and saw me in a football game."

One second stretched into two.

Cassidy leaned forward. "Daniel Price was Marcus's agent," she said quickly. "They met when Marcus first came to Houston."

Quinton didn't say a word. He didn't have to.

Cassidy caught the look immediately. A sharp, silent correction. *Not now.*

She stopped mid-sentence and leaned back, color rising in her cheeks. The room went still. She learned quickly, and she'd just learned that the answer was not as important as the delivery. Mo was trying to gauge her new client.

Cassidy chastised herself for interfering again without thinking. Quinton had told her about Mo and the need for her as second chair. She had agreed but didn't realize how much it would sting to feel the pecking order change in the meeting.

Mo didn't react at all. She didn't look annoyed or amused. She just waited, eyes back on Hale, patient as a judge.

Hale cleared his throat. "Yeah," he said finally. "The scout told Daniel Price about me. Price watched my games for a while, then asked me to come to camp in Houston. He became my agent when I left Hawaii and moved here. It happened so fast, I needed someone right away and one of the other players was using him."

He paused again, choosing his words carefully. "I didn't have much. No friends or family looking out for me, no real understanding of contracts or money. Price showed up at the right time."

"In what way?" Mo asked.

"He said he could help," Hale looked strained. "Said he believed in me. Took me to dinner. Talked about protecting my future."

Quinton watched him closely. Hale's voice was steady, but

there was something rehearsed about it. Like he'd told himself this version enough times that it almost felt complete.

"He negotiated my first contract. Handled endorsements. Media stuff. All the things I didn't want to think about."

"And how long did that relationship last?" Mo asked.

"Years. Longer than it should have."

Cassidy shifted beside Quinton but stayed silent this time.

"What changed?" Mo asked.

Hale hesitated again. This time it was more pronounced.

"People change. Success changes things."

"That's true," Mo said evenly. "But not always in the same way for both people."

Hale's eyes flicked up to hers, then away.

"He started making decisions without consulting me. It was as if he owned me and my career."

Mo nodded. "Did you ever try to end the relationship?"

"Absolutely."

Quinton caught it. So did Mo.

"And?"

"And it wasn't easy. Price didn't like being told no."

Silence settled again.

Mo opened her pad, wrote a single word, then closed it. "All right. I'll fill in the gaps with Quinton and Cassidy."

Mo looked at Quinton as if to say, *I'm done.*

Quinton ended the meeting. "That's enough for today."

Hale looked relieved and uneasy at the same time.

As they stood to leave, Quinton met Mo's eyes.

As they walked out, Quinton glanced back at Hale, who was already being escorted away.

The story he'd told was true. But it wasn't complete, and the two seasoned attorneys knew it. Whatever Hale was still hiding lived somewhere in that pause before he'd answered the very first question.

Quinton could tell that Cassidy knew something had changed. It wasn't anything anyone said. It was the way Quinton and Mo walked a half step ahead of her, already talking in low voices. Not excluding her. Just moving with such intention.

Quinton had been clear. He'd told her the Hale case was bigger than it looked, that he was bringing Mo in to help. Second chair. Someone with trial scars she didn't have yet.

Cassidy had nodded then. Said she understood. Said all the right things. Now, it appeared that maybe she hadn't fully realized the pecking order. She looked as if she'd been slapped.

Cassidy slowed near the exit doors, checking her phone, letting them drift a few feet ahead. Somewhere down the hall, a door slammed. The sound followed them like punctuation.

Quinton wanted to ease her along. He knew what it felt like to be a baby lawyer in a tank of sharks. He also knew that the best way to learn was the hard way. She hadn't been wrong. Just premature. A shortcut where patience mattered. And Quinton's look had landed harder than he'd intended.

Quinton had explained to Cassidy that bringing Mo Powers in would be a relief. Less pressure. Another mind in the room. Someone to shoulder the weight.

Of course, Quinton would want Mo there. They had history. Victories. Losses. He had history with Cassidy too. Just not as much.

She caught up to them near the elevators.

Mo was saying something about Hale's hesitation, about the first pause being the one that mattered. Quinton nodded, already filing it away.

Cassidy listened, silent this time. She straightened her shoulders.

Quinton glanced back at her. Just a look. Checking in.

She met his eyes and nodded once. *I'm good.*

Quinton acknowledged her and held the door for them to exit into the Houston heat. She had brought in the client, this was true, but if she was going to share the room, she was going to earn it.

And next time, he knew she wouldn't speak until it was time. He knew she knew it, too.

Quinton and Mo said goodbye to Cassidy and took separate cars to his office.

The first cup of coffee was back in Quinton's conference room, that was starting to look like a trial war room, with boxes of files and charts on easels. Both attorneys sat amidst the chaos quietly in thought until Mo cracked open a file and Quinton followed.

It wasn't until the building had gone silent and the city outside Quinton's window had settled into its evening hum that Mo finally spoke.

"You noticed it too."

Quinton looked up from the file. "The pause?"

"Yes."

She reached into her bag and pulled out the legal pad she'd carried into the jail. It was folded now, pages bent at the corner, like it had been used and put away without ceremony.

She slid it across his desk and opened it to a single page.

One word sat in the middle of the paper, written cleanly, deliberately.

OWNED

Quinton stared at it. Not surprised. Just confirmed.

Mo tapped the word and said, "He didn't hesitate because

he didn't remember. He hesitated because he was deciding how much truth he could survive."

Quinton exhaled slowly. "Or how much he was willing to entrust to us. He's still protecting something."

"Or someone. Or his past."

That landed harder.

Quinton looked up. "Any ideas how to get it out of him?"

"We're going to have to earn it. That's the job."

12

Quinton had been to the gym for three days in a row, trying to relieve a nagging feeling of unease. When swimming failed to work, he began to get the itch for a card game. It started as a low thrum in his gut, the kind of restlessness that chlorine and laps couldn't wash away. He'd tried. Swim, shower, stretch, beer. He was still wired. On the third day, he gave in.

By eight that night, he was on the road, headed north. The new casino, Cherokee Nation, just across the Oklahoma state line, had been on his radar for weeks. It was a very long drive, but that cut both ways. His chances of running into someone he knew was slim.

Word was they had a private poker room tucked behind the usual floor games. Real stakes. Real players. No tourists chasing thrills as there were in the main room, only serious gamblers.

He walked through the open casino floor with its jangling slot machines, through the public poker area, and to the back where a host guarded the door. Tall guy in a black vest chewing on a toothpick that moved from one corner of his mouth to the other like a clock hand. No small talk. Just a glance at Quinton's attire, his hands holding his tray of chips, and a nod toward the red velvet curtain.

Quinton called for luck. *Baby needs a new pair of shoes.*

The high-stakes room was quieter than expected after the mayhem of the main casino. It was smoke-free, dimly lit, with just enough playing from the overhead sound track to muffle casual conversation. Eight seats were at the table. Seven filled and one open. He slid in without a word.

The dealer was a woman in her fifties, tan face like creased leather, fingers fast and sure. She wore a black visor with the emblem of the casino low over her brow and had a sharp, no-nonsense way of pushing chips across the felt. Her name plate read *Martha*.

To her left, a heavyset man with silver rings on every finger stared at the flop like it owed him money. Across the table, a bearded man in a navy suit sipped dark liquid through a straw and blinked too often. Two seats down, a woman in a red blazer and gold bangles had a stack as tall as a coffee cup and a stare that said don't waste my time.

Quinton bought in and took a deep breath as Martha dealt. The cards settled something in him.

First hand, he got a king-jack off suit. Middle position. He limped in, saw the flop, a king of spades, four of hearts, ten of clubs. He checked. Red Blazer came on with a strong raise. Quinton folded. No heat yet.

Second hand, ace and eight of diamonds. Small blind. Called the big bet. Flop came down with two hearts and a diamond. Ace, seven, queen. A little action followed. Quinton stayed in through the turn and picked up a second diamond. The river brought the ten of diamonds. He held his poker face as he realized he had a flush.

He bet half the pot, just enough to invite the fish. Navy Suit took the bait. Called. Quinton turned over his cards. Martha pushed the chips his way. First win of the night.

By the fourth hand, the rhythm took over. Time folded. The tension in his shoulders eased. The game became the only thing that existed. Reading hands, watching for hesitation, listening for the silent breath that came before someone got bold.

Quinton pulled king-king on the button. Raised to eight hundred. Two calls. Flop: nine, king, two, rainbow. Trips. The other players checked around. He checked, too. Turn came a seven. Silver Rings put in two thousand. Quinton smooth-called. River brought the three of hearts. Rings shoved. Quinton called. Ring's full boat beat his trips. Quinton exhaled, sat back, watched the dealer scrape in his stack.

"Nice hand," Red Blazer said.

Rings just grunted.

That's when Quinton noticed the man. He was standing near the bar at the edge of the room, just outside the pool of light cast by the chandelier. Not watching the game. Watching him. Maybe.

Quinton held his poker face. He settled into his chair, reached for his drink, and scanned the green felted table like nothing had changed. But the air had shifted. The game kept going. Bets were made. Cards fell. Now, Quinton wasn't just watching the players. He was waiting to see what the man did next.

The watcher had a ballcap pulled low over his brow and a fuzzy mustache. Quinton recognized a disguise when he saw one. He had become an expert when he had first gone on the run from New York to Reno. He wished he'd worn a disguise today, but the oppressive heat had influenced his attire. Assuming he wouldn't encounter anyone in Oklahoma who knew him was a big mistake. One he wouldn't make again.

The game was ruined and he was distracted. He finished the hand before him and asked to color up. By the time he retrieved his chips and headed toward the bar, the stalker was gone.

The lights of the Cherokee Nation Casino faded in his rearview mirror, swallowed by the black stretch of Oklahoma highway.

Quinton told himself it was nothing. A man in a casino. A look that lasted half a second too long. That was all. But his hands stayed tight on the steering wheel as he eased his car onto the road. The radio was tuned to classic rock. "Highway to Hell" by AC/DC was blasting.

The night air felt different out here, heavier somehow. The casino had been noise and neon and slot machines. Out here there was nothing but dark pasture and the thin beam of his headlights carving a tunnel through it.

He checked the rearview mirror. Just black road and two distant headlights cresting a hill.

You're being paranoid.

He turned the radio off and drove a few miles in silence. The hum of the tires on asphalt sounded louder than it should have. His pulse had not quite returned to normal since he'd locked eyes with the man near the high limit room.

He could still see him. Late forties, maybe older. Clean cut. Not drunk, or smiling, or gambling. Watching. There was something familiar about him. *Maybe.*

Not the casual glance of a curious stranger. Not recognition from television coverage of the Hale case. It had been something else. A stillness. A measuring.

Quinton adjusted the mirror again. The same headlights

behind him now. Closer. He shifted lanes. The headlights shifted too. His jaw tightened.

"Coincidence," he muttered to the empty car.

He eased off the accelerator. The headlights slowed. A thin ribbon of sweat crept down his back.

Don't do this. Don't spin up ghosts.

He signaled and took the next exit abruptly, tires whispering over the reflective paint. A lonely gas station sat at the corner, fluorescent lights buzzing over two pumps and a darkened convenience store.

He pulled in without using the signal. The headlights continued past the exit without hesitation. Gone.

He stayed parked under the light for a full minute, engine idling. Nothing turned around. No car circled back. No slow roll through the lot. Still. The feeling didn't leave.

He checked his phone. No new messages or missed calls from Anna. No texts from Mo or Cassidy. No updates from Dart.

Houston felt a thousand miles away. He merged back onto the highway and drove south. The farther he went, the more isolated he felt. The Oklahoma night bled into North Texas darkness. Occasional eighteen-wheelers roared past, shaking the car as they overtook him. Every time one came up fast in his mirror, his heart spiked.

He kept replaying the moment in the casino. The man had not looked surprised to see him. He had looked like he expected to.

Quinton flexed his fingers on the steering wheel.

You're not that important.

Except he was. Not to the world. But to someone.

He checked the mirror again as traffic picked up. The lights of an SUV three car lengths back. Steady. Not passing. Not falling away. His stomach turned cold. He slowed slightly. The

SUV slowed and other drivers passed them both. He accelerated. The SUV matched him.

Quinton waited until the next stretch of empty highway, then punched the accelerator hard enough to feel the engine strain. The car surged forward. Wind noise increased. The SUV behind him lingered for a moment, then began to shrink. It wasn't following. It simply had cruise control. Quinton slowed. The SUV eventually passed him, driver oblivious, music thumping faintly through closed windows as it disappeared into the night.

Quinton swallowed. He hated this. He hated that he could not tell the difference anymore between instinct and trauma.

He rolled down his window slightly. Warm air slapped his face, sharp and real.

By the time he drove into Central Texas, the sky had deepened into that pitch-black that only exists far from cities. No moon. Sparse stars.

His headlights flickered across road signs and reflective posts. He checked the mirror again. Empty.

Hours later, Houston finally rose on the horizon, a faint orange glow against the sky. The closer he got, the more the world felt normal again. Traffic increased. Lanes multiplied. Familiar billboards loomed. The city had weight. Presence. Noise.

He exited onto the Loop. Traffic thin. Red brake lights blinked in uneven lines ahead of him. He blended in, just another driver.

He forced himself to stop checking the mirror every ten seconds. Then checked it anyway. Quinton exhaled slowly.

You are unraveling.

When he reached his neighborhood, the streets were quiet. Trees lined the sidewalks. Porch lights glowed warmly. Ordinary life. He drove past his house once without turning in. Just to see. Nothing unusual. No idling car. No figure standing on the sidewalk. He circled the block anyway.

When he finally pulled into his driveway, he did not immediately get out. He scanned the street. The houses. The dark windows across from him. He killed the engine. The silence pressed in. For a moment, he just sat there. Then he slid out and locked the car. The click of the lock sounded too loud. He moved quickly to the front door, keys ready before he reached it. Inside, he locked the deadbolt. Then the secondary lock.

He stood in the foyer, listening. The house hummed softly with the air conditioning. The refrigerator kicked on in the kitchen. Normal.

He moved room to room, turning on lights. Checking windows. Peering through blinds into the street. He didn't see anyone.

When he finally reached his bedroom, he paused at the window. Parted the curtain slightly. Across the street, a car rolled slowly past. Not stopping. Not slowing. Just passing. He told himself that was all it was. A car passing. Still, he watched until its taillights disappeared around the corner. Only then did he let the curtain fall.

He did not sleep easily. Being on high alert for hours driving home did not subside quickly. Every distant engine made him sit up. Every flicker of light through the blinds made his pulse spike.

Somewhere in the back of his mind, steady and insistent, a single thought repeated itself: The man in the casino had not been surprised to see him. He had been following, and he seemed familiar.

13

The courthouse was already humming with tension by the time Quinton and Cassidy stepped off the elevator on the fourth floor. Mo had begged off to take care of one of her regular clients. Lawyers hurried past with armfuls of files, clerks rolled carts laden with exhibits, and somewhere down the hall a judge's gavel cracked like a gunshot. People's lives hung in the balance. Everyone felt it.

Quinton pushed open the door to the small attorney conference room they'd been assigned. It was an undersized space with a dented table, a temperamental AC vent that ticked like a metronome, and a window that looked directly into a brick wall. Just another day in Harris County.

Cassidy dropped two overstuffed binders on the table. "Nice of Durant's office to finally cough up their supplemental discovery."

Quinton nodded. "Yep. Classic Sawyer Durant. Hold it as long as possible and pray we miss something."

A deputy opened the door, ushering Hale inside. He wore a county jumpsuit, chains at his wrists and ankles, but his expression was sharper than the day before. Fear was still there, but stoic. Bracing, because he knew what was coming.

Hale sat. "You said there was something new."

Quinton took a slow breath. "Yes. Durant dropped it on us this morning. Something he claims 'just came in' from the digital forensics lab."

Cassidy opened the binder and slid a printed screenshot across the table.

Hale's eyes widened. "What is that?"

"A timestamped ping from your phone. From the night of the murder."

Hale's mouth fell open. "No. No, that's wrong. My phone was at my house. I was home. You have my building's security logs."

Cassidy pushed the page toward him on the table. "We do. But this shows your phone connected briefly to a public Wi-Fi node on the way to Price's townhouse at 10:17 p.m."

Hale shook his head violently. "That can't be. I wasn't there. I didn't go anywhere near Daniel's house that night."

Quinton steepled his fingers. "Is there any reason at all your phone could have pinged a router in that area?"

"No! It didn't leave my place. I was watching the storm coverage and trying to get through all my game tape before the power flickered off."

Quinton studied Hale. "Durant is calling it 'digital presence.' He'll argue you drove by. That you went to confront Price. That the storm gave cover."

Hale stared at the screenshot as if willing it to dissolve. "Someone must have taken my phone. Or cloned it. Or spoofed something. Because that is not my phone."

Quinton watched him carefully, reading every flicker in his eyes. Fear. But there didn't seem to be deceit.

Cassidy tapped another page. "And there's more. They've

matched the time of the ping to a gap, one they highlighted, between the texts you sent to others from your phone."

Quinton nodded. "They're trying to say that the gap was because you were driving to see him."

Hale covered his mouth with his hand. "No... no... this is twisted. This is manufactured."

Quinton's jaw tightened. "We agree. And the timing, Durant sitting on this. That's strategic. He waited as long as possible without incurring the wrath of Judge Blaylock."

Cassidy pursed her lips grimly. "This is the cleanest piece of circumstantial evidence they've produced. Not conclusive. But persuasive if they frame it right."

Hale's voice was barely a whisper. "Can they do that? Use something that isn't true?"

Quinton nodded. "Yes. They can present it if it's real. But we can attack it."

Hale looked at him desperately. "How?"

"By proving what they have isn't what they think it is." Quinton flipped the page. "There's one oddity. The ping lasted less than three seconds. That's unusually short for a device truly in range and engaged."

Hale leaned in.

"We're pulling in an expert. Someone who will explain to the jury how unreliable these micro-pings can be."

Hale closed his eyes, gathering himself. "This is too much. Every time we talk, there's something new and worse."

Quinton softened his voice. "That's why we stay ahead of them. Durant is trying to give the appearance of inevitability."

Hale took a shaky breath. "Do you believe me?"

Quinton met his eyes but didn't respond.

Cassidy's tone was low and solid. "Of course we do."

Outside the door, the bailiff called for all attorneys to assemble in Judge Blaylock's court for the pretrial docket call.

Quinton stood, gathering the new pages. "Let's go deal with Durant. And let's see what else he thinks he's hiding."

Quinton knew the truth: This was only the beginning, and Sawyer Durant had just shown his teeth.

Later that day, Quinton's office felt tighter than usual, the heavy air pressing against the windows. Files lay open across the conference table, and the overhead light hummed like it was nervous.

Dart shoved the door open with his elbow, carrying a Whataburger bag in one hand and a giant soda in the other.

"Man, you look beat. Durant rainin' on yo' parade again?"

Quinton gestured at the door. "Close it. You need to see this."

Dart kicked it shut, the sound echoing. "A'right then. Hit me."

Quinton slid the supplemental discovery packet across the table. "They dropped this on us in the second package. Claims it 'just came in' from HPD's digital forensics unit."

Dart set his soda down and squinted at the folder like it might bite him. "Digital forensics? What kinda mess we talkin'?"

"A ping from Hale's phone."

Dart's eyebrows shot up. "A ping? Where?"

"Near Price's townhouse. Public Wi-Fi node. Timestamped at 10:17 p.m. the night of the murder. Three seconds."

Dart let out a low whistle and finally picked up the packet. "Three seconds ain't much... but ain't nothin' either."

"It's flimsy but adds to the evidence."

Dart took a drag on the soda. "Yeah. Flimsy's still evidence if a jury's squintin' at it the right way."

Quinton crossed his arms. "Exactly, but Hale says he wasn't there. Actually, he says the phone wasn't there."

Dart looked up sharply. "You sure about that? 'Cause this right here says maybe he was drivin' by at least."

"Says he didn't go anywhere near Price's place."

"They all say that," Dart shook his head. "Look, I ain't sayin' the man's a saint, but he might be hidin' the truth."

"True. Durant's gonna wave this around like he found the Holy Grail."

"The jury won't like it."

Quinton felt irritation flare in his chest. "I know, and it's late to be turning it over now. Hale says he's not lying."

Dart shrugged. "Hey, maybe he ain't. Maybe he is. Ain't my job to believe him. My job's to verify."

Quinton stiffened. "Are you suggesting he killed him?"

"I'm suggestin'," Dart said, pointing with the packet, "that storm night, he texts all these people, then there's a big ol' gap in the messages. His phone pings by Price's house. No forced entry. Door gets opened by someone he knows. You stack that up, it ain't exactly sunshine."

Quinton nodded. "It's circumstantial, but we both know circumstantial's just the warm-up band for 'guilty,' if Durant plays it right."

"Yep."

Quinton paced to the window, staring at the slick streets below. He hated this, being on defense before the trial even started.

He turned back. "I need you to investigate this ping. Hard."

Dart cracked his neck. "What you want? Router logs, Wi-Fi node specs, maybe who the damn thing belongs to? I can dig through all that."

"Yes. All of it. And look into interference from the storm,

device cloning, MAC spoofing. Any way this could have been faked or misread."

Dart smirked. "So, you're thinkin' somebody set him up?"

"I'm thinking that nothing about this case is lining up clean. Durant sitting on this until now? That's not incompetence. That's strategy. I also want you to dig deeper into the way these sports agents get their clients. How and why."

Dart gathered the copies, stuffing them into his bag. "A'right, I'll pull the threads. But listen, if I find somethin' ugly? Somethin' that points right at him?"

Quinton met his eyes. "Then you tell me. All of it."

After Dart left, the office felt colder, the case heavier. Quinton stared at the three-second ping printout laying on his desk. The evidence, stacked neatly on the table, didn't give a damn what he believed. And with juries, he knew phone data was tricky. Folks believe it because it's shiny. He knew he'd be fighting an uphill climb if it was real.

14

———————

Silver Jamail, looking radiant, arrived precisely on time. She always did.

The years had softened nothing. Her silver hair was swept back neatly, her posture still perfect, her presence capable of silencing a room without effort. The kind of woman who never raised her voice because she never had to.

Quinton stood when she entered. He walked to her and took both of her hands in his. His fondness for her was evident.

"Hello, Silver."

"Quinton," she squeezed his hands, warm but measured. "You look thinner."

"Occupational hazard."

Quinton had been mentored by Silver Jamail at the request of Q's father, Judge Sirus Bell. Suffice it to say she was complicit in Quinton's fraud on the State Bar of Texas and City of Houston without knowing it. She had been a close friend and cohort of Judge Bell before he died and after his death, she shared the co-trustee position with Quinton under his last will and testament.

Quinton acknowledged the history, and the warmth they shared over it, but knew they would never be close in the way that caused intimacy and whispered secrets.

Silver smiled, then rested her hand on the shoulder of the young man beside her.

"This is my grandson, Evan."

Evan Jamail stepped forward awkwardly and shook hands with Quinton. He was tall, broad-shouldered, dressed like a college kid who had grabbed the nicest thing he could find. His eyes darted around the office taking measure of the room and following the lead of his grandmother.

Quinton gestured toward the chairs. "Have a seat."

Silver remained standing for a moment, taking in the office. She noted the smaller footprint but acknowledged the understated furnishings. She approved without saying so.

Then she sat. "I wouldn't come to you unless I trusted you completely. And I wouldn't bring Evan unless he needed more than a good lawyer."

Quinton looked at Evan. "Tell me what this is about."

Silver turned to Evan and nodded her consent for him to answer.

Evan cleared his throat. "My girlfriend, Monica, and I had a fight in my dorm room. We were arguing. It got a little out of hand. She started recording me on her phone. I didn't know it at first, then she said she was going to call the cops and play it for them."

"And?" Quinton said.

"I knocked the phone out of her hand," Evan admitted quickly. "I didn't think. It just happened."

Silver's expression didn't change, but Quinton saw the tension beneath it.

Evan sensed it too. "She ran into the hallway crying. Campus police showed up."

"And the accusation?"

Evan hesitated.

"She told them I tried to strangle her."

The words landed hard.

Quinton studied Evan carefully. Not the panic. Not the fear. The sincerity beneath both.

"Did you touch her neck?"

"No," Evan said, almost too quickly. "I swear. I never did that. I wouldn't."

Evan gave Silver a beseeching look. Silver leaned forward. "There were documented marks. Redness. EMS was called."

"Did they call the local police?"

"Yes, but there were no witnesses. No one in the dorm came forward to even complain of noise."

"Which won't stop them from charging."

"Yes. That's how I got arrested. They let me go to my grandmother's."

"I went to the arraignment and bail hearing to get him out that day, but I can't handle the case past this point. We need someone with criminal law experience. We need you."

Quinton acknowledged the compliment with a nod. "There is a strong inclination to believe the woman in this situation."

Evan's head snapped up. "But I didn't do it. I admit to hitting her hand to knock out the phone. That's all."

"That's not the issue."

Evan looked genuinely confused.

Quinton leaned back. "You're about to learn something unpleasant. Accusations like this don't require proof the way you think they do. They require timing. Framing. And a story someone wants to hear."

Silver watched her grandson closely. "He doesn't understand. He was raised to believe that honesty resolves conflict."

Quinton gave a faint smile. "It should. Unfortunately, it doesn't always."

Evan frowned. "She was mad. That's all. It was stupid stuff. We'd been fighting all day."

"I understand, but stupid stuff becomes motive. Especially when someone feels embarrassed. Or threatened. Or decides they need leverage."

"I'm starting to see that."

Quinton addressed Silver. "What did you think of the girl?"

"I've never met her."

Evan looked at Silver. "It wasn't that serious a relationship."

"What was the fighting about?"

Quinton waited. Silence had always been one of his better tools.

"I wanted to break up. She came over to get her things from my dorm room and then picked a fight. She wouldn't leave. I got a box and started putting her things into it. That's when she started the recording, I think."

"Have you spoken to her since? Apologized? Maybe she was just hurt and wanted revenge."

Evan shifted in his seat. "No. I haven't seen her. You think she'd take an apology?"

"I think it's too late to try. People lie most convincingly when they believe they've been wronged, even if they weren't."

Silver's lips pressed together.

"Campus police documented it as domestic violence. He was charged with assault with a deadly weapon."

Quinton kept his voice even. "Control will slip out of Evan's hands unless we take it back."

He picked up his legal pad and wrote a few notes. Monica's name, Evan's comments. Naive came to mind as he was documenting the meeting.

"Evan. From this moment forward, you don't try to explain

yourself to anyone. Not friends. Not professors. Not administrators."

"But—"

"No buts. You don't fix this by being reasonable. You fix it by being prepared for anything."

Evan nodded, shaken.

"If she contacts you, you don't respond. If anyone asks you questions, you say one sentence: *I'm represented by counsel.* Then you stop."

Silver placed her hand over Evan's.

"He's never dealt with someone who weaponizes emotion."

Quinton met her eyes. "Learning the hard way."

Silver studied him for a long moment. "You'll take the case?"

"Of course I'll take it."

Evan exhaled in relief. Silver did not.

15

———

Quinton sat at his desk, alone and surrounded by stacks of motions and a half-empty coffee cup. He was reading the same sentence in a case file for the third time when someone pounded on his outer office door hard enough to shake the frame.

Quinton went through to the reception area and saw Dart standing beyond the glass doors. He turned the key at the bottom of the right side and opened it.

"Hey, Dart. Why didn't you use your key?"

Dart barged in, cheeks flushed from the humidity outside, a Big Gulp in one hand and a folder in the other.

"I left it in the car downstairs. Besides, I learned a long time ago not to surprise people late at night. Even friendly ones."

"Well, come on in."

They both moved past Anna's empty desk into Quinton's inner office.

"I got somethin' for you," Dart said, dropping into the chair across from Quinton's desk without waiting for an invitation.

Quinton sat. "Tell me."

Dart slapped a folder on the desk. "First off, I didn't figure this out alone. I ain't a tech guy. Just what I learned in PI school. Hell, I can barely send a PDF without breakin' somethin'."

Quinton raised an eyebrow. "That sounds accurate."

"Yeah, well." Dart jerked his chin toward the reception area. "Anna hooked me up with her buddy. Some cyber-whatever dude that fixes systems for corporate folks. Name's Miles. Real smart. Talks fast. Kinda jittery. Wears them tiny round glasses like he's in a hacker movie."

Quinton tried not to smile. "Okay. What did Miles find?"

"So, I bring him the router logs the prosecution gave us," Dart said, leaning forward. "Miles takes one look and goes, 'Oh yeah, this is garbage.' Just real blunt, like he was insulted someone printed it for him."

Quinton opened the folder. "Garbage how?"

Dart scratched his jaw. "Well, I ain't gonna pretend I understood all his mumblin'. He kept sayin' stuff like packet drift and signal ghosts and auto-handshake errors. The gist is this: The ping ain't reliable. Router's too old, storm messed it up, and it coulda logged Hale's phone last time he was in the area then got hung up. It might have happened without him bein' anywhere near Price's house or that salon on that night."

Quinton looked sharply at him. "Salon?"

"Yeah, that's the real kicker," Dart said, warming up. "Miles tells me the only way to know for sure is to see the actual router. The hardware. So, I go down there. He told me it was Luna's Luxe Cuts in Sharpstown. It's on the way to Price's townhouse." He smirked. "Fancy name for a rundown place with purple walls and a picture of Dolly Parton taped to the register."

"And the router?"

"Oh, man." Dart shook his head. "Thing's sittin' on a windowsill, covered in hair and spray dust, plugged into a power strip with a lava lamp. Barely hangin' on. Looks like it came free with a box of cereal and might catch on fire any minute."

Dart opened his phone and showed Quinton a photo of the mangy device.

Quinton's brows lifted. "Did you speak with the manager?"

"Yep. Lady named Missy. Sweet as pie, talked my ear off. She lives in the back of the salon. Says the power flickered on and off all night durin' the storm. Router kept rebootin'. Miles told me every time it turned back on, it broadcast this wide-open signal tryin' to reconnect to anything it ever saw before. He said that's typical for outdated equipment."

Quinton sat forward, interest sharpening. "Which means?"

"Means Hale's phone coulda been miles away, sittin' on his damn coffee table, and the router still might've grabbed its little handshake from the past and logged it for a couple seconds. Not in current time. Like an echo of a prior connection."

Quinton exhaled, stunned but relieved. "Dart, that gives us a plausible alternative explanation. And a simple one."

"Simple-ish," Dart held up a finger. "That tech guy, Miles? He can explain it clean. Real clean. Said he's testified before. Loves tellin' juries how old tech screws stuff up. He'll break it down so even the folks who don't know Wi-Fi from pickle ball can get it."

"How much?"

"He's workin' up a bid. Says he'll give you the Anna Van Buren discount."

"Whatever it costs, it's worth it. So, you're sure the ping isn't solid?"

"Hell no. Damn thing's like a drunk without his glasses tryin' to read a license plate durin' a hurricane. Durant's makin' it sound fancy, but it's junk."

"Circumstantial evidence. Not so solid."

"Exactly." Dart took a big swig through the straw in his drink.

Quinton nodded slowly, then decisively. "We can use this. If the jury believes our witness, Miles, the prosecution loses their clean timeline."

Dart leaned back, satisfied. "Exactly. And Missy said the storm knocked her whole block goofy that night. Miles says even if Hale *had* been drivin' somewhere nearby, there's no way to prove the router still grabbed his signal. Ain't proof of nothin'."

Quinton closed the folder. "Good work. Really good."

Dart shrugged, though he was clearly pleased. "Hey, I just talked to the people who knew what they were doin'. But thanks." He stood and tossed the empty cup in the trash can. You want Miles to come in sometime? He said he'd love to yammer about this stuff. Actually, seemed excited."

"Yes. We'll need him. I'll let you know when I'm ready."

"Alright then. I'll line it up." Dart reached the door, paused, and glanced back. "This don't clear Hale completely, but it sure pokes a hole in Durant's big bad theory."

Quinton nodded. "Big crack. And cracks are how we make the whole damn wall come down."

The attorney meeting room in the Harris County courthouse always felt like it had been carved out of concrete and forgotten. Gray walls, fluorescent lights too bright to think under.

Quinton waited until a guard brought Hale in. He looked bigger than the room allowed. His broad shoulders hunched slightly, jaw tight, eyes alert in the way Quinton was coming to recognize as learned vigilance rather than arrogance.

Hale sat across from him. "You said there was news," Hale's voice was low. Controlled.

"There is." Quinton opened his folder and slid a single page across the table. "This is about the phone ping. The one Durant claims put you near Daniel Price's house the night he was killed. It may be a reason."

Hale's eyes narrowed, not with hope, but caution. "How?"

"Dart tracked down a tech expert. Then, he went to a salon near Price's place. The shop has the Wi-Fi router the State's relying on."

Hale frowned. "I've never been in a salon near Daniel's house."

"You didn't need to be. The equipment is old. Cheap. It has echoes of past connections."

Hale exhaled slowly. "So that ping doesn't mean I was near his place that night."

"Not definitively, but it means your phone might not have been."

Hale nodded once. "Might not? I told you already, I was home."

"I need more than that. Walk me through that night again."

Hale looked down at his hands, then clasped them together. "The storm was bad. Flood warnings everywhere. I didn't go out. I heated up leftovers. Ate half of it. Watched the game footage until the power flickered."

"Your phone?"

"On the kitchen counter. Charging. I remember because when the lights went out for a second, it buzzed like it lost connection."

"Did you leave the apartment at all? Trash? Car? Balcony?"

"No," Hale said firmly. "Didn't even open the door."

"Any windows?" Quinton pressed.

Hale thought for a moment. "I stood near the living room window. Just watching the rain. That's it."

Quinton nodded. "Okay."

"Are they still going to say I was there?"

"They'll try. But now we can counter it."

Hale stared at the paper. "So, my phone could've been sitting on my counter."

"Yes."

"And it still shows that ping."

"Yes."

Something shifted in Hale's expression. Not relief exactly, but the loosening of a coil that had been wound too tight.

"I kept replaying it. That night. Thinking there had to be some moment I forgot. Some slip."

Slip is a strange word to use, Quinton thought.

"I believe you. But belief doesn't win trials. We need a clean, credible story. Details make it clean."

Hale looked up. "Their timeline—"

"—just cracked," Quinton finished.

The guard knocked twice on the door.

As Quinton stood, Hale added quietly, "Cassidy said you were the best lawyer."

Quinton paused, hand on the door and grinned. "She was right about that."

But as he stepped into the hallway, the feeling returned, that the case was still shifting, still hiding someone else's hand behind the evidence. Waiting.

16

———

Quinton stopped for coffee on his way to the office at his favorite brewhouse. He ordered a dark, hot cup from the brewmaster and found an empty table near the window, the morning light filtered through the glass in long, golden stripes. He pulled out his phone, scrolling through emails, sifting through text messages, always half expecting to see something like a name, a threat, a reminder that he wasn't as invisible as he hoped.

Anna had sent him a draft of the Evan Jamail campus police report as an attachment to an email. He decided to wait and review it when he got to the office.

A lovely young woman sat at a table over, typing away on a sleek laptop with a glowing piece of fruit on the back. Her hair fell in loose waves around her face, and when she looked up, her hazel eyes met his. She smiled, a warm, effortless thing that sent a rush of something dangerous through his chest. His breath hitched.

Quinton liked the look of her. More than he should. And worse, she seemed to like the look of him, too. His gut clenched, an icy dread cutting through the moment. The coffee he'd been anticipating turned bitter in his mouth before he even took a sip.

Not again. It always started like this. A glance. A connection. The possibility of something real. And then it ended in blood, in loss, in another life ruined just because they had the misfortune of knowing him.

He could still see Joannes's face in the courtroom, her eyes wide with terror as the gunfire shattered the world between them. Before that, in New York, his best friend and protege, Michael, had taken a bullet meant for him. He hadn't deserved that. Neither of them had.

Quinton jerked his gaze back to his phone, his fingers tightening around the device as if that alone could anchor him. He forced himself to breathe, to push away the sharp-edged memories that threatened to drag him under.

He had always been prone to self-reliance from the time as a young man in Houston with a single mother, but at this stage, he felt so lonely.

When his name was called, he stood too quickly, nearly knocking his chair askew. He grabbed his coffee, his movements sharp, controlled. On the way out, he purposefully avoided looking at the woman again. For her sake, she needed to forget their eyes ever met.

Quinton stepped out of the coffee shop into the late afternoon heat, the bell above the door jangling once before falling quiet behind him.

He thought of the woman. She'd been sitting alone by the window, sunlight catching the drape of her hair and rim of her mug, a paperback by John Grisham open but unread.

He'd turned away first. It wasn't disinterest. It was discipline due to regret.

Quinton adjusted the file tucked under his arm and scanned the street out of habit.

Two lanes of traffic. Parked cars, nose to curb. A delivery truck idling at the corner, exhaust ticking in the heat. He crossed toward his car.

That was when the engine roared. A dark SUV burst from a side street, too fast, wrong angle, tires screaming as it cut across traffic. A horn blared. Someone shouted.

Quinton stopped short. Just long enough to recognize intent. The truck jumped the curb. It missed him by inches.

The oversized side mirror clipped his shoulder, spinning him sideways as air and noise exploded around him. He hit the pavement hard and rolled, skin burning through his sleeve.

The truck didn't slow. It fishtailed back into the street, clipped a parked sedan, and vanished through the intersection against the light. For a beat, the world was noise. Brakes, horns, a woman screaming somewhere behind him.

Quinton pushed himself up from the grime, pulse slamming in his ears. His car sat ten feet away, untouched. The concrete where he'd been standing was scarred with rubber streaks and fresh paint chips.

An accident, the rational part of his brain offered. His body refused it. He somehow reached his car, opened the door, and slid into the driver's seat, locking it automatically. His shoulder throbbed.

Across the street, the coffee shop door stood open. The pretty woman was there now, one hand pressed to her chest, eyes locked on him.

"You okay?" someone on the sidewalk called. Quinton nodded once and looked away.

He started the engine, then froze. On the passenger seat lay a folded card. He stared at it, breath shallow. Quinton picked it up slowly and unfolded it. Two words, written in block letters with deliberate pressure.

TOO SLOW.

His jaw tightened. The driver hadn't tried to kill him. Whoever it was had wanted him to feel it. They wanted him to understand that distance, locked doors, and caution weren't enough. That someone had opened his locked car and left a message.

Quinton dropped the note onto the seat and pulled into traffic, eyes already working mirrors, intersections, reflections. Old instincts snapped into place. In the rearview mirror, the coffee shop shrank away. The woman was still standing there, small now, already part of a life he couldn't afford to touch.

This was why. The reason he could not know anyone. Whatever had just entered his world wasn't interested in chance encounters or collateral damage. He had a wave of nostalgia for his life in New York. "Only The Lonely" by Roy Orbison began to play on Sirius XM. If he had noticed, he might have laughed. Maybe.

Someone was spreading fear, and they had accomplished their goal.

The note lay folded on the passenger seat now, where he had found it. He had not put it in his pocket. He wanted to see it. To make sure it was real.

He drove without direction, through lights he did not remember turning green. Past storefronts he did not register. A left where he normally took a right. A right where he should have merged onto the freeway.

His mind replayed the moment at the coffee shop. The paper resting there like an accusation.

He always locked his car doors. *How did someone get in? It's not that hard if you know what you're doing. Who knows what they're doing?*

He checked the mirrors again, though he had been doing that every thirty seconds. A white SUV two cars back. A sedan drifting in the next lane. Nothing steady. Nothing obvious. No truck. Still.

He drove on in a kind of muted haze. Streets shifted from commercial to residential without his noticing. The buildings lowered. Trees thickened. Lawns widened. The city noise thinned into neighborhood quiet.

He did not realize where he was until he slowed for a familiar curve in the road. The magnolia tree came into view first. Broad leaves. Heavy branches. Taller than he remembered. He lifted his foot from the accelerator.

The house sat exactly where it always had. White brick. Blue shutters. A shallow porch with two steps and a railing he had replaced the year he bought it. The azaleas along the walkway were trimmed differently now, neater, less wild than his mother had kept them.

He had purchased the house in the Heights for her the year he won his first big case in New York. The first year the verdicts came in heavy and fast. The year his name began to circulate in Manhattan corridors with a mixture of admiration and resentment.

He had wanted her safe. Close to doctors. Close to neighbors who would look in on her. He had wired the money from a conference room overlooking the Hudson, then flown down to surprise her with the keys.

She had stood in the driveway and cried, one hand over her mouth, the other gripping his sleeve as if she might float away.

He recalled the times she'd scrimped and worked to give him as much life as she could. He eased the SUV to the curb now, engine idling.

She had lived here until she died a few years later. A stroke in the front bedroom. He had been back in New York at the time. Quick, the doctors said. Merciful.

He had visited regularly before her death. Flights down for holidays. Weekends when the noise of New York grew too loud. He would sit at her kitchen table, telling her about judges and juries and cases she half understood. She would nod, proud but practical. A crucifix hung on the wall in most rooms. Her deep faith on display.

"Are you eating enough?" she always asked.

"Yes, ma'am. It's the swimming. I keep it up to manage the stress."

"How much stress?"

"Don't worry, the exercise works."

Following the funeral and reception, he had stood on this same street while the last of the cars pulled away. After sorting the estate, he had locked the door behind him and left Texas without looking back. He had not returned. Not for years.

Not until he came back searching for Q. He had to have help. Someone, anyone. He had needed to find his childhood friend. The one person who knew him before law school, before New York, after Byron's death became a headline.

Of course, he had not found Q. He had found Judge Bell instead. Q's father had aged into authority the way some men age into bitterness. The first time they met again, the judge's eyes had glimmered with excitement. He was thrilled to have a connection to Q, even if it was only from a visit with his son's best friend, Byron.

"You always did run far," the judge had said. "I wondered if you would ever circle back."

Circle back. Full circle. Quinton stared at the house now, at the front window where his mother used to stand when she heard his rental car in the driveway. He could almost see her silhouette; hand raised in a small wave.

He felt so lonely. So very alone. He missed her smell, her sweet voice, her perfect pimento cheese recipe and how she smiled when he asked for more. She always wanted a grandchild. How could he ever risk bringing a wife, much less a child, into his dilemma. Would he forever be alone?

The note on the passenger seat caught his eye. He gulped then looked at the house again. Different curtains. A child's scooter tipped on its side near the porch. New life inside walls that once held his mother's laugh, her cough, the smells of the wonderful nourishment he relied on.

He felt the old weight settle in his chest. The one he had buried under court filings and cross-examinations and a new name.

Someone had opened his car door. Close enough to place a message that said they knew where he was, where he went, who he was and that they could get to him at any time. His grip tightened on the steering wheel.

A car passed behind him, slow enough that he felt its presence. He checked the mirror. A man glanced over, curious at the SUV idling in front of a house that was not his.

Ordinary. Probably.

He put the vehicle in drive but did not press the gas. For a moment he let himself sit there, suspended between then and now. Between the son who bought this house out of pride and love, and the man who returned under a different name, hunting ghosts.

Then he eased away from the curb, watching the magnolia tree growing smaller in the rearview mirror.

17

Quinton assembled the team in the conference room with Anna sitting in the corner taking notes. Mo, Cassidy, Dart, and Quinton sat around the table sorting through documents and tapping on their laptops.

Quinton looked up from a folder he had open. "Okay. Today, we begin to sort the facts and plan our strategy on the Hale case."

"Dart and Anna's friend, Miles, have put a hole in the prosecution's biggest piece of evidence by knocking out the phone ping, but there's a lot of circumstantial bits left for us to tear down."

Mo looked around the table. "Our biggest problem. If it wasn't Hale, then who was it?"

Dart grunted. "We have to do their job for them and find the real killer?"

Mo nodded. "The jury sure would feel better if they had somebody else to pin it on."

Cassidy joined the discussion. "Have anyone in mind?"

Quinton gestured. "No, but Hale might. I'd like for you and

Mo to head over to the jail tomorrow and brainstorm with him. See if anyone pops up as a possible suspect. Did Price piss off anyone else he was representing? Did Hale see anything unusual when Price was around the team?"

Mo nodded. Cassidy nodded. "On it."

"I'll visit with Coach Brown of the Wildcatters and see if he can shed any light on Hale's behavior."

Dart cleared his throat. "What do you wan' me to do?"

Quinton pointed to the front of the room. "Work with Anna to set up some erasure boards and start with the list of circumstantial evidence. Then, we'll start picking at the list one at a time."

"Okay. Glad we got a plan."

As the room began to prepare to leave, Quinton held up his hand. "There's one last thing, and it doesn't leave this room."

It was as if a wet blanket had been thrown over all of them.

"Price had discovered that Hale is gay."

Cassidy sucked in a breath. Obviously, Hale had not told her as promised. "Is that what you didn't want to go into before?"

"Yes, and I'm sorry about that. I needed to make sure it needed to be revealed. Now, I think it does. Price was holding Hale hostage with the information, and it needs to go into your thinking as you evaluate the case. However, I don't want anyone to research anything that could lead to the prosecution finding out. So far, there's no evidence that they know."

Mo looked stricken. "What if they do?"

"That's why I'm telling you. If they spring it on us, I don't want you all to be caught by surprise."

"Was he out and dating?"

"Barely. He apparently had a few close friends, but nothing too public."

"How did Price know?"

"Caught him coming home from a date one night, so Hale says. There might be more to it. Hale says Price had him followed and investigated. If those records were in Price's townhouse, we'd have received them by now. So, who was the investigator and where are the records, if any?"

Dart looked at his notes. "There's nothing in the financials that shows he was paying a PI. Might have been cash off the books."

"Dig deeper, but cautiously."

18

Quinton had an appointment with Hale's coach at the Wildcatters' headquarters located on the Loop between his office and east of downtown Houston. He hoped it would shed some light on the situation between Hale and Price and maybe open the door to some insight about Hale and the type of man he was.

Quinton presented his driver's license at the main gate to GulfTex Stadium and was instructed to park in the visitors' lot by the entrance to the corporate offices. With the season over and the players on partial leave until summer training at The Greenbriar Sports Complex in West Virginia, there were few cars in the parking lot and little activity on the campus.

Quinton placed a lanyard with a visitor's pass around his neck and grabbed his briefcase. He went to the door marked with the Wildcatters' logo and the word Office, as he'd been instructed.

He had spoken to Cassidy at length about Hale to become familiar with his disposition, but he wanted more nuance into the man and how he operated.

Quinton knew from Dart's research that the team Hale played for in Hawaii was not the NFL. It was not even close. The stadiums were smaller, the budgets thin, the crowds loyal but limited. Scouts came rarely, chasing someone else besides Hale. Everyone knew where he stood on the food chain. He was good enough to dominate on Saturdays and invisible on Sundays.

What he did have was a reputation for violence. Hale played linebacker the way a storm hits an island. Fast off the edge. Relentless through the gap. He did not just tackle. He arrived. Quarterbacks felt him before they saw him. Coaches warned opposing offenses to account for number fifty-two, even when they knew it would not help.

He led the semi-pro league in tackles. He broke plays that were drawn up as touchdowns. He forced fumbles when hands were already reaching for the ball. He played like someone who knew he was running out of chances.

The call from the mainland did not come during the season. It came after. Quiet. Almost casual. An assistant defensive coach with the Houston Wildcatters had been sent west to evaluate a different prospect. That prospect left the game early with a hamstring issue. Hale stayed on the field and drew his attention.

The film did not lie. The scout watched Hale shoot gaps that should not have existed. He watched guards miss assignments because Hale had already moved. He watched linemen double him and still fail to slow him down.

The Wildcatters were rebuilding on defense. They needed speed. They needed aggression. They needed someone cheap enough to take a chance on with the cap line approaching.

Hale was invited to camp. He arrived in Houston with no guarantees. Training camp was brutal. Veterans tested him. Coaches ignored him. Roster math worked against him.

It was reported that Hale did not complain. He did not talk. He hit. Every drill became an audition. Every rep looked like it might be the last one he would ever get. He learned the playbook faster than expected. He stayed late. He asked questions without ego. When he made mistakes, he corrected them quickly. The Wildcatters decided to keep him on.

Preseason games gave him his opening. He forced a fumble on a kickoff unit. He stuffed a third down run on a goal line stand. He chased down a quarterback who thought the edge was safe.

Broadcasters started saying his name more often. Hale came off the bench like weather. Sudden and disruptive. Someone in the booth said it first. Here comes the Halestorm. Local announcers picked up the moniker Halestorm as a joke at first, then the storm references stuck. Wind. Rain. Pressure. Momentum. Every big hit added to it.

The nickname stuck. Fans loved it. Reporters loved it more. A last name that begged for metaphor. A style of play that earned it.

By the time final cuts came, the decision was simple. Hale made the roster not because he fit a scheme but because he changed momentum. The Wildcatters' defense gained an edge they had not planned for. Energy. Fear. Uncertainty.

Hale became a starter faster than anyone expected. He earned it snap by snap. The Halestorm was no longer a novelty. It was a problem offenses had to plan around.

In the reception area, Quinton shook hands with Coach Brown. "I won't take long. I know you're busy."

Zack Brown was a large man with a head full of hair and thighs as big as watermelons. Quinton knew he had played defense back in the day before he turned to coaching. Quinton wasn't starstruck, but something close. He walked through the hallways of awards and photographs of great football players and tried to keep his mouth from gaping open.

"No problem. Come on back. Would you like some coffee or a Dr Pepper? Water? I'd offer Topo Chico, that's my favorite, but as you've probably heard, there's a shortage, and we're all out."

"No, thanks. Look at all these trophies. Do you ever get used to it?"

Brown chuckled. "Not really. It's a lot to ignore." He pointed to a chair in a conversation pit and sat on the sofa across from Quinton.

"As I told you on the phone, I'm here to see if there's anything you know that will help my client. He speaks highly of you."

Brown paused for a long moment. The Wildcatters' logo blurred on the wall behind him. He sat with his hands folded, the way he always did when he chose his words carefully.

"I do not pretend to understand what Marcus Hale is dealing with right now, but I do know the athlete. And I know the kind of player he has always been."

He paused, eyes dropping for a moment before he looked back up at Quinton.

"By the time Marcus Hale left Hawaii, he had already learned a hard truth about defensive football. Talent alone was not enough. It never had been. What mattered was violence with purpose and the willingness to keep moving when the rest of the field wanted you to stop."

Quinton studied the man. *Was this insight or publicity hype?*

"From Hawaii to Houston, from obscurity to Sunday nights, Hale did not arrive quietly. He arrived like the Halestorm. Fast. Relentless. And impossible to ignore."

"As a person or as a player?" Quinton wanted to ask if Coach Brown knew or suspected Hale was gay, but he didn't dare.

"That is not just how he played. That is how he lived every day in this building. First in. Last out. Accountable. Respectful. He earned the name Halestorm because he brought everything he had to every snap, and he never backed down from hard work. It breaks my heart to see him in trouble with the law. I believe in due process. I believe the truth will come out. And until it does, I will stand by him."

"Any insight into what motivated him?"

"More like drove him. Most guys in the NFL play for family, or love of the game, or even the money. Hale played from a deeper place. I was never able to fully put my finger on what or where his drive came from, but it was profound and intense."

Interesting. "Was it sinister or sporting?"

"I have no idea."

"If I need a character witness, can I count on you?"

"Absolutely."

After a few more questions, it was a quick wrap-up. *Don't hang around when you get what you're after.*

19

The legal team reconvened in the war room at Quinton's office to bring the parts of their assignments together.

The late-afternoon light through the glass doors had turned gray and flat, pressing against the glass. Traffic murmured below. Inside, the air carried the smell of coffee that had gone cold.

Quinton locked the outer office door himself. That alone told everyone this was not a casual meeting.

Cassidy was in the chair to Quinton's right, blazer off, laptop on, legal pad already half full. Mo claimed the seat across from her, posture straight, pen aligned with intent. Dart leaned against the wall near the window, one ankle crossed over the other, a Big Gulp sweating onto a coaster Anna had slid beneath it without comment.

Anna stood in the corner near the credenza, tablet in hand, fingers moving quietly. She knew when to manage things and when to disappear into the background.

Quinton didn't sit. He rested his palms on the table and looked at each of them in turn.

Mo Powers was first to speak.

"We went to the jail," she said, sliding her notebook toward the center of the table. "Hale was more focused today. Less defensive."

Cassidy nodded. "He'd clearly been thinking. Maybe got some sleep."

Quinton sat, leaning back in his chair. "And?"

Mo did not look at Cassidy before answering. "He reported that Daniel Price had other clients who were unhappy. In particular two of the Wildcatters. A rookie wide receiver who claims Price steered him into a bad endorsement deal. Really hurt his reputation. And a veteran linebacker whose contract negotiations stalled after Price pushed too hard. He never got another chance."

Dart shifted in his chair. "That common knowledge?"

Mo responded. "Within the team, but not publicly. Hale said the locker room had been tense the week before the murder. Price had shown up at practice unannounced. Twice."

Quinton's brow furrowed. "That unusual?"

"Hale said agents don't usually hang around the facility unless they're closing something or scouting for new clients."

Anna's pen scratched faster.

"Hale said he knew there were problems on other teams, but he didn't have names."

Quinton looked at Dart. "It's already on my list."

Mo flipped a page in her file. "There's more. Hale said Price had been arguing with someone in the players' parking lot three nights before he died. Hale couldn't see who it was. Just heard raised voices."

Dart lifted a brow. "Convenient."

Cassidy shot him a look. "He didn't offer it until we pressed him. That makes it less convenient."

Quinton tapped his finger against the arm of his chair. "Did he recognize the voice?"

Mo fielded the question. "No. Only Price's."

Quinton looked around the room for the next bit of information.

Dart leaned forward. "All right. My turn."

He set the Big Gulp on the coaster again and pulled a sheet of paper from a file folder.

"I ran down those two disgruntled clients. The rookie's broke. The endorsement deal tanked. But he's in California this week. Confirmed. Flight records and team media appearances."

"Solid alibi?" Quinton asked.

"Solid enough for now."

"And the veteran linebacker?"

Dart shrugged. "He's got motive. Price was tryin' to force him into a trade. It didn't work out, and the guy was left with no team at all. The guy's built like a tank and doesn't scare easy. Teammates say he'd fight you to your face, not in a house in the dark of night."

Quinton allowed himself the smallest smile. "Not all killers look like killers."

Dart grinned. "Fair enough. I'm working on his alibi."

Mo turned a page in her notebook. "There's something else. Hale said it was common knowledge that he and Price weren't getting along."

Cassidy stiffened almost imperceptibly. "He said no one knew the details. Price suggested Hale owed him loyalty."

The room quieted.

Anna stopped writing.

Quinton's jaw tightened. "Did Hale elaborate?"

Mo fielded the question. "No. He shut down."

Quinton leaned in. "All right. That might explain why police zeroed in on Hale. If they heard about the discord."

Dart muttered, "There it is."

Quinton ticked off the reasons on his fingers.

"Public argument history. Control issues. Financial leverage. It's still not wrapped and tied with a bow." Quinton folded his arms. "But, here's the problem. All of that cuts both ways."

Dart tilted his head. "How so?"

"If Price was exerting control, and he was squeezing Hale, that could be motive. But, if there was more than one player at odds with him, why is Hale the one on trial?"

Anna resumed writing. Cassidy swallowed.

Mo's eyes sharpened. "So, we widen the circle. Show the discord was not unusual to Hale."

"Exactly. Even with the alibis, it shows a pattern of bullying. We don't just defend Hale. We expose Price."

Cassidy looked uncertain. "We have to be careful not to look like we're smearing a murder victim."

Quinton agreed. "We won't smear. We'll contextualize."

Dart gave a low chuckle. "Sounds like lawyer talk for takin' him apart politely."

Quinton ignored the comment. "Anything on forensics?"

Dart shook his head. "Nothing new since the phone ping. They're leanin' heavy on circumstantial and narrative. They want a story the jury can swallow."

Mo closed her notebook. "Then let's give them a better one."

Quinton stood and walked to the window overlooking the Loop. Brake lights streaked red beneath him. The city moved, indifferent.

"Here's where we are," he said without turning. "Police focused on Hale because he's visible. Because he had motive that fits on a headline. Because he's big enough to look dangerous. And because Price is dead and can't contradict anything. Dead men tell no tales."

He turned back toward the table. He pointed at Dart. "Dig deeper into Price's client list. All of it. Not just the big names. Assistants. Business managers. Anyone who might have felt cornered."

Dart nodded. "On it."

He turned to Mo and Cassidy. "Get into Price's financial records. I know Durant's office is holding something back. If there's anything there, I need to know now. Not in the middle of trial."

Everyone wrote their assignments down. "Send everything through Anna for the case file."

Anna looked up from her pad. "Do you want me to organize this by suspect matrix?"

"Yes," Quinton said. "Motive. Opportunity. Exposure risk. And who benefits most from Price being dead."

Dart looked up from his computer. "You mean other than our client?"

Cassidy froze, then closed her laptop. The team began gathering their papers.

"Let's get our story straight and meet again on Monday."

As they stood, Dart paused at the door. "You think we're missin' somethin' obvious?"

"Yes, I do. I feel it in my gut."

20

Dart stood in the doorway of Quinton's office, hands shoved into his jeans pockets. He took one look at Quinton's face and knew this wasn't a casual check-in.

"You got a new mess?"

"Yes. New client. College mess. Which means it's already worse than it looks."

Dart stepped in and nudged the door shut with his foot. "Those are my favorite. Everybody panics; nobody documents right."

Quinton slid a thin file across the desk. "Evan Jamail. Alleged assault and attempted strangulation. Campus police handled the initial response."

Dart raised an eyebrow. "Jamail?"

"Silver Jamail's grandson."

Dart whistled low. "That Jamail."

"That Silver," Quinton paced. "Which means this stays clean. No shortcuts. No assumptions. Budget is unlimited. She loves the kid."

"What do you want first?"

"Everything. But in the right order."

Dart sat, picked up a pen and legal pad and took notes.

"Campus police records. Full incident report. Dispatch logs. Body cam. Supplemental narratives. Any photographs, even the useless ones."

Dart appeared skeptical. "Campus cops are allergic to outside scrutiny."

"Which means they'll overcompensate in their paperwork. Sloppy certainty. I want it."

Dart nodded. "Got it. I may have to bribe some people to get the records."

"Do it but watch your back. No paper trail. Next, court records. And, we don't trust that Silver remembered to tell me everything. We need arraignment transcript. Bond hearing notes. Conditions of release, if any. Statement of charges exactly as filed. Not summarized."

"You're looking for drift," Dart said.

"I'm looking for inflation," Quinton said. "Language gets stronger every time it's retold."

Dart grinned. "Strangulation cases love adjectives."

"They love fear words. Pressure. Breath. Panic. Hands. I want to know who introduced them and when. Witness or cops?"

"Do we have a list of witnesses?"

"Start with what's in the campus files. I'll get the rest from the prosecution."

"Got it."

"I want it all. Hallway statements. RA report. Anyone who claims they heard something but didn't see anything. Especially those."

"Because they always remember more later."

"Because they're coached into it."

Dart shifted his weight. "You want the girlfriend's statement too, I assume."

"Every version. Initial oral statement. Written follow-up. Any edits. Any add-ons. Timestamps matter."

Dart nodded slowly. "College kid case. He probably thinks truth wins."

Quinton didn't smile.

"He's naive. And the system eats naive people alive."

"You think she's lyin'?"

"I think she's escalating. Those are different things. One is emotional. The other is strategic."

Dart considered that. "You want me to try to talk to her on the sly?"

"Not yet. We can't interfere with a witness or a complainant."

"Timeline?"

"Yesterday. This is still malleable. Once it hardens, it gets political."

Dart headed for the door, then paused. "Anything else?"

Quinton thought for a moment.

"Yes. See if campus security pulled hallway footage. Even if it doesn't show the room. I want entry times. Exit times. Who came running and who followed."

Dart nodded and stood. "Fear spreads."

"And narratives follow it."

Dart opened the door. "I'll shake the trees."

As he stepped out, Quinton added, "Dart?"

Dart turned and grinned.

"This isn't about proving Evan innocent. It's about proving the accusation unreliable."

Dart's grin faded. "Different war."

"Same battlefield."

After Dart left, Quinton sat down at his desk and opened Evan's file again. Young. Unprepared. Already labeled.

Outside, the city kept moving, indifferent as ever. Inside, Quinton started building the only thing that ever mattered in a case like this. The record.

21

The following Monday, Quinton reconvened the team to follow-up on the strategy meeting he'd held the week before. Each took the same seat as the last time, with Anna sitting in the corner taking notes.

Quinton stood, rolled his neck to get the kinks out and started.

"We're not meeting with Hale yet. That's intentional. This is where we say the things we can't say in front of him."

Cassidy nodded once. "We need a story that doesn't sound like spin."

"We need a story that explains the evidence better than the State's does," Mo added.

Cassidy started by summarizing her and Mo's conversation with Hale about who might have wanted Price dead to refresh everyone's recollection.

Next, Mo did what she did best, strategized. "At this stage, there are three possible areas to explore."

Quinton inclined his head. "Three alternate theories?"

Mo nodded. "Of sorts. We've settled on the three most plausible ideas. We'll try them out on you, then we'll tear down the weak ones ourselves before we choose what we'll take to court."

Quinton looked thoughtful for a full minute. "I like this plan. Let's begin."

Mo motioned to Cassidy, who went to the front of the room where Anna and Dart had set up an easel with an erasable board on it. She wrote: Theory One - Financial Fallout

"Daniel Price wasn't just an agent," Mo said. "He was a middleman with his hands in too many pockets. Athletes, investors, side deals. Somebody loses money, somebody panics."

Quinton folded his arms. "You're thinking a financial dispute escalated."

"Or a cleanup," Dart said. "Someone decides Price is more dangerous alive than dead."

Cassidy frowned. "That leans toward a professional hit."

"Not necessarily professional," Dart replied. "But deliberate."

Mo shook her head slowly. "The downside to this theory is that the scene doesn't support that. Too much rage at the murder scene."

Dart conceded with a nod.

Quinton tapped the table once. "We keep it on the board for now."

Below Theory One, Cassidy wrote: Theory Two - Misplaced Suspicion

Mo leaned back. "The State's version. Hale snaps. Personal motive. Private confrontation."

Cassidy exhaled through her nose. "Cops jump to conclusions."

Quinton tapped his pen on his legal pad. "Which ignores everything we know about Hale's and Price's intentions. Not enough motivation. Coach Brown told me Hale was not motivated by money and he had no family around. If he intended to kill Price, we don't know why."

Dart shook his head. "It's too convenient. Cops stumble upon Hale and stop looking for the real killer."

Quinton pointed at the board. "We've used this theory in other cases. It's a good one, but not great for this scenario."

Mo drew a line through her notes. "It doesn't survive much scrutiny."

Quinton didn't hesitate. "In summary, Hale is the easiest suspect, cops are lazy. Let's keep that one on the list too."

Cassidy wrote under Theory Two: Theory Three - The Other Client

The room shifted when Quinton read it off the board.

Mo straightened. "This is my favorite one." She stood, paced once, then stopped. "Price made a career out of leverage. Contracts, secrets, reputations. He represented people who had far more to lose than Hale."

Cassidy nodded slowly. "And he wasn't subtle about reminding them."

Dart picked up the thread. "With Hale's help, we've already identified three more former clients who accused Price of unprofessional tactics. Threats. Pressure. They all have alibis, but there may be more."

Mo leaned forward. "A disgruntled client explains the crime scene. Emotional. Personal. Uncontrolled."

"And it explains the timing," Quinton said. "Price could have been escalating pressure. Someone thought killing him would end the threat. This theory relies on Price being exactly who the evidence shows he was."

Mo tapped her pen on her front teeth. "And it lets us introduce names. Documents. Patterns of behavior."

Quinton sat down. "People with motive and opportunity who aren't sitting in a jail cell."

"So, which one do we like best?" Mo pointed at the board.

Quinton thought for a moment. "We eliminate the first. Too speculative. The second collapses under its own weight. We build on the third."

Cassidy closed her pad. "We'll still need to be careful not to victimize the victim."

"We won't. We'll put his conduct on trial."

Anna scribbled more notes.

The room went quiet for a moment.

Then Quinton said, "Good work. Now let's find the client who may have finally pushed back."

Dart looked at the board. "I'll keep digging."

Cassidy nodded. "I'll help you."

Mo nodded. "And I'll start shaping how we present it."

Quinton nodded once. "This is the defense. Now we prove it. Only one problem, it's exactly the case against Hale. Someone who was being squeezed by Price and decided to fight back."

The entire team froze and looked at him.

22

D art sat at the conference table in the war room at Quinton's law firm, a beam of late-afternoon sunlight slicing across the stacks of case files. He'd been clicking through public record databases for hours, looking for anything on Hale before he'd blown into Houston and became the Halestorm.

He started by digging deeper into Hale's background in Hawaii. His pre-NFL history checked out clean, almost too clean. Recruiting rankings. Combine stats. A spotless trail from his first snap at a Division I program in the Aloha State to his signing bonus with the Wildcatters.

But everything before age sixteen was practically blank.

No social media accounts under his name, or any variation of it. No tagged photos from middle school or youth leagues, or proud-parent Facebook posts about peewee championships. No newspaper clippings. No local awards banquets. Nothing.

It wasn't that the records were sealed. They just didn't seem to exist.

Dart leaned back in his chair and stared at the screen, the

blue glow reflecting off the empty Big Gulp cup on his desk. Kids with Hale's size and speed didn't come out of nowhere. They were noticed early. Chased. Tracked. There were camps, coaches, grainy photos taken on borrowed phones. Even the kids who didn't want attention still left footprints.

Hale had none.

Dart opened the bookmarked immigration research portals he'd learned about during his PI licensure classes. These were the ones an instructor called 'boring but gold.' He typed Hale's name into the search bar with variations of spelling and date ranges. For a moment, nothing. Then the screen populated.

A set of immigration documents dated years back. Dart clicked, pulse ticking up. A faded digital scan loaded. It was a humanitarian-processing file tied to the name Marcos Hale. He clicked and up popped a picture of a young man. Hard to identify.

He squinted at the photo attached to the file. Almost child-like Asian features. Devoid of polish, lacking vitality and life force, free from everything but bone and will.

The date of birth jumped out at him next. It didn't match the age on Hale's Texas ID or his Hawaiian ID. According to the record, this Marcos Hale was five years older than Halestorm claimed to be. No reason or details for redaction or refugee status.

He clicked around trying to go deeper but met a dead end. Either there were no more related documents, or they were blocked from public view.

Maybe it wasn't him. There must be more than one Marcus Hale.

Dart sat back for a long moment after the screen went blank. The immigration record stayed open in the corner of the monitor like something that had wandered in from the wrong story.

Maybe not the same man. Maybe just another Marcus Hale. Still. Odd.

Dart printed the screen anyway. He went down the hall to the work room where the printer hummed and spit out the page in slow jerks. Dart picked up the paper and studied the photograph again.

Young face. Hollow eyes. Hard to connect with the linebacker who flattened linebackers on Sunday afternoons.

Dart grabbed the page and walked down the short hallway to Quinton's office. The door stood half open. Quinton looked up as Dart entered.

"Whatcha got?"

Dart set the page on the desk.

"Something strange."

Quinton slid the paper closer.

A long silence followed while Quinton studied the immigration file.

"Marcos Hale?"

"Yep. A Marcos Hale, but is it our Marcus Hale?"

Quinton pointed to the date of birth and did the math. "Five years older than our client."

"Yep."

Quinton leaned back and looked at Dart.

"Where did this come from?"

"Immigration processing file."

"Public?"

"Barely."

Quinton looked again at the photograph.

"Hard to tell if that is Hale."

"Picture taken years ago."

"Before Hawaii?"

"When he arrived, I think."

Quinton tapped the page with one finger.

"Anything before that?"

"Nothing. Not a single proud-parent post anywhere."

"That alone is suspicious."

Dart nodded.

"Kids like Hale get noticed early. Coaches brag."

"Yes, and parents brag more."

Quinton turned the paper sideways and studied the picture again. "What happens after this immigration entry?"

"Hawaii. School. Football."

"Direct jump."

"Yep."

"No explanation in between."

"Nope."

"What happens when you try to open the rest of the file."

"Nothing."

"Blocked?"

"Looks that way. Or, maybe there's nothing else there."

Quinton nodded. "Any aliases show up?"

"None that I found."

"Time to bring in help."

Dart already knew the answer.

"Miles."

"Yes. Get with Anna and she'll set it up."

Dart folded his arms. "If that is Hale, someone changed the age."

"Or changed the story."

"Yep."

Quinton slid the paper back across the desk.

"Dig deeper."

"How far."

"Everything before Hawaii. Do not tell Cassidy yet."

"Agreed."

"If this is him, there is a reason his past disappeared. She may or may not need to know."

Dart headed for the door.

Quinton spoke again.

"Dart."

Dart turned.

"Expect unpleasant answers."

"Unpleasant answers are my specialty."

Dart left the office with the paper in hand, already thinking about which door Miles might know how to open.

23

───────

Quinton arrived at his gym off San Felipe and checked in at the reception desk. He swam regularly, especially when under stress, and there was the nice bonus that he could eat all the fried food and pimento cheese he wanted and still maintain his weight.

He offered a nod to the woman at the front counter, barely hearing her cheery, "Y'all have a good swim." The familiar sounds of the club settled around him.

He moved straight to the locker room. The air inside was dry and cool, with a faint bite of chlorine. He opened his locker, methodically unbuttoned his shirt, hung it up, then did the same with his slacks. His movements were automatic. After slipping into his blue Speedo, he pulled his goggles over his head and down around his neck and stepped into shower shoes. He grabbed a towel and went to the back of the locker room through the door that led to the pool.

That's when the smell hit him. Chlorine. Clean and sharp. It triggered something deep in his bones. Discipline, memory, control. That old version of himself in New York, clawing through depositions and twelve-hour prep sessions, had leaned on swimming to stay sane. It still worked most of the time.

He walked to the edge of the pool and paused. No crowd at this time of day. A few swimmers moved like seals in the far lanes, stroking and turning at each wall. The surface of lane one rippled gently, open and waiting. Quinton adjusted his goggles, sat on the side of the pool, and slipped into the water like a whisper. It closed around him. Cool, clear, still.

He pushed off the wall and started slowly. One arm, then the other, breathing every third stroke. The rhythm anchored him. He let the water carry the clutter away.

Thoughts of the case came back in slivers. Had Hale actually murdered Daniel Price? Quinton couldn't imagine his doing such a dastardly deed, but that wasn't his problem. Whether his client was guilty or innocent, he needed a defense. He needed the puzzle pieces to start falling together. Let that one steep for a minute.

Next, he turned his mind's eye to Evan's assault case and Silver Jamail. He didn't want to disappoint her, but there was a lot of evidence stacked against the kid.

Quinton sliced through the water, building speed.

There was that damn recording. So prejudicial. Could he get it thrown out? Probably, but his goal was to get the charges dismissed before the full-blown circus that would ensue if they had to go to court.

He flipped at the wall and powered into another lap. The pool blurred. His mind sharpened. Each stroke matched a move in his head as his cases blended in his subconscious.

Right arm—discredit the witness.

Left arm—undermine the tape.

Breath—drive home the alternate theory.

Kick—focus on what mattered.

Glide—don't overplay the hand.

By the time he eased to a stop at the wall, chest heaving, arms warm and fluid, he felt it. Centered. Ready. Dead calm.

He knew what to do next for both clients.

Dart didn't sit at the table. He leaned against the wall near the window, arms crossed, eyes half-lidded like he was bored. Anyone who didn't know him would have missed his careful attention to detail.

Quinton knew better.

Silver Jamail had brought Evan in and had just left. The door clicked shut behind her, and the room changed temperature. Quinton had insisted that he get some alone time with his client. Silver had been reluctant at first but knew it was inevitable. After a few minutes of standard case review, she finally departed.

Quinton turned to Evan.

"This is just us now. You, me, and Dart. I've asked him to listen. Not to judge. Not to interrupt."

Dart lifted his cup in a mock salute. "I be furniture."

Evan managed a weak smile, but he was obviously terrified. Quinton waited until Evan settled back into the chair. His right knee was already bouncing.

"I'm going to ask you questions I didn't ask before. Same rule as last time. Don't protect anyone, especially not yourself."

Evan nodded. "Okay."

"So, you and Monica had been fighting. Start from the beginning."

Evan took a breath. "We'd been fighting all week. Little stuff. Monica thought I was pulling away."

"Were you?"

"Probably. Yes. I was going to break up with her. It was getting too intense."

"She was in the dorm a lot?"

"Most nights until the last week before we broke up."

Quinton nodded. Dart didn't move.

"Anyone ever complain? Noise?"

"The RA did once. A while back."

"How long?"

"Maybe two or three weeks."

Quinton wrote. Dart's eyes stayed on Evan's hands.

"Night of the argument. Who else was around?"

"People in the hall. The usual. Doors opening. Closing."

"Roommate?"

"I have one. Jake. He wasn't there."

Dart's head tilted slightly.

"Where was he?"

"Study group. He stayed away when Monica was over to give us some privacy. He has a girlfriend."

Dart's eyebrow twitched. Just once.

"Tell me about the argument. The moment it changed."

"She baited me. She said I was cheating on her, which I wasn't. She kept pushing until I was cursing and threatening to kick her out the door. I lost my cool and swore at her. I couldn't let her go on. You heard the tape."

"Yes."

"Then she said she was calling the cops. I asked what for, and she said that I had assaulted her. Hit her. Then she said she was recording me and they'd believe her."

"What next?"

"She held up the phone with the red recording light on, and I told her to stop."

"And when she didn't?"

"I knocked the phone out of her hand."

"With what? Closed fist?"

"My hand. More like a swat. I didn't hit her. I just wanted her to stop recording me. I wasn't thinking. I was so mad."

Quinton nodded. "Where did the phone land?"

"On the floor. Near the bed."

Dart glanced at Quinton, then back to Evan.

"Did you block the door at any point, preventing her from leaving?"

"Not intentionally. I was near the door, but there was room to go around me."

"Did you grab her?"

"I grabbed her wrist when she pushed past me. Just for a second."

Dart shifted his weight.

"Why?"

"I thought I could reason with her. Calm things down. But it was too late. We'd both said too much."

"Did you, at any point, slap her with an open hand or hit her with your fist?"

"No. Absolutely not."

"Did you push her against the wall or any furniture?"

"No."

"Did you ever touch her neck?"

"No. Never."

Silence followed.

Dart let it stretch. Quinton let it stretch.

"Did Monica have a temper?"

Evan hesitated. "I don't want to make her sound worse than she was."

"I'm not asking you to. I'm asking about behavior."

"She escalated when she was upset. Fast. Crying to yelling. She'd throw stuff."

"What stuff?"

"Pillows. A cup once, but she said she missed me on purpose."

"Ever threaten you?"

"Not physically."

"Ever threaten to call the police?"

Evan paused. Longer this time.

"Yes. Once. A couple weeks before. The day the RA came down because of the noise."

Dart's eyes sharpened.

"What did she say?"

"She said if I 'lost it,' or hurt her, she'd have proof."

"Had she recorded you before?"

Evan nodded. "Maybe. I think so."

Quinton closed his notebook. Evan looked even more terrified.

"We need to be very careful in our approach to your defense. We cannot attack her. We don't call her vindictive. We don't call her a liar."

Evan's jaw tightened. "But I didn't do anything. She is lying."

"I hear you. That doesn't change how this has to be handled with victims."

Evan's voice cracked. "I'm the victim."

The words landed hard.

Dart spoke for the first time.

"No one's saying you aren't. We're just saying the system is biased. Law enforcement hasn't seen a lot of arrests where the aggressor is the female."

Evan looked at him, startled. "How can we convince them? What can we do?"

Dart went back to mute mode and Quinton took over again. "What I'm listening for is whether your story changes when Silver is not present."

Evan swallowed. "Does it?"

Quinton shook his head. "Not so far."

Dart watched Evan carefully.

"To defend you, we find the soft spots. Timing. Witnesses. What was said before the police arrived. What others may have seen or overheard."

"Jake might help. He's seen her get angry before."

"That matters. Tell him Dart will be contacting him for an interview. Don't coach him."

"I won't. He's a good guy."

Dart nodded once. Quinton wrapped it up.

When Evan finally left and the door closed behind him, Quinton exhaled.

"He's not lying," Dart said.

Quinton agreed. "No."

"He just unprepared for life," Dart added.

Quinton looked down at the file.

"Naive. Those are the easiest people to destroy. Time to get into the accuser. See what you can dig up on Monica. Be careful. We can't appear to be harassing the complaining party. After that, see what the roommate has to say."

"Expecting any surprises?"

"Always."

"On it."

24

After a hard swim, Quinton returned to the war room at his office for the Hale case. Someone had left the lights on though no one else was there. The long conference table sat in the center of the room, its surface crowded with legal pads and binders. Half-erased notes were written on whiteboards perched on easels from earlier strategy sessions. Someone had left a chair pulled out, as if the meeting had only paused instead of ended.

He crossed to the huge pane glass stretching across the expanse of the room. Below him, the Loop curved around downtown Houston. Evening traffic slid past in uneven ribbons of red and white. He did not really see it. He was listening to the building instead. The soft hum of the HVAC. The distant elevator chime. The kind of quiet that settled only after everyone else had decided the day was over. It was the silence that, for him, followed unfinished work.

Quinton moved to the table and spread the discovery out again, aligning the pages with methodical care. He had already read them. More than once. Still, he moved slowly around the table as he reviewed them, stopping here and there, picking up a document only to set it back down.

There should be more.

The prosecution had produced enough to justify the arrest. Phone records. A timeline. Statements that pointed in a single, narrow direction. What it had not produced was just as telling.

They did not overreach.

That bothered him.

Prosecutors with a clean case pressed their advantage. They flooded defense counsel with paper, daring them to drown in it. This was the opposite. Everything here was curated. Intentional.

He returned to the window, folding his arms as he looked down again, this time seeing his reflection faintly layered over the city lights.

Discovery tells you two stories. What they give you and what they hold back.

If the prosecution had uncovered evidence that complicated its theory, it would still have to disclose it. But the way this file was built suggested something more deliberate.

They know more than they are saying. More than they're sharing.

Either they had information that did not fit the narrative and were still deciding what to do with it, or they had made a conscious choice to frame the case around Hale and leave everything else untouched.

Quinton stepped away from the glass and circled the table again, slower now, his eyes tracing the edges of the file rather than its contents.

Price did not live a simple professional life.

An agent with that many clients accumulated leverage. Secrets. Favors. People who preferred their names to never appear in print. Yet the discovery treated Price as if he existed only in relation to Hale.

Quinton straightened and folded his arms. The theory settled with uncomfortable clarity. The prosecution was not building a case to explore the full scope of Daniel Price's life. It was building a case designed to hide it.

Dart climbed the narrow stairs to Miles's apartment two at a time. The hallway smelled faintly of burnt coffee and overheated electronics, the scent of a man who lived mostly inside his machines. The faded digital scan of the humanitarian-processing file tied to the name Marcos Hale had led Dart to a dead end and he needed help.

The door stood half open, expecting company.

Miles sat at a long table crowded with monitors. Four screens glowed in the dim room, lines of code sliding past like rain.

"You going to stand out there breathing my air or come in?"

Dart stepped inside.

"I need some more help."

Miles leaned back in his chair and turned. "That narrows it down." Miles watched him a moment. "More phone pings? Police database you're not supposed to see?"

"No."

Miles waited.

"I need a man's lost past."

That got his attention. Dart had withheld the name of the client when Miles had done the phone ping research. Now, he needed to reveal it.

"Define past."

"Before he became a superstar."

Miles spun back to the keyboard.

"Name?"

"Marcus Hale."

Keys began clacking.

"Linebacker. Houston Wildcatters. Currently sitting in Harris County jail accused of murdering his agent. Hard to miss that one. Grew up in Hawaii."

Dart leaned against the wall. "Look before Hawaii."

Miles searched for a while. Databases opened and closed. Immigration records. Athletic registries.

Then he stopped typing.

"That's strange."

"What?"

"There's nothing on the surface. Somehow, he's been anonymized."

"Anonymized? Is that a word? Dig deeper. Try immigration records. There's a humanitarian-processing file."

Miles dug. "Found it."

"That's where I reached a dead end. Can you go any further?"

More databases opened. Aid networks. International relief groups. Refugee processing systems.

Then Miles froze.

"Well."

"What."

Miles enlarged a document.

"First official record of Marcus Hale anywhere. Medical intake file."

"Where does it say he came from?"

"Thailand."

Dart pushed off the wall and stepped closer. "Thailand?"

Miles scrolled through the intake notes.

"Male intake. No passport. No identification. Multiple injuries."

The room went quiet.

Miles opened another file.

"Seems the kid, Marcus Hale, applied for asylum and asked for legal identification so he could stay in the States."

Dart stared at the screen.

"Why?"

"Doesn't say. Sanitized."

"Date?"

"About eight years ago."

Miles kept searching.

"There's about six months after that where he disappears again. Then suddenly he appears in Hawaii playing football."

Dart did the math on his fingers. "Only, he's five years younger."

"Gave him a few more early years."

"Someone helped him," Dart said.

"Looks like it. Probably governmental, based on the grant of asylum."

Dart studied the screen a long moment. "Why would he want to appear younger?"

Miles searched further. "Looks like he got a GED and entered junior college. Maybe he wanted to fit into that age group."

Dart paused. "Maybe he needed to make up for some of the education he lost before he arrived in Hawaii."

"Gave him more football playing years in school."

Dart waited until the office emptied before he went to see Quinton again.

Not because what he had to say was explosive, though it was. Because it was fragile. The kind of theory that could collapse if you said it too loudly too soon.

Quinton sat at his desk with a legal pad covered in tight angular notes. He looked up immediately.

"You've got something."

"I've got smoke. Maybe fire."

Quinton leaned back. "Talk."

Dart sat across from him.

"Hale came into Hawaii out of the blue. There's something back there, but Miles and I can't get to it."

Quinton waited.

"You may have to ask Hale to get to the bottom of it. Where was he and what was he doing before he sailed into Honolulu?"

Quinton stared out the window.

Dart tapped his pen on the desk.

Quinton exhaled. "Hale told me something."

Dart waited.

"He said he would never be owned again."

The words hung between them.

Quinton rubbed a hand over his face. "We keep this quiet for now."

Dart agreed.

Quinton thought of Hale. Did he escape something before he manifested like a spirit in Hawaii? No one knows a man's secrets.

25

Quinton waited in the attorney client meeting room, the cold air crawling up his sleeves the way it always did in that concrete box. The metal table was scarred with initials and hash marks. The plastic chairs were designed for discomfort. Somewhere down the corridor a steel door slammed, then another, the sound echoing like a warning.

He had come alone. No Mo. No Cassidy. No Dart. Just him seeking whatever truths Marcus Hale had decided to bury.

The guard brought Hale in without ceremony. Shackles at the wrists. No expression on his face. He sat across from Quinton and rested his cuffed hands on the table as if he were settling in for a spell.

Quinton studied him a moment. The strength was still there. Even in jail clothes. Even stripped of the Halestorm myth. But there was something else now. A tightening around the eyes. The fatigue of a man who knew the story was turning against him.

"Is there new evidence?"

"Nothing from Harris County. This is from us."

He opened the folder and slid a photocopy across the table.

A ship manifest. Faded ink. Marcus Hale entering Hawaii.

Hale looked at it but did not touch it.

"You want to tell me about that."

Silence. Only the hum of the lights overhead.

"I told you about Hawaii."

"You told me about football in junior college."

Hale's jaw tightened.

"You came into Honolulu as a deck hand. No passport trail before that. No family listed. Just a name on a cargo ship out of Bangkok."

"That was a long time ago."

"It becomes today if the prosecutor finds it."

Hale leaned back, the chair legs scraping faintly against concrete.

"I was thirteen."

"You were older than that," Quinton said. "Immigration estimated seventeen."

Hale did not argue.

"You jump ship?"

A slight nod.

"Why?"

A long pause.

"Because I thought I was safe in Hawaii."

Quinton let the words sit between them. He did not rush to fill the space.

"You go from undocumented deck hand to junior college student, then enrolled at a Division I program. Walk on. Scholarship. That does not happen by luck. How?"

Hale stared at his own name on the paper as if it belonged to someone else.

"I slept on the beach for a while. Worked kitchens. Carried

plates. Learned English. There was a recreation league. A high school coach saw me play."

"And."

"He let me practice. Said if I wanted real football, I needed papers. Said if I could get eligible, he would help."

"You got a GED?"

A nod.

"Then community college?"

"Yes."

"You were undocumented?"

"Not for long."

"Somebody fixed it?"

"Somebody helped."

"With immigration?"

"With everything."

Quinton watched him carefully.

"Men do not rise that fast without someone taking an interest."

Hale's eyes lifted. Calm. Guarded.

"I was a good athlete. I worked hard."

"That, I believe."

Another steel door slammed in the distance.

"You walked on after junior college at Hawaii State and earned a scholarship," Quinton said. "Full ride. Boosters. Alumni."

Hale said nothing.

"Is that where Daniel Price found you?"

The name changed the air in the room.

Hale's hands curled slowly against the metal tabletop. Not rage. Control.

"He came later."

"But he knew how you had come to be in Hawaii."

"Yes, but I didn't know that at the time."

"He knew you had no family here. No roots. No one to contradict a story about you."

Hale did not answer.

"Marcus, this matters. If someone thought you owed them because they helped you stay, it's important."

Hale's breathing slowed. Measured.

"I earned my spot. Every yard. Every class."

"I am not questioning your work."

"Then what are you questioning?"

"I am questioning whether the help came with a price."

Hale looked at him then. Direct. Unblinking.

"Everyone expects something."

The words were flat. Old.

"He liked stories. He liked telling people he found talent in unlikely places."

"And did he?"

"Yes."

Quinton was losing patience. "You do not get to shield me from your past. My job is to protect you. But I cannot defend the version of you that starts at kickoff. I need the one that started on that ship."

Hale looked back down at the manifest.

"I thought if I ran far enough, it would not follow."

"The truth always follows."

"That's all I can tell you."

"If you won't tell me everything, I can't defend you. That's our deal."

"I can't."

Later, in his office, Quinton contemplated the relationship between Hale and Price.

Price had exercised leverage over Hale. That much was clear. He also had an ugly past. Contracts, threats, secrets wrapped in nondisclosure agreements and quiet payoffs. Price collected people the way some men collected watches. Wound them tight. Owned them. Sold them when they stopped shining.

Hale had been one of those watches.

Quinton leaned back in his chair and closed his eyes. Fear had a smell. Quinton had learned that early in his career. It didn't always look like panic. Sometimes it looked like control stretched too tight, like a man holding himself together with discipline and silence because the alternative was unthinkable.

Self-defense wasn't just about fists and knives. Sometimes it was about escaping from cages you couldn't see.

Quinton picked up his pen and wrote a single word on the yellow pad beside the file: Motive with a question mark. He underlined it once.

The prosecution, with their present case, would argue greed, rage, entitlement. A star athlete finally snapping when he realized his money and fame couldn't buy silence. It was clean. Easy. Juries liked clean, but they could look past it.

But, and it was a big but, if they found out about Hale's sexual orientation, the motive came alive. It would suck the air out of Quinton's case. How would they find out? No one in the world of national sports had ever put the picture together. The scrutiny on public figures was high, and Hale had managed to skirt the spotlight on his personal life.

How could they know if Hale didn't tell them? And, what about the past? The part Hale would not share?

26

———

Quinton had an appointment at the prosecutor's office. The elevator ride up felt longer than it was, as Quinton juggled both cases in his mind and tried to breathe.

Quinton carried Dart's file on Evan Jamail under his arm, the paper heavier than its weight. He'd already read it twice. Once for facts. Once for tone, then discussed it with Dart to get the nuances of the research.

The prosecutor's office occupied a clean, glass-walled floor. Efficiency without warmth. Intentional.

Allison Dale's name was etched on the frosted door, followed by:

Assistant District Attorney

Family Violence Division

She stood when he entered. Early forties. Composed. Navy suit. No wasted motion.

"Quinton Bell. I was wondering when we'd cross paths."

"Hello, Allison. I haven't had a lot of family violence cases. Thanks for seeing me on short notice."

She gestured to a chair but didn't sit right away. Power move. Subtle.

"You wanted to talk about Evan Jamail?"

"Yes. And about whether we can resolve this before it becomes something neither of us recognizes."

She smiled faintly and took her seat. "That's optimistic."

Quinton set the file on the table but didn't open it. "You've reviewed the campus police reports?"

"Yes. Multiple times."

"And the inconsistencies?"

"The allegations," she corrected.

Quinton acquiesced. "Fair enough. Then you know there were no marks other than the ones on her neck and a small red circle around her wrist. No other bruises or scratches. No medical findings otherwise. No corroboration by any witness."

"All of which," Allison said calmly, "is entirely consistent with strangulation cases."

Quinton studied her face. She believed that. Or at least she believed she needed to.

"Evan admits to knocking the phone out of her hand and grabbing her wrist. That's reckless. It's not violent strangulation."

"It's assault. Add the use of hands as a deadly weapon and it's a third-degree felony under Texas Penal Code Section 22.01."

"I'm aware."

"The offense is punishable by two to ten years in prison and fines up to ten thousand dollars."

Quinton leaned back. "That's a lot to put on a young man. This is a college lover's argument that got out of hand. It could ruin Evan's life. He's from a good family and is doing well in school. It's she said, he said."

Allison folded her hands. "It's an allegation of family violence by strangulation."

"She's not his family," Quinton said.

"She's an intimate partner," Allison replied. "Texas law doesn't require a ring."

Silence settled between them.

Quinton broke it. "What are you actually looking for here, Allison?"

She held his gaze. No flinch.

"I'm looking at a political environment that doesn't allow me to quietly dismiss cases like this anymore."

There it was.

"Every family violence case that gets pled down gets scrutinized. By advocacy groups. By supervisors. By people who've never tried a case but know how to tweet."

Quinton nodded slowly. "So this isn't about Evan."

"It is, but it's about precedent, and perception."

"You don't believe he's a danger?"

"I believe," Allison said carefully, "that letting a well-connected young man walk away from a strangulation allegation looks exactly like the thing we've been accused of doing for decades."

Quinton let that sit.

She filled the silence. "I know who his grandmother is. That doesn't help him."

"I didn't expect it to. I expected fairness."

She sighed. "Fairness is aspirational right now."

Quinton opened the file at last. "Then let's talk resolution. Deferred adjudication. Counseling. No admission to strangulation."

Allison shook her head. "Not on the table."

He tried another tack. "Assault by contact? Class C misdemeanor. Anger management."

She didn't hesitate. "No."

"Disorderly conduct. Mutual argument. Dismissal after six months."

Allison met his eyes. "Quinton, if I let him off easily, I get dragged. If I push this forward, I get praised for taking abuse seriously."

"And if the case collapses?"

"That happens later. Behind the scenes. After the message is sent."

Quinton closed the file.

"So you're willing to risk an innocent kid's future to protect your optics."

"I'm willing to let a jury decide whether he's innocent."

"This will ruin him. Even if you lose."

She didn't argue that.

"The climate," she said softly, "ruins people. I just work inside it."

Quinton nodded once and opened the door.

As he stepped into the hallway, he understood something he hoped to avoid.

This case wasn't about truth.

It wasn't even about justice.

It was about weather.

And storms didn't care who was caught in them.

27

Quinton and Hale were back in the attorney client meeting room in the jail that had no windows. The narrow-wired glass in the steel door blurred the movement of guards passing in the corridor. The air carried the sharp scent of something old and hard to scrub away.

It was just the two of them by Quinton's design. He had some hard questions to ask of Hale and Cassidy didn't need to hear them.

Hale sat forward, not touching the back of the chair. The orange fabric of the jail uniform pulled across his shoulders when he moved. His hands were locked between his knees, fingers laced tight enough to blanch the knuckles.

"Are you still my lawyer?"

Quinton placed his file on the table and left it closed.

"We need to pick up from our last conversation about how you came to be in Hawaii. Are you ready to tell me what happened before then?"

"I don't know if I can."

Quinton backed off a bit to see if he could ease him into the story.

"You mentioned before there were parts of your past you never put in the notes you gave us."

A single nod. Controlled. Precise.

Quinton did not hurry him. He had learned that when truth finally forced its way up, silence was often the only thing keeping it intact.

Hale fidgeted. "I did not lie. I just stopped before I got to that part."

"Understandable, but now it's time to let that out. Then, we'll decide who needs to know. I won't reveal it without your permission."

Hale drew in a breath that sounded scraped raw. "I did not grow up with a football in my hands or parents in the stands. No normal childhood."

His gaze fixed on a scuff mark on the concrete brick wall.

"I'm still not sure of my real name. I vaguely remember a woman I think was my mother. I think she called my name Chaiwat. But it could be my imagination. I don't remember a father at all. My best guess is that I was taken or sold from Singapore or the Philippines because I knew some English, even at that age."

Quinton held the silence.

"I was taken young. Seven, eight. I don't know exactly. Moved around. Different islands. Different names. Places where no one asks questions if you keep your head down."

Quinton remained still, but his jaw hardened.

"It was a trafficking ring. Boys. Girls. We were inventory. That's what they called us."

A slow heat rose in Quinton's chest, but his tone remained even. "You do not have to walk through physical details you would rather leave alone."

A breath that almost passed for a laugh. "I have lived with the details for years."

A cart rattled faintly beyond the door. Then quiet again.

"There was a brothel. Near the water. Nothing flashy. Just another building. Customers came and went. We workers stayed. We lived there, if you can call it living."

His fingers flexed once, then tightened again.

"I was small. Malnourished. Weak. I looked younger than I was, and that made me valuable."

Quinton held steady, eyes on him.

"The worst part was not the pain. It was the waiting. Not knowing who would come through the door. Not knowing what version of yourself would survive the night."

The camera dome reflected a warped image of them both.

"I learned how to disappear. How to shrink. How to leave my body without leaving the room."

Silence stretched thin.

Hale took a breath. "But bodies change. Boys grow into men."

Quinton nodded.

"I was growing up. Taller. Broader. Stronger. I could not stop it. I ate scraps like everyone else, but my body kept growing. Then I helped it along. Stole food. Ate whatever I could find in the kitchen. Moved crates to lift weight when no one was watching."

A faint shake of his head.

"I once tried to lift a car. Just to see. I developed into something unmistakably adult. I was not a boy anymore. Whether they liked it or not."

"And I assume they did not."

His mouth pressed thin. "No. And, it got worse. They started sending me the violent ones. One of them tried to remind me who was in charge. Same routine. Same door closing behind him."

For the first time, Hale's eyes rose to meet Quinton's.

"For once, the man hesitated. This time, things shifted."

Quinton did not move.

"He observed me. The size. The way I filled the room. He still came at me. Habit, maybe. Fear too. Maybe he sensed something in me."

Hale's hands trembled now, though his voice remained level.

"I did not plan it. I just stopped being afraid first."

No description followed. None was necessary.

"You ran."

A small nod. "I didn't know where I was going. Only that I could not stay."

Quinton held the space.

"I followed the water. A dock. Cargo being loaded. I climbed aboard and hid. They either couldn't find me or decided not to look."

"Where did you go on the ship?"

"First, Myanmar, then Laos and Cambodia. I changed ships a few times when we docked at different ports. First, I hid and stole food. Later, I worked when they needed a hand. I did not give a name. I did not ask questions."

"And Honolulu."

"The last ship docked there. My first time in the United States. I chose the name Marcus Hale because it was the name of the owner of the last ship I was on. I stepped off that boat and never looked back."

The room felt smaller with the weight of it.

"I found people who looked like me. Asian. Mixed races. They helped without asking why. I learned how to be normal.

How to hit someone wearing pads instead of running from them."

A breath.

"Football let me be strong and part of a team without being owned."

Silence again, heavier now but cleaner.

Quinton leaned forward another inch.

"You survived something no child should endure. You did more than escape. You reinvented yourself."

Moisture gathered in Hale's eyes but did not fall.

"I didn't tell anyone because I was afraid. Afraid they would see me as damaged. Or worse, try to own me again."

Quinton's voice firmed, steady as concrete.

"No one owns you. Not then. Not now. Not ever again."

Hale held his gaze.

In a room built for confinement, something loosened.

Hale murmured, "For the first time, I believe that."

28

———

Quinton left the jail with a lot to think about. Hale's confession left him questioning everything about the human race and what people were capable of doing to each other. He walked toward his car in the parking lot in a fog.

The explosion wasn't loud at first. It was pressure.

A concussive shove that punched the air out of Quinton's chest and folded the parking lot inward, sound arriving a beat later like it had been dragged behind the blast. His gray Range Rover erupted in a violent bloom of fire and glass, the rear quarter panel lifting, twisting, then slamming back down as if the vehicle itself had tried to jump free.

Quinton went down hard.

His shoulder hit asphalt. His head snapped sideways, cheek scraping rough pavement. The world rang, high and shrill, like a struck bell that wouldn't stop vibrating. Heat rolled over him in waves, sharp and oily, carrying the unmistakable smell of burning rubber and fuel.

No. No no no.

The street and buildings vanished.

For a split second he was back in the courtroom with Joanne. The first gunshot cracking through. Wood-paneled walls closing in. The low hum of voices.

Someone screamed. A chair went over. Plaster exploded behind the witness stand, white dust filling the air like smoke. Quinton remembered the way his body had reacted before his mind did. Ducking, covering Joanne and Mo, heart hammering so hard it felt like it would rupture something essential.

"Get down!" someone shouted. Or maybe it had been him.

The judge leaning forward and firing his .44 Magnum into the gallery. The blood on his hands. Too final.

Back in the parking lot, Quinton curled instinctively, forearms over his head, knees pulled in tight. His hands were shaking uncontrollably, fingers flexing and locking as if they'd forgotten how to follow orders. His breath came in fast, shallow pulls that didn't reach his lungs.

The Range Rover burned ten feet away. Flames licked out from beneath the hood, climbing the windshield in orange sheets. Glass rained down in glittering arcs, scattering across the painted parking lines. The alarm wailed briefly, then cut off in a sudden, unsettling silence.

He tasted copper. His vision tunneled, the edges darkening while the center pulsed and throbbed. The smell—burning plastic, scorched wiring—layered perfectly over memory. Too perfectly.

This wasn't just fear. This was a switch being thrown.

Footsteps echoed across the lot. Running away. That registered somewhere deep, through the panic. These footsteps were deliberate. Fast. Already retreating.

Quinton forced his eyes open. Blood was oozing into the right one.

The blast pattern was wrong. Tight. Focused. The surrounding cars were damaged but intact, their windows cracked, bodies scorched but not destroyed. The Range Rover had taken the hit squarely. Right where he'd parked it.

Scraps of paper, trash, and ash fluttered down and landed nearby.

A hand touched his arm. His stomach dropped so hard it felt like he might blackout.

"Sir?"

Quinton reacted without thinking, swinging his elbow up defensively, heart slamming. He stopped short when he saw the woman crouched beside him, hands raised, face pale.

"I'm sorry. I didn't mean to scare you. Are you hurt?"

Her voice sounded distant, warped, like it was coming through thick glass.

"I..." His throat locked. The words wouldn't come. The courtroom surged back again, layered over the parking lot now. Blood on tile. Joanne's body beside the defense table. Someone crying behind him, over and over, oh God. Oh God.

Sirens wailed somewhere beyond the courthouse walls.

Quinton pressed his palms flat against the asphalt, grounding himself. Name what's real. Name what's now.

Fire. Smoke. The courthouse facade looming overhead. His Range Rover burning. His phone laying face down, screen cracked. A message he couldn't read.

The rough grit under his hands. The ache in his shoulder. The heat on his face. The familiar, creeping certainty that this wasn't random.

A uniformed officer knelt beside him as more patrol cars skidded into the lot.

"Sir, can you tell me your name?"

Quinton swallowed hard.

"Byron. No, Quinton Bell," he said. His voice sounded hoarse, scraped raw, but steady enough.

The officer paused. "Stay still. An ambulance is on the way."

"I can get up." But he couldn't stand. Instead, he sat up and looked at what was left of his SUV. At the controlled burn. At the ghosted message in the air now smudged with soot.

"Someone knew exactly where I was."

The officer studied him. "Let's get you checked out."

Quinton tried to get up. "My bag. In the car. My go bag."

"I'm afraid anything that was in the vehicle is gone, sir."

As they helped him to his feet, the courtroom receded, leaving behind its echo.

He returned to present time, to the unwelcome knowledge that this wasn't over. That someone had just taken careful measurements of his habits, his timing, his scars.

Quinton didn't know who had done it. But he knew one thing with absolute certainty. This wasn't meant to kill him.

It was meant to frighten him, and it had worked.

———

Detective Broussard arrived like a bad memory.

Not running. Not rushing. Just that familiar, unhurried saunter that said he already knew the worst part and was mostly irritated he had to confirm it. He ducked under the yellow tape, took in the smoking wreckage of Quinton's Range Rover, then let out a low whistle through his teeth.

"Mais la," he muttered. "You really do like to make a statement, don't you, Counselor?"

Quinton sat on the edge of the curb with a blanket draped over his shoulders, several butterfly bandages were holding together a cut on his forehead. A paper cup of water was sweating in one hand, his cracked cell phone in the other. He looked up slowly. "Good to see you too, Broussard." He slid his cell phone into his pocket.

The detective crouched in front of him, joints popping like old wood. He smelled faintly of coffee and gun oil.

"You got a habit," Broussard said, shaking his head. "Every time I turn my back, you done wandered into some fresh mess like a crawfish in a bait bucket."

"Nice to know you missed me."

Broussard snorted. "Missed you? Cher, I been hopin' you'd take up stamp collectin' or golf or somethin' quiet. Instead, I get you blowin' up cars in courthouse parkin' lots like it's Mardi Gras."

Quinton glanced past him at the charred shell of the SUV. "Wasn't exactly on my to-do list."

"No?" Broussard raised an eyebrow. "'Cause from where I'm standin', trouble keep findin' you like you sprinkled yourself with shrimp boil."

He stood, pulling out a small notebook, flipping it open with a practiced thumb. "All right. Let's get this over with so they can get you to the hospital."

"I don't need a hospital."

The attendant looked at Broussard as if to say, *He sure as hell does.*

Broussard looked down at Quinton. "You gonna tell me why someone tried to kill you this time?"

"If they'd wanted me dead, I think I would be."

"Then who'd want to scare the hell outta you today?"

Quinton took a breath. His hands were steadier now, but only just. "I don't know who did it."

Broussard made a small, dismissive noise.

"That's all I've got."

Broussard stared at him for a long beat, eyes sharp, unreadable. Then he sighed and rubbed a hand over his face. "Mon dieu. You always say that right before things get real interesting."

He flipped a page. "Timeline. You walk out of the court-house, heading to your car. Then boom. That about right?"

"Yes."

"You stop anywhere? Talk to anybody? Take your sweet time admiring the scenery?"

"No."

Broussard scribbled. "You been getting threats?"

Quinton hesitated.

Broussard's pen stopped mid-stroke. He looked up. "A-ha. See? That little pause right there? That's the sound of you lyin' by omission."

"I didn't say no."

"Non. You said nothin'. Which is worse."

He leaned closer, voice dropping. "Listen to me, cher. Every time you decide to carry the weight alone, folks end up bleeding or shot. And I get stuck explaining it to people who don't enjoy my accent."

Quinton swallowed. "I didn't recognize anything specific. Nothing concrete."

"Uh-huh." Broussard straightened again. "And I'm the King of Acadiana."

He snapped the notebook shut. "This wasn't random. My boys say the blast was tight. Controlled. Just enough oomph to make you dance without sending you to the morgue."

"That's what I thought."

"Of course you did." Broussard sighed. "You always thinking three moves ahead, then act surprised when somebody else does the same."

He glanced around the lot, lowering his voice. "Let me tell you something, Bell. Somebody knows you well enough to know fear works better than funerals."

Quinton's jaw tightened.

Broussard noticed. He always did. He tucked the notebook back into his jacket. "You gonna do me one small favor?"

"What's that?"

"Stop pretending you're just unlucky." Broussard pointed toward the smoking wreck of the SUV. "Luck don't plan timing down to the minute. Somebody stirred this gumbo special, and you the main ingredient."

Reporters were starting to gather at the edge of the lot, cameras lifting like vultures.

Broussard took a step back. "I'll need a formal statement later. Somewhere quiet. Somewhere without fireworks."

He paused, then added, "And, Quinton?"

"Yes."

"If you remember *anything*. A face, a voice, a bad smell that don't belong. Don't marinate on it. You call me. Right away."

Quinton nodded.

"'Cause I swear, cher, if I gotta pull you outta another mess like this, I'm gonna start charging you rent."

He turned and walked off, muttering to himself. "Courtroom shootouts. House fires. Car bombs. Lord, help me, I shoulda stayed fishin'."

Quinton watched him go, the weight of it settling in his chest. He decided he'd go for a few stitches after all.

Whoever had done this hadn't just rattled him. They'd pulled Broussard back into it too. It was bad enough that Broussard was part of the prosecution of Hale, now Broussard was back in his personal life.

Quinton had helped Broussard's nephew a while back when he'd gotten into trouble with the Galveston police for vandalism. He'd hoped it would cause Broussard to cut him some slack if he had more trouble. It hadn't worked. It seemed to Quinton that Broussard was too close to him and knew too much about him. He'd have to remedy that.

29

———————

Price's townhouse sat quiet under a fading wash of light. Officer Gere was supposed to be sent by the DA's office to allow access. He was late.

Quinton and Dart met outside and waited for Officer Gere to arrive. Dart leaned against his truck like he owned the block, Big Gulp in hand. He took one look at Quinton standing there on the sidewalk and stopped mid-sip.

"Well damn," Dart said. "You lose a bar fight with a lawn-mower or somethin'?"

"Nothing that concerns you."

Dart barked a laugh. "Oh, it concerns me. You out here lookin' like you got dragged behind a pickup down Westheimer, that concerns me plenty."

A car rolled past. Quinton didn't watch it.

"I tripped."

Dart blinked, eyes never leaving Quinton. "You tripped?"

"Uneven pavement."

Dart shook his head. "Man, you got singe marks. Pavement don't singe."

Quinton finally glanced at him, just long enough. "It was an unfortunate event."

"Oh, an event," Dart said. "Like a charity gala? Little wine, little cheese, little spontaneous combustion?"

Quinton looked back out at the street. "You're being dramatic, smartass."

"I'm being accurate. That your car that got cooked the other day at the courthouse?"

"So, you heard about that."

Dart leaned in a little. "Yeah, I heard. Why didn' I hear it from you?"

Silence.

Dart straightened, rubbed a hand over his mouth. "Lemme guess. You 'tripped' and the ground just exploded up under you."

Quinton's jaw tightened just a fraction. "It's handled."

"Handled?" Dart let out a low whistle. "Handled like how? 'Cause from where I'm standin', somebody tried to turn you into a french fry."

Quinton shifted his weight, gaze still forward. "I'm fine. Maybe you've been eating too much fast-food."

"Yeah. You look great. Little crispy, little shaken, but yeah, real fine." He tilted his head. "You forget, I know about you and trouble from way back."

Quinton's expression didn't change.

Dart grinned, but there was no humor in it. "Man, don't play me."

"Broussard's looking into it."

Dart gestured at Quinton. "This is you gettin' a message."

Quinton didn't respond for a beat. Then, flat, "Then message received."

"A'right. You wanna play it like dat, we play it like dat."

Quinton said nothing.

Dart gave him one last look. "And hey... if you plannin' on gettin' yourself killed, at least leave me a note. I want to be out of town."

Officer Gere arrived, giving Quinton a reprieve from Dart's interrogation. He unlocked the door and pushed it open. He gestured for the two to enter and took his place standing guard outside the door, where he immediately opened his phone and sunk his brain into screentime.

Quinton stopped just inside and surveyed the space. The room still bore the shape of it. A dark red stain soaked into the hardwood, bleeding into the edge of a Persian rug that had been left in place. Not red anymore. Brown. Fixed. Permanent.

Dart stepped in behind him, pulling the camera from his bag.

"Good," Dart said quietly. "They preserved it."

Quinton nodded. "For the jury."

Dart began shooting. Wide angles first. The entry. The living room. The rug. The stain from multiple positions.

Click.

Click.

Quinton moved slowly, eyes scanning past the obvious.

"This is where it ended."

"Yeah. Bloody."

They moved through the living area, careful not to disturb anything. Dart documented. Quinton read the space. No paper. No files. No trace of a man who dealt in leverage. He knew the police had the laptop because the contents were part of discovery. Nothing about Hale in there or Price's time in Asia with his charities.

Quinton stopped near the built-in shelving along the wall. Decorative books. Art objects. He slipped his hand around the edges of things looking for something to click or maneuver.

"Where is it?"

Dart glanced up. "What?"

"His records. Contracts. Notes. Financials. He didn't run everything off memory."

"Police would've taken it."

"We've got discovery. There's nothing like that in it."

Dart's expression shifted slightly.

"Either it's gone, hidden, or stored somewhere else."

Quinton shook his head. "Hale said he kept the reports from the PI. Probably had his other records, too."

"Then it's here," Dart said.

"Maybe." They examined all the furniture and cabinets, then moved upstairs. The bedroom looked normal.

Dart kept photographing. Angles. Edges. Details.

Quinton stood at the desk. He opened the drawers. Sparse. Very little paperwork, no flash drives or journals.

"Nothing unusual."

Dart didn't answer. He was scanning now, slower. Less about documenting, more about reading. Quinton checked the dresser, closet, and bathroom. Nothing.

"What are you thinking?"

"Digital. If he's not leaving paper, maybe he's keeping it small."

Quinton turned. "Then where?"

Dart walked the perimeter of the room, eyes moving from floor to wall to furniture. He paused in the far corner.

A simple floor lamp stood there, not plugged into the wall. Black metal. Minimalist. Forgettable.

Dart crouched. "Maybe the cops unplugged the lamp?"

"What?"

Dart tilted the lamp slightly, testing its weight. He set the camera down and lifted the base carefully, turning it over. Nothing obvious. Then his thumb traced along the underside seam. He stopped.

"There," he said.

Quinton held a finger to his lips for quiet, stepped closer, and pressed a recessed edge. A narrow panel shifted open just enough to reveal a micro flash card inside.

Quinton let out a quiet breath. "Jesus."

Dart slid it out carefully, holding it between two fingers.

"Want to bet these are the records?" he whispered.

Quinton took it, staring at something so small possibly carrying something so large.

"Photograph it," he said.

Dart picked up the camera again, documenting the lamp, the seam, the compartment, the card in Quinton's hand.

Click.

Click.

Dart straightened and hissed. "Cops missed it."

"They weren't looking for it," Quinton replied.

A beat passed. "What you gonna do wit it?"

Quinton didn't answer right away.

He looked at the card in his hand.

"If we turn it over now, they decide what it means before we do."

Dart's jaw tightened. "It's evidence."

"Evidence of what?"

Silence stretched between them. The whispering made the conversation more intense.

"Are we crossing a line?" Dart glanced at the card. Then back at Quinton.

"We're holding it. For now."

Another beat.

Dart nodded once and looked toward the stairs. They assumed Gere was still outside the front door.

Quinton took a plain white envelope from the desk drawer and slipped the card into it.

Dart took one last photograph of the room, the lamp, the place no one had thought to look, then put the lamp back in the circle on the carpet where it had stood and left it unplugged.

Click.

They turned to leave.

Downstairs, the stain remained.

Upstairs, the truth had been small enough to hide in the base of a lamp, and maybe important enough to change everything.

Quinton locked the door to his office. Not out of habit. Out of instinct.

He sat and placed the letter-sized envelope on his desk, the micro card inside. Something that small shouldn't carry such weight.

He pulled a card reader from his drawer and plugged it into his laptop. For a moment he looked at the envelope, then opened it. Careful. Deliberate.

He slid the card into the reader with a soft click and waited.

The screen blinked once, then populated. Folders. Organized. Labeled.

He scrolled down looking at the names until he got to Hale and clicked it open. Dates, timestamped entries, and locations all listed in a summary from a PI. At the bottom of the second page were notes.

"...subject arrived 21:14..."

"...male occupant confirmed..."

"...departed 08:32 following overnight stay..."

"...pattern consistent with ongoing same-sex relationships..."

"...subject exhibits no attempt to conceal behavior in private settings..."

Quinton's jaw tightened. He clicked into the next folder marked Hale Photos. Obviously taken with a long lens. Grainy, but clear enough. Hale in a car. Hale at a doorway. Hale entering. Hale with another man on a balcony, close enough that there was no ambiguity in the posture, the familiarity. Hale kissing him.

There were dozens more, and Quinton did a quick click through. There were more of the same with different men. Quinton leaned back slowly.

"You were right. They followed you," he said under his breath.

He opened a file titled Hale Reports. Private investigator letterhead with a full report from each encounter. Expanding on the summary with more detail.

Quinton exhaled, slow. *Leverage. Blackmail.*

He sat there for a long moment, the glow of the screen reflecting in his eyes, then scrolled and clicked into another directory marked Asian Charities. He opened and scanned several files.

Some official records in the names of several international corporations. Some unofficial records. Minutes from Board Meetings. A charitable foundation operating in Southeast Asia.

Financial documents. Internal logs. Rotations. Clients. Payments. Dates that stretched back years.

Another folder caught his eye: Myanmar Border Operations. Quinton clicked.

A new series of documents opened in tight, orderly rows. Ledger sheets first. Fuel purchases. Satellite internet contracts. Generator maintenance logs. Security invoices tied to compounds just across the Thai border. At first glance it looked like the back-office paperwork of some remote aid project, the kind of infrastructure support a foundation might quietly provide.

Then he opened the internal memoranda beneath it. The language changed. Passport holds. Labor quotas.

Shift rotations tied to English fluency, typing speed, and successful conversion rates.

Twelve-hour blocks became sixteen. Red notations marked disciplinary actions for workers who failed to meet targets. Food restrictions. Isolation. Escalation protocols.

Quinton went still. These were not shelters. They were fortified compounds. Buildings stocked with educated captives lured into Thailand with promises of lucrative office jobs, then moved over the Myanmar border, locked inside, and forced to sit at computers around-the-clock running scams on victims halfway across the world.

The evidence revealed that refusal brought beatings, starvation, electric shocks. The paperwork was clinical in a way that made it worse, reducing human misery to metrics, percentages, and maintenance costs.

His eyes moved lower. Price's foundation money was threaded through every page. Shell entities. Utility payments. Internet infrastructure. 'Outreach grants' that were nothing more than the financial lifeline keeping the compounds operational.

A slow, controlled breath left Quinton. Price had not just preyed on weakness. He had built systems for it.

The pattern was bigger than Hale. Bigger than Thailand. Bigger than Houston. Control, scaled into an industry.

For a moment Quinton sat motionless in the dim light of the office, the glow from the laptop reflecting in his eyes, and understood with cold certainty that Daniel Price's focus had never been sports. It was finding markets for human suffering.

With a sickening feeling, he opened another folder marked Personnel Routing. His jaw tightened. He clicked deeper. The room seemed to contract around him.

These locations included Thailand and Chiang Mai, then south toward the ports.

The names were foreign to him, but the pattern was unmistakable. Rotations. Client lists. Housing transfers. Youth intake numbers disguised as outreach metrics.

Children. Mid-teens. Sold and moved under the cover of foundation work.

Quinton stared at the screen, pulse pounding now.

Then he saw it. Chaiwat. The name Hale's mother had called to him in his memory of her. Not Marcus Hale. The name buried in the islands and the years before football and money and fame. Chaiwat.

The air left his lungs. Price had known.

Not just about Hale being gay. About all of it. Where he had come from. What had been done to him? Who had owned pieces of his life before he ever set foot in Hawaii?

He opened a file marked Cargo. There they were. The names of those sent to work in the Asian brothels, including Chaiwat. Entry upon entry. Some full names, some only first or last. The addresses of the brothels were included showing where each of the humans were shipped. Cold. Systematic. Devastating.

Price was tied to foundations that appeared to be charities. Funding shelters. Outreach programs. But it was all smoke and mirrors hiding the evil of buying and selling the most vulnerable of the world.

Quinton let out a quiet, humorless breath. The evidence sat there on the screen like a lie everyone had agreed to believe.

Hale wasn't just being watched in Houston. He had been

cataloged long before. Owned. Bought and sold again and again.

Quinton moved to the window, staring out without seeing anything. He closed his eyes for a brief second, then opened them again.

If someone did that to me, maybe I'd kill him too.

30

In a lesser part of Houston, Seamus Devlin sat on the stained mattress in the rundown room he'd paid cash for, the kind of place where the clerk didn't bother with names and the walls carried more secrets than any guest who'd passed through would ever know. Neon light from a nearby liquor store's sign flickered through the blinds, painting the room in pulses of red and blue like a warning he couldn't escape.

He leaned over a spread of papers scattered across the bed: Photocopies of Tua Dannon's sentencing, articles about the trial, and a dozen notes scribbled in Devlin's jagged handwriting. His eye kept snagging on the same line in the federal report:

"Confidential cooperating witness. Identity sealed."

Devlin's throat tightened.

He'd heard whispers back east that Tua Dannon was looking for him. No one said why. No one ever knew Dannon's reasons. The man didn't share his concerns. He eliminated possibilities.

Devlin swallowed hard. He didn't know if Dannon was after

him because of the mess he made in Houston during Joanne's trial or because Dannon thought he had given information to the Feds. Either case was not good.

He had *not* talked to the Feds. Devlin was pretty sure Quinton was the rat. If he could talk to Dannon without getting shot, he'd tell him that Quinton was in Houston hiding in plain sight. But Dannon wouldn't care about distinctions. He'd kill them both just to make sure.

"Doesn't matter what I did," Devlin muttered. "It matters what he thinks I did."

He paced the small room, boots thumping against the thin carpet. Every time the neon light stuttered, it felt like a bullet whizzing past his ear.

He sat again, staring down at the name he'd written across the top sheet in thick black ink: QUINTON BELL. Devlin jabbed his finger against it.

Devlin leaned back, breath shaking. "Bell put me in this position. No contacts, no money, no way to get back into Tua Dannon's good graces. It began with Byron Douglas, and it will end with Quinton Bell."

The idea steadied him. But he needed a plan.

"How do I pin the stink on him?" Devlin murmured. He paced again, thinking. "Could forge records, plant something in that fancy new house of his. That would just bring in the cops or maybe make Quinton run again."

He paced faster now. He stopped moving and pressed both hands to the wall, head bowed.

"Kill him," Devlin whispered. "Then leave behind breadcrumbs. Make sure Tua Dannon finds out, lay low for a while, then try to get back into his good graces."

He went back to the bed, staring again at Dannon's mugshot. The fear returned. Cold, crawling, insistent.

If Dannon believed Devlin was a traitor, Devlin had no life

left to salvage. But if Devlin could convince Dannon that Quinton Bell had given the information he must have gleaned from his client, Killian, and talked to the FBI, then Devlin might buy himself the one thing he'd been chasing for months: Redemption.

Bell's the perfect target. Too clean. Too righteous. Nobody will question it once he's dead. Maybe he could make it look like Witness Protection. Byron's death in NYC had been planned by the Feds in exchange for his testimony against Dannon. Devlin couldn't be sure it had been, but Dannon might believe it.

He stuffed the papers into his backpack with trembling hands. He reached up and switched off the lamp, plunging the room into darkness. The neon light still flickered across the floor in violent reds and blues like a heartbeat counting down.

Devlin lay back on the bed, staring at the ceiling, planning every step of how to kill and frame Quinton Bell, and how to make Tua Dannon believe that he deserved a second chance.

31

———————

Dart did his research on Evan Jamail's case carefully. He did not start from the assumption that Monica had lied. That was the mistake people made when they wanted a story to resolve too cleanly. Dart started with a quieter question. Not whether she was cruel, but whether she was capable. Did she have a predisposition to cause this type of trouble?

Her current online presence was immaculate. Thoughtful captions. Soft attitude. She presented herself as attentive, empathetic, warm.

The charm seemed real. Was there discipline behind it?

Dart scrolled backward. Before college. Before Evan.

The photos changed gradually. Group shots where she stood slightly apart. Smiles that did not quite reach her eyes. Extra weight that disappeared abruptly during her last two years of high school.

He found older posts that had never been deleted, only buried. A public thread from a small-town Facebook page, preserved the way those places preserved everything.

In high school she had written that 'people either control

199

the story or live inside someone else's.' That was the line that stayed with him. She was a journalism major, and this was probably what prompted the career choice.

Dart broke into private records next. It was not difficult.

Scholarship archives. Public attachments. Letters of recommendation that were glowing but precise. One letter from a guidance counselor described prolonged social isolation during adolescence. Bullying was not named directly, but the language was suggestive.

School attendance records showed gaps. Counseling referrals appeared twice. A nurse visit from junior year mentioned complaints of neck soreness attributed to stress. No incident report. No allegation. Just the notation. Dart did not draw conclusions. He documented and expanded his notes.

In an archived high school newspaper feature, Monica was quoted as saying she had learned early to advocate for herself because no one else would. She mentioned being teased in middle school for her weight and clothes. She said it made her stronger. It made her watchful.

He composed his records into several files for Quinton's use.

On campus, Dart had not asked about Monica directly. He asked about noise complaints and hallway activity. About who people remembered.

The resident advisor had spoken carefully. She described Monica as persuasive and emotionally intelligent. Someone people wanted to help. Someone who framed her experiences in terms of safety and power.

A hallmate had filled in another detail without realizing its weight. She said Monica came out of the dorm room after the fight, upset but composed. She said Monica went to the bathroom before calling anyone. The hallmate saw no evidence of an attack.

Dart highlighted that sentence in his notes.

He spent another hour in the online college campus records. He did not search for scandal. He searched for patterns.

Two years earlier, during her freshman year, Monica had filed an informal complaint against three girls on her floor for what she described as targeted exclusion. The report referenced group chats she was not included in and whispered conversations in common areas. The complaint was resolved with a mediated conversation. No formal finding. No discipline.

Dart found the mediation summary. It described Monica as articulate, calm, but deeply hurt. It also noted that the other students appeared confused by the accusation. They described ordinary roommate friction. Differing friend groups. No overt bullying. No threats.

Again, Dart documented his findings.

There was also a counseling intake form, disclosed through a records release. In it, Monica described a lifelong feeling that others were aligning against her. She used phrases like, "They turn people on me" and "I can feel when someone is building a case." The counselor had noted hypervigilance. A tendency to scan for signs of betrayal. No diagnosis attached. Just observation.

Dart did not speculate. He highlighted the language.

Then, he summarized and evaluated: "She's got a habit of thinking folks are teaming up on her, even when it's just regular arguing. Every little disagreement turns into somebody trying to take her down. She runs to authority quick. Don't wait. Don't cool off. Straight to filing something. And when she tells it, she's calm. Put together. Like she knows exactly how it's supposed to sound."

He leaned back in the chair and stared at the report. Then added: "If someone believed others were building a case against her, or about to reject her, she might build a case or reject them first. If someone equated vulnerability with leverage, she might understand how visible injury changes the balance of power."

Dart closed the file. He had documented a possible pattern. Ammunition for Quinton to use as he wished.

In Quinton's inner office, Dart spread the documents across the small round table in careful rows. The conference room was still reserved as the war room for the Hale trial and there was no space left, so he made do.

Dart did not dramatize it. The story spoke louder than he could. He laid it out.

Quinton remained standing as he read, moving around the circular table one step at a time. He read first from the earlier files.

High school disciplinary records. Counseling summaries. A prior campus incident report from a different university. A withdrawn Title IX complaint. The scholarship letter. The nurse's intake note and statements from the resident advisor. Lastly, Quinton scanned the counselor's note. *Patient presents with somatic symptoms during periods of perceived rejection. Reports throat tightness, difficulty breathing when anxious.*

He set it down slowly. "How did you get this?"

Dart grimaced. "Don't ask. It's obvious she's paranoid and she learned early that reports of physical abuse plus the right narrative gets people on her side."

Quinton walked to the window, hands in his pockets. Traffic moved below, unaware.

"So, you're saying she doesn't have to be a mastermind. She just has to know what the system recognizes."

Dart leaned back against the credenza. "Pretty much. That's

the point. The defense mechanism was there long before Evan came into the picture."

Quinton moved farther around the table and reopened the recent medical report.

"The marks. They were consistent with pressure, not force."

"Right. No deep tissue damage. Just surface redness. Coulda come from Evan's hands. Coulda come from her own grip during a panic spiral."

"Interesting, and sad."

Dart held up a hand. "Can we argue she strangled herself?"

"No. We argue that she might have a documented history of interpreting anxiety and physical distress as assault. We show that pattern. Let the prosecution draw their own conclusion."

Dart grunted.

"If the prosecution sees this as a pattern of escalated claims under stress, they have room. They can downgrade. They can decline. They do not have to accuse her of lying. They can say the evidence does not support criminal conduct beyond a reasonable doubt."

"And Evan gets a break."

Quinton completed the circle and flipped again to the first high school file.

"What triggered the original accusation?"

Dart answered without hesitation. "Her girlfriend reported that her debate partner had started seein' someone else."

Quinton exhaled. "And here, Evan told her he wanted space. Texts show that on the night before the incident. She said she thought he was seeing someone else."

Dart nodded. "She's not a villain. She's a confused and damaged kid who learned that accusation equals safety. Who knows what might have happened to her before high school. I'd guess something pretty bad. She probably didn't feel safe in most situations."

Quinton's voice softened. "Maybe she still doesn't. And if she believes her stories, even better for the prosecution. Bad for us, delusional witnesses are the hardest to cross."

Dart gathered the files into a neat stack and put them back into the folder.

"What's the play?"

"We present the prior recantation. We present the withdrawn complaint. We present the counseling notes on somatic symptoms. We do it clinically. No judgment. No theatrics."

"And?"

"And we ask the prosecutor one question: Are you certain this is the first time she has mistaken anxiety for assault?"

Dart gave a low whistle. "That'll move the needle?"

"She does not need to be proven a liar. She only needs to follow a pattern. And patterns are reasonable doubt."

<hr>

Quinton waited until Allison Dale spoke first.

"You asked for this meeting. Make it worth it."

Quinton slid one document across the table. A timeline Dart had prepared showing the issues experienced by and at the hand of Monica from earliest to most recent. He keyed each of the entries to supporting evidence marked from one to thirty-four.

"All of this predates Evan. Or occurs before law enforcement engagement in the dorm."

Allison frowned. "You're attacking the victim?"

"No. I am showing contamination."

Allison flipped through the supporting evidence. "This is hardly conclusive. We still have him on tape."

"Maybe, but she may have recorded him until she caught him at his worst. If we must go further, we will subpoena her phone and any other recordings. I assume you haven't done that."

"No."

He turned the page and pointed to the statement from the dorm witness.

"It's possible that the allegation crystallized after she left the dorm room. Not during the event. That makes the charge unstable. If this goes to trial, I am entitled to present alternative explanations for perceived physical symptoms. That opens doors neither of us wants opened."

Allison exhaled slowly.

"You would put her on the stand?"

"I would have to. And once that happens, this stops being a prosecution and starts being a referendum. This girl needs help, and Evan needs to grow up and use better judgment in selecting women to date."

She looked at the file again.

"You're right. This is not a good case."

"It never was."

Allison closed the folder.

"I am dismissing. Insufficient evidence." She paused. "Quietly."

Quinton nodded. "Quiet is good."

The next week, the charge disappeared without press, without explanation, without apology. Evan Jamail never returned to court. Silver was grateful.

Sometimes winning meant leaving no footprint at all.

32

———————

The courtroom on the tenth floor of the Harris County Criminal Justice Center filled long before Judge Robert Blaylock entered.

The holes where the bullets had struck the walls during Joanne Wyatt's trial had been patched and painted, the plaster smoothed so carefully that a casual observer would never know gunfire had once ripped through the courtroom.

Yet Quinton still knew exactly where the rounds had hit. To the reporters and spectators filling the gallery today, the courtroom looked orderly and ordinary. To Quinton, the room still remembered.

This was also the room where, months after that shooting, Quinton had stood and felt the walls closing in, the noise draining out of the air as the first wave of PTSD had taken hold.

Press occupied most of the gallery. Cameras were not allowed inside, but sketch artists worked quickly, charcoal sliding across thick paper as they captured the players at the tables. A low murmur floated through the room like the sound before a storm.

Quinton sat in the first spot at the defense table next to Mo. Hale was flanked by Mo and Cassidy. The broad shoulders that swallowed quarterbacks on Sunday afternoons now seemed slightly folded inward inside a conservative gray suit. Hale stared straight ahead, jaw set, hands clasped together on the polished wooden table.

Behind Hale sat several members of the Houston Wildcatters' organization, including Coach Brown. Fans had slipped in among the spectators. A few wore jerseys under jackets. Everyone watched Hale's side of the room.

Quinton, a legal pad in hand, turned and moved his eyes slowly across the crowd. He wore his first day of trial navy suit with upbeat tie. Not stuffy, not flashy.

Across the aisle, District Attorney Sawyer Durant took the lead seat. His assistant, Mark Benavides, was back. Durant arranged several rust-colored accordion folders in precise order beside his laptop. The DA carried the quiet confidence of a man who had tried a hundred cases in the same courtroom. He dressed conservatively, dark suit, striped tie. Boring in Quinton's estimation, but juries liked their prosecutors serious.

At exactly nine o'clock the bailiff, George Grant, stepped forward. He had been with Judge Blaylock for more years than either could count, their military background and disciplined lifestyle bonding them.

"All rise."

Judge Blaylock entered through the door leading to his private chambers and took the bench. The black robe settled over him in the high-backed chair on the raised dais. The courtroom rose as one.

"Be seated."

The chairs and benches creaked as everyone sat.

Judge Blaylock looked down over the rim of his reading glasses at the twelve citizens occupying the box to his left.

"Good morning, ladies and gentlemen of the jury. As you know, this case concerns the death of Daniel Price. The defendant, Marcus Hale, stands charged with capital murder which involves premeditation. You are about to hear opening statements by both the prosecution and the defense. I want to admonish you, opening statements are not evidence. They are an outline of what each side expects to prove. The prosecution will open first, as they have the burden of proof. You may take notes, but you should satisfy yourselves, as the trial progresses, that each side has kept their promises."

Judge Blaylock turned toward the prosecution table.

"Mr. Durant."

The district attorney rose smoothly and walked to the center of the well. He faced the jury with hands folded loosely in front.

"Thank you, Your Honor. Ladies and gentlemen of the jury. Good morning. Thank you for being here and for giving your precious time to honor the long tradition of civic duty in our judicial system. Today, the people are trying Marcus Hale for violations of the Texas penal code, involving the willful, deliberate, first-degree murder of Daniel Price. The people will prove beyond a reasonable doubt that Marcus Hale killed poor Mr. Price with planning that is called premeditation or malice aforethought. We will do so by calling to the stand witnesses who will make this assertion clear."

The jury exhaled and settled in for the long haul.

"The prosecution will show that on that fateful evening, Daniel Price was murdered inside his townhome on Bellaire Boulevard."

Durant paused.

"We will show that Daniel Price and the defendant, Marcus Hale, were business partners. Daniel Price acted as the defendant's agent and manager. Their relationship covered millions of dollars in contracts and endorsements."

Durant paced slowly in front of the jury box.

"The prosecution will show that the relationship between these two men had begun to deteriorate. Financial disputes had arisen. Control of future earnings had become the subject of bitter disagreement."

Durant turned slightly toward the defense table.

"The prosecution will show that earlier on the afternoon of the murder, a neighbor heard a heated argument between Marcus Hale and Daniel Price."

Durant lifted a hand toward the witness stand.

"You will hear from Sheryl Benton, who lives next door to the victim. Mrs. Benton heard raised voices and threats. She heard Daniel Price and another man arguing loudly enough that the words carried through the open window of her residence."

Durant allowed the words to settle in the quiet courtroom.

"The prosecution will show that only a few hours after that argument Daniel Price was found dead. We will show that at the time of death, Marcus Hale's telephone was confirmed to be in the exact location of Mr. Price's townhouse. We will show Mr. Hale's fingerprints in the townhouse."

Durant clasped his hands again and stepped closer to the jury rail.

"The prosecution will show financial pressure. The prosecution will show anger. The prosecution will show stalking by the defendant. The prosecution will show a confrontation that escalated into violence."

Durant paused one final time.

"And at the end of this trial the prosecution will ask you to return the only verdict the evidence supports. Guilty."

Durant held his gaze on the jury for a moment then returned to counsel table.

A murmur rippled briefly through the spectators before fading again.

Judge Blaylock turned toward the defense table.

"Mr. Bell."

Quinton stood slowly and walked to about the same spot Durant had occupied moments earlier, just a bit closer to the edge of the rail separating the well from the jury.

"Ladies and gentlemen," Quinton began quietly, "Mr. Durant would have you believe that Marcus Hale's life is simple."

Quinton glanced briefly back toward the defense table.

"A football star. A powerful man. A man who lost his temper and killed his agent."

Quinton shook his head.

"But life is rarely that tidy."

Quinton paced a few steps across the floor.

"Marcus Hale did not argue with Daniel Price that afternoon. You will hear that argument described, but my client was not visually identified. Sheryl Benton is a nice woman, with a good heart. We assume she did hear voices that afternoon, possibly an argument. But when police asked Mrs. Benton to visually identify my client in a lineup, she was unable to do so. Mrs. Benton is what is called an earwitness. An earwitness is a person who testifies about something that they heard and did not see, someone who has firsthand knowledge of an event only from hearing that event. This type of identification has been proven to be very unreliable."

Quinton knew he had the jury's full attention.

"You will hear from experts who place my client's phone at the scene of the crime, but you will hear my witness tell you why that is a mistake. You will hear their experts tell you his fingerprints were in Mr. Price's townhouse, but they will not be able to tell you when they were placed there, only that my client had been in the townhouse in the past."

Quinton let that settle for a moment.

"What you will not hear is from anyone who saw Marcus Hale enter Daniel Price's house that night. You will not hear of the location of the murder weapon. You will not hear of a motive substantial enough to cause my client to commit murder."

Quinton lifted one finger. "No eyewitness."

Another finger. "No physical evidence tying Marcus Hale to the killing."

A third finger. "No motive."

The jury hung on every word.

Quinton spread his hands slightly and looked slowly across the jurors.

"In addition, assuming that Mrs. Benton has perfect hearing, Mr. Durant would like you to assume that if Marcus Hale argued with Daniel Price earlier that day, that Marcus Hale must have returned later that night and committed murder."

Quinton shook his head again.

"But assumptions are not proof. Layers of possible misidentification strung together with other elements to prove something that is not factual is called circumstantial evidence."

Quinton rested his hands behind his back.

"This case contains noise. It contains speculation. It contains a tragic death."

Quinton glanced briefly toward Hale.

"What it does not contain is proof beyond a reasonable doubt that Marcus Hale committed this crime."

Quinton looked back at the jury.

"When all the evidence is presented, the defense will ask

you to return the only verdict that justice allows." Quinton paused. "Not guilty."

Quinton returned to the defense table.

Judge Blaylock looked out across the expectant courtroom.

"Ladies and gentlemen of the jury, we will take a short break then proceed with the presentation of evidence."

After the break, the attorneys returned to their respective places in the courtroom, gladiators ready for battle with Judge Blaylock setting the rules of engagement.

"Call your first witness."

Durant rose from the prosecution table. "The prosecution calls Officer Sam Gere."

The handsome, young uniformed police officer stepped from the side benches and walked to the witness stand. Gere raised one hand while Bailiff Grant administered the oath, then settled into the chair.

Quinton recognized the standard procedure that most prosecutors followed, calling the first officer on the scene to lay out the case in broad strokes for the jury. True to form, each witness who testified would expand and emphasize different parts of the prosecution's case, making it easy for the jury to follow the story Durant wanted to tell.

Durant approached the lectern. "Please state your name and occupation for the jury."

"Sam Gere. Patrol officer with the Houston Police Department."

"How long have you served with HPD, Officer Gere?"

"Three years."

"Were you on duty the evening Daniel Price was found dead?"

"Yes."

"Did you respond to a residence on Bellaire Boulevard that evening?"

"I did."

"Officer Gere, were you the first officer on the scene?"

"Yes, I was."

"What brought you there?"

"Dispatch received a call reporting an unresponsive male inside the residence."

"Who made that call?"

"A neighbor. Sheryl Benton."

Durant walked slowly toward the witness box.

"When you arrived, what did you observe?"

"The front door was partly open. I announced police presence and entered to check on the welfare of the occupant."

"And what did you find inside?"

"A male lying on the living room floor."

"Did you later learn the identity of that man?"

"Yes. Daniel Price."

"Was Daniel Price alive when you found him?"

"No."

Durant paused.

"What did you do next?"

"I secured the residence and contacted Dispatch to report a possible homicide. I requested detectives and crime scene personnel. While I waited, I went next door to interview Sheryl Benton, the neighbor who had discovered the body."

"After that, who arrived in response to the call to Dispatch?"

"Detective Clive Broussard."

"We'll hear from Detective Broussard later. For now, give us your version of what happened when the detective arrived."

"We walked through the residence together. I explained

what I observed when I first entered and pointed out the condition of the room."

Durant glanced down at his notes.

"Officer Gere, during that initial walk through, did you observe any items in the room that appeared significant?"

"Yes."

"What did you observe?"

Gere shifted slightly.

"There was a Houston Wildcatters baseball cap on the floor near the sofa."

A faint stir moved through the gallery.

Durant continued. "Anything else?"

"A broken table near the entry in the foyer. The table had blood on the leg."

Durant let that sit for a moment.

"Anything further?"

"Yes. A pool of blood that spread on the floor near the victim."

Durant turned toward the jury.

"After that walk through, who assumed responsibility for the investigation?"

"Detective Broussard."

Durant stepped back.

"Thank you, Officer Gere. No further questions."

Judge Blaylock looked toward the defense table. "Mr. Bell. Your witness."

Quinton rose and walked to the lectern.

"Officer Gere, when you conducted the initial walk through of the home, you said you saw a Houston Wildcatters baseball cap on the floor."

"Yes."

"Did the cap have anything in or on it that tied it to my client, Marcus Hale?"

Gere hesitated slightly. "Not that I could tell."

"Was there anything else in the home that belonged to Mr. Hale?"

"Not that I could identify."

"No wallet?"

"No."

"No phone?"

"No."

"No identification of any kind?"

"No. At that point, there was nothing visible that directly connected Mr. Hale to the scene."

"And you did not see Marcus Hale at the house that evening?"

"No."

"You did not see him enter?"

"No."

"You did not see him leave?"

"No."

Quinton turned slightly toward the jury.

"When you left the scene that night, there was nothing connecting my client to that house."

"Correct."

"No further questions."

33
———

"Mrs. Benton, earlier that same afternoon, did you hear anything unusual coming from Mr. Price's home?"

"Yes."

"What did you hear?"

"Two men arguing in the yard."

"Could you hear what they were arguing about?"

"Some of it. It sounded like they were yelling about money."

"Was the argument heated?"

"Yes. Very."

"Did you recognize either of the voices?"

"I recognized Daniel's voice."

"And the other?"

"No. I didn't recognize the other voice."

Durant nodded.

"Mrs. Benton, were you later asked by police to participate in an identification procedure?"

"Yes."

"What kind?"

"They first showed me several men in person and asked if I could identify the man whose voice I heard."

"Were you able to do that?"

"No."

"Why not?"

"I never saw the man arguing with Daniel. I only heard him."

Durant continued.

"After that, a few days later, were you asked to participate in another procedure?"

"Yes."

"What kind?"

"A voice lineup."

"How did that come about?"

"Detective Broussard came back for a second interview and asked me if I thought I could recognize the voice."

"Explain that second lineup for the jury."

"I listened while several men read the same sentence. I was in another room and could only hear their voices."

"And did you recognize one of those voices?"

"Yes."

"Whose voice did you identify?"

"Marcus Hale. He was voice four."

Durant allowed the answer to settle over the courtroom.

"So your identification of Mr. Hale is based on the voice you heard during that argument?"

"Yes."

Durant nodded.

"No further questions."

He returned to the prosecution table as the quiet scratching of reporters' pens filled the room. Quinton sat motionless for a moment, watching the witness, already measuring how fragile a voice alone might sound to twelve people asked to decide a man's fate.

Judge Blaylock gestured toward the defense table. "Your witness, Mr. Bell."

Quinton stood and approached Mrs. Benton. He gave her a warm smile that the jury could see and spoke in a low, kind voice.

"Good afternoon, Mrs. Benton."

She appeared afraid of him. "Good afternoon."

"You've lived next door to Mr. Price for some time, correct?"

"A couple of years."

"And during the time you've lived there, you've come to know many of the neighbors on your street?"

"Yes."

Quinton began to charm her. "You strike me as someone who keeps an eye out for the neighborhood."

She gave a small, uncertain smile. "I try to."

"You notice when things are out of place."

"Yes."

"When a car is unfamiliar or someone doesn't pick up their mail. When a neighbor hasn't been seen for a while."

"That's true."

"And that's what brought you to Mr. Price's home that evening. The lights you thought were on."

"Yes."

Quinton nodded gently. "I'm sorry you had to witness that. It must have been very upsetting."

"It was."

"You also told the jury you heard two men arguing that afternoon."

"I did."

"That argument took place outside Mr. Price's house?"

"Yes."

"You were inside your own home at the time?"

"Yes."

Quinton stepped a little closer.

"Mrs. Benton, from your living room window, can you see Mr. Price's front yard?"

"Yes."

"And his front walk?"

"Yes."

"In fact, you can see quite a bit of activity around his house from that window."

"I suppose so."

"But on that particular afternoon, you didn't see the two men arguing."

"No."

"You only heard them."

"That's right."

Quinton tilted his head slightly.

"You didn't go to the window to look?"

"No."

"You never actually saw the two men together."

"No."

Quinton paused, letting the answer sit in the quiet courtroom.

"Mrs. Benton, do you wear glasses?"

"Yes."

"Were you wearing them that afternoon?"

She hesitated.

"No. I don't think so."

"So even if you had looked out the window, your vision would not have been as clear as usual."

Durant shifted slightly at the prosecution table.

"That's correct."

"Weren't you curious about the ruckus in your neighborhood?"

"Yes, but I didn't want to miss my show."

"You had the television on?"

"Yes. *The Young and the Restless*. It's my favorite."

Quinton's tone remained courteous.

"Mrs. Benton, may I ask your age?"

"Seventy-eight."

"And like most of us, some things change a little with time."

She nodded cautiously.

"Yes."

"Vision sometimes changes."

"Yes."

"Hearing sometimes changes as well."

Another small pause.

"Yes."

"Do you wear hearing aids?"

"No."

"Did you recently have your hearing checked?" Quinton returned to the defense table and picked up a folder containing research Dart had done on Mrs. Benton's recent audiometry test.

"Yes."

"You've noticed your hearing isn't quite as sharp as it once was."

She looked down at her hands.

"That's fair."

"You sometimes ask people to repeat themselves."

"Sometimes."

Quinton consulted the damning file. "Did you have your hearing checked ten days before the date of the murder of Mr. Price?"

"Yes. But..."

Quinton interrupted. "Thank you. So just to be clear for the jury. The only thing you relied on to identify anyone was a voice you heard from inside your house."

"Yes."

Quinton nodded politely.

"Thank you, Mrs. Benton."

He returned to the defense table without another word. Behind him, the courtroom had grown noticeably quieter, the certainty that had filled the room during the prosecution's questions now replaced with something thinner and far less solid.

Durant jumped to his feet. "Redirect, Your Honor?"

"Proceed."

Durant approached the witness stand with measured steps.

"Mrs. Benton, defense counsel asked you several questions about your eyesight and your hearing."

"Yes."

"Do you want to finish what you were saying about your hearing test?"

"Yes, I did have it checked, but the doctor told me I was in normal range."

"Very good. Now, I want to focus on what you actually heard that afternoon. The two men arguing. Were they speaking softly?"

"No."

"How would you describe it?"

"They were yelling."

"Loudly?"

"Yes."

"So even though you were inside your own home, and the television was on, you could hear the argument."

"Yes."

Durant nodded.

"And that is how you were able to recognize Mr. Price's voice."

"Yes."

"And, later, you were able to recognize Mr. Hale's voice in the lineup?"

"Yes."

Durant gave a small, satisfied nod and stepped back from the lectern.

"No further questions."

Judge Blaylock looked toward the defense table.

Quinton remained seated, his pen resting loosely between his fingers. He did not stand.

"Very well. You may step down, Mrs. Benton."

The witness gathered her purse and descended from the stand.

The courtroom settled again, but the earlier certainty had faded. Durant's questions had steadied the witness for a moment, yet the jurors still carried the image Quinton had left them with.

A woman who never saw the men. Without her glasses. A woman whose hearing was no longer what it once had been. And yet, she had picked out the only suspect in the voice lineup.

"The prosecution calls Dr. Bart Kowalski."

The side door opened and a tall man in a dark suit stepped forward. His hair was clipped short and steel-gray at the temples. He moved with the quiet efficiency of someone used to courtrooms and worse places than courtrooms.

The bailiff administered the oath and the good doctor sat.

"Please state your name and occupation for the jury," Durant said.

"Dr. Bart Kowalski. I'm the Harris County medical examiner."

"How long have you held that position?"

"Eight years."

"And before that?"

"I served as a forensic pathologist in Dallas County."

Durant nodded.

"Did you perform the autopsy on Daniel Price?"

"Yes, I did."

"When was that performed?"

"The morning following the discovery of the body."

Durant approached the screen that had been positioned beside the jury box.

Judge Blaylock held up a hand. "Just a moment, Mr. Durant."

"Yes, Your Honor."

The judge turned to the jury. "Ladies and gentlemen. You are about to see several graphic photographs taken during the autopsy of Mr. Price. They may be difficult for you to look at, but it's important in understanding this part of the evidence. Please prepare yourselves."

Quinton frowned at Mo. They had argued in the judge's chambers for over an hour trying to get the photos excluded as inflammatory and unnecessary to the case. They had even offered to stipulate to the nature of the cuts and gashes on the body. Durant had won the argument and Judge Blaylock had allowed them in.

Durant clicked a small remote and a photograph of Daniel Price with gashes across his chest appeared onscreen. He was naked except his private parts were covered by a small white towel.

Several jurors gasped.

"Doctor, without getting overly graphic, can you explain the nature of Mr. Price's fatal injuries?"

Kowalski folded his hands.

"Mr. Price died from several gashes to the upper torso."

"A sharp force injury?"

"Yes."

Durant paced slowly.

"Doctor, when investigators first arrived at the scene, was there an initial belief about what type of weapon may have been used?"

"Yes."

"What was that?"

"A knife."

"And was that your conclusion after performing the autopsy?"

"No."

"What changed your opinion?"

"The depth and shape of the wound tract."

Durant leaned slightly closer.

"Please explain that for the jury."

"The wound was far deeper and wider than what a typical knife would produce. The bone damage was also significant."

"You ruled out a standard knife?"

"Yes."

"What type of instrument would be consistent with the wound you observed?"

"A heavier bladed tool."

"Such as?"

"Possibly a hatchet."

Durant paused.

"Doctor, could it also be consistent with a small axe?"

Kowalski nodded.

"Yes."

Durant turned toward the courtroom clerk.

"Your Honor, the prosecution would like to publish State's Exhibit 3."

Judge Blaylock nodded. "You may."

The screen changed from the autopsy photo to one taken from social media. Several young men stood shoulder to shoulder inside a neon-lit venue. A rack of wooden targets hung on the wall behind them. Each of the men held an axe.

Marcus Hale stood in the center, smiling broadly. One arm slung around a teammate.

The caption beneath the photo read:

Halestorm's birthday at Axeperience! The boys hooked him up with his own axe!

A murmur moved through the gallery.

Durant let the image linger before speaking again.

"Dr. Kowalski, you see the object Mr. Hale is holding in that photograph?"

"Yes."

"What is it?"

"A small throwing axe."

"Doctor, based on your examination of the wound, could a weapon like that have caused the injury that killed Daniel Price?"

"Yes."

"Would it be consistent with the damage you observed during the autopsy?"

"Yes, it would."

Durant turned back toward the jury.

"No further questions."

The screen went dark.

At the defense table, Quinton leaned back slightly in his

chair, eyes still on the photograph that had just disappeared. The jurors had seen exactly what Durant wanted them to see.

A weapon. And a smiling man holding it. The courtroom erupted and reporters vigorously scribbled notes.

Judge Blaylock banged his gavel. "Order. We'll recess for today and begin tomorrow with cross-examination, Mr. Bell."

There wasn't a lot Quinton could do; it was almost five and Judge Blaylock had made up his mind. Too bad the last thing on the jury's mind was Hale with a weapon in his hand.

34

The office was quieter than usual that night. The courthouse day had drained them all. Half-empty takeout containers sat open on the conference table beside a pile of chopsticks, hot sauce and soy sauce packets. Outside the windows the downtown lights glowed through the glass like a distant second city.

Quinton sat at the head of the table with the medical examiner's report spread open in front of him.

Mo leaned back in her chair, rubbing her temples. Dart stood near the window with his arms folded. Cassidy sat forward with her laptop open, scrolling through notes that no longer seemed to matter.

Quinton tapped the report with the end of his pen. "Read this again."

Cassidy looked down.

"Sharp force trauma. Probable instrument meat cleaver or hatchet."

Quinton nodded.

"Anything else?"

She scanned the paragraph again.

"No."

"No axe," Mo said.

"No axe," Quinton agreed.

Dart grunted from the window.

"Durant turned a hatchet into a birthday present."

Cassidy stared at the screen of her laptop as if the answer might still appear there.

"I should have found that photograph."

No one answered immediately.

She looked up.

"It's public. It's on social media. It shouldn't have been hard to find."

Dart shook his head.

"I didn't find it either."

Cassidy rubbed her forehead. "I ran searches on Hale's name, on the Wildcatters, on Price, on the bars where they went to celebrate victories. Nothing like that popped up."

Dart looked over at Quinton. "I should have asked Miles to scrape their accounts. He would have pulled every photo those guys ever posted."

"Social media hides things. Algorithms bury posts. People change privacy settings."

"That photo didn't look buried," Cassidy said. "Durant had it ready like a present under the tree."

Mo gave a dry laugh.

"He probably had an investigator looking for something exactly like that."

Dart looked frustrated. "I shoulda thought of it."

Quinton looked around the room at the three of them. The fatigue showed in all their faces. Cassidy's eyes were rimmed red from too many late nights. Mo's legal pad was filled with cramped handwriting that slanted lower with every page. Dart looked like he had been awake since last week.

"We're all tired," Quinton said.

Cassidy shook her head. "That's not an excuse."

"No," Quinton said evenly. "It's reality."

He slid the autopsy report back into the folder and stood. "That's enough for tonight."

They all looked at him.

"Go home."

Mo hesitated. "You sure?"

"Yes."

Dart was already reaching for his jacket. Cassidy lingered a moment longer.

"I'm sorry, Quinton."

He gave her a tired smile.

"You're doing fine."

She studied him as if she wasn't entirely convinced, then finally nodded and followed the others toward the door. A few minutes later the office was silent again. Quinton sat back down at the conference table and opened the medical examiner's report once more.

Cleaver. Hatchet.

He tapped the page with his pen and stared at the words in the quiet office.

The pool was nearly empty when Quinton arrived at the gym. The overhead lights reflected across the surface in long white ribbons. Chlorine hung faintly in the air.

Quinton dropped his towel on a chair and slid into the water. Cold at first. Then steady.

He pushed off the wall and began the slow rhythm that had

carried him through a hundred long nights before. Stroke. Breathe. Stroke. Breathe.

The day in the courtroom followed him into the water. Axe.

The photograph had been perfect for Durant. Bright lights. Smiling athletes. Marcus Hale holding the small throwing axe like a trophy.

A birthday gift.

Quinton turned at the wall and pushed off again.

Stroke. Breathe.

But the medical examiner had not said axe. Cleaver. Hatchet.

The words drifted through his mind as he swam the length of the pool again. He slowed slightly, letting the water glide along his arms as the rhythm shifted from exercise to thought. The perfect zone.

The autopsy report had been clear. He had read it half a dozen times that night in the office. Nothing about an axe. Durant hadn't started with the photograph. If he had, he could have had the medical examiner add the axe as a possible weapon. No, he found the picture after the autopsy report had been completed.

Too late.

Quinton pushed off again, slower this time. Stroke. If Durant had possessed that photograph before the autopsy, it would have been in the report.

But Durant had not been able to ask it that way because it wasn't there. Instead, he had built the category first to try to get it in without the jury noticing it was missing. Cleaver. Hatchet. Then introduced the photograph. After discovery had been exchanged.

Which meant Kowalski had never examined that axe or the picture of the axe. Never measured it. Never even knew it existed. Durant had walked into the courtroom with a picture and built the connection.

Quinton finished his laps and leaned his arms on the edge of the pool, breathing slowly.

That was why the question had been so careful. Could a weapon like that cause the injury? Yes.

Because any axe could. Any hatchet. Any cleaver. The photograph wasn't science. It was theater.

In court the next morning, Quinton rose without hurry, buttoned his coat, and walked to the lectern as though the photograph on the screen had meant very little to him.

"Good morning, Doctor."

"Good morning."

Quinton eased into his questioning, setting up the good doctor for the squeeze.

"You testified yesterday on direct that the injury to Daniel Price was not, in your opinion, caused by an ordinary knife."

"That's correct."

"And that, after the autopsy, you believed the wound was more consistent with a heavier bladed instrument."

"Yes."

"Something like a meat cleaver."

"Yes."

"Or a hatchet."

"Yes."

"But, you did not mention an axe in your autopsy report, did you?"

"No, but I said like a meat cleaver or hatchet."

"Okay, Doctor. What is the difference between a hatchet, a meat cleaver, and an axe?"

"Well, for one thing, they all have different depths of impact when used to strike. Also, the hilt on each one is made of different materials causing the hilt to go into the wound, following the strike of the blade."

Quinton nodded once.

"So, did you evaluate these different weapons based on your experience as a medical examiner?"

"Yes."

"In detail?"

"Of course."

"If so, then why did you not include an axe as the possible murder weapon in the autopsy report?"

"Well, I was speaking generally about chopping instruments."

Quinton pulled photographs of several chopping instruments from a file, dropped a copy on the prosecutor's table, and approached the judge. "May I offer Defense's Exhibit 8?"

Judge Blaylock took a quick look at the exhibit and handed it to Bailiff Grant. After it was marked, Quinton took it over to Dr. Kawalski and handed it to him. He took it as if it might bite him.

"So, Doctor, you said a chopping instrument," Quinton repeated. "Because tools designed to chop come in different forms. A full axe, the kind used to split logs, has a long handle and generates tremendous swing force. A hatchet is smaller, shorter handled, but still wedge-shaped and capable of deep cuts. And a meat cleaver, the kind used in a kitchen or butcher shop, carries a heavy rectangular blade that can chop through bone with a straight downward strike."

He paused, letting the distinction settle over the room.

"When you examined Daniel Price, Doctor, you could not say a chopping instrument or axe caused those wounds, could you? Only that the injuries were consistent with a hatchet or cleaver."

The doctor hesitated.

"That is correct."

Quinton turned slightly toward the jury.

"So, when Mr. Durant asked you about the axe in that photograph, you were not saying that you could identify that particular axe as the murder weapon."

"No."

"Did the investigators find an axe when they searched Mr. Hale's home and locker at the stadium?"

"No."

"So, you have not examined that particular axe."

"No."

"While you were doing the autopsy, did you use the photograph to estimate the length of the blade or the hilt on the axe?"

"No."

"So, you can't tell this jury that the axe in the photograph killed Daniel Price."

"No, I cannot."

"Did you know about this photograph at the time of the autopsy?"

"No."

"And, were you made aware of this photograph prior to your testimony?"

"Yes, I was."

"So, you've only added the word axe to your testimony to give credence to the photograph, have you not?"

"I said hatchet or meat cleaver. It's almost the same thing. You're mincing words."

"Almost, but a man's life is at stake here. Don't you think details are important?"

"Well."

"You can only say that an object of that general type could have caused the injury."

"That is correct."

Quinton took a step closer.

"And when you say general type, you mean there are multiple possible instruments that fit your findings. And you only testified yesterday about an axe because the prosecution showed you that photo."

"A small hand axe could fit."

"And other similar chopping tools as well."

"Yes."

Quinton let the words settle.

"So your testimony does not identify one unique weapon."

"No."

"It gives a category."

"Yes."

"You were not offered a murder weapon to compare against the wound."

"That's correct."

"You did not test the blade in the photograph."

"No."

"You did not measure it."

"No."

"You did not examine its edge, its weight, or its condition."

"No."

"In fact, for all you know, the object in that social media picture may never have left the axe-throwing venue."

Durant rose halfway. "Objection. Calls for speculation."

"Withdrawn," Quinton said easily, before Judge Blaylock could rule.

He turned back to the witness.

"Doctor, let's keep it simple. You have no forensic basis to connect that specific axe in that photo to Daniel Price's death."

"That is correct."

"You cannot tell this jury it was that axe, a hatchet, or a meat cleaver."

"That's correct."

"And if police never recovered the actual weapon, then from a medical examiner's standpoint, your job is limited to describing what kinds of instruments are medically consistent with the wound."

"Yes."

"When the jury saw that birthday picture yesterday, that was not science, was it?"

Durant was on his feet again. "Objection."

Quinton dipped his head. "No further questions."

Quinton had not proven the axe was not the murder weapon, but he had caused the jury to doubt the prosecution. They'd tried to pull a fast one, and juries did not like that. Score one for the defense. One more piece of circumstantial evidence cast in reasonable doubt.

35

The air inside the Harris County jail never changed. It carried the stale scent of disinfectant and body odor and something metallic beneath it all.

Hale sat at the narrow steel table in the attorney client meeting room, hands clasped, forearms resting on cold metal.

Houston was stretching toward football season, and the tiniest promise of fall was breaking through the Texas heat in the nighttime.

Inside, Hale was waiting. He wasn't the only one. Protestors carrying signs and shouting slogans had started to congregate daily on the courthouse steps. 'Free the Halestorm' and 'Hale is Innocent' were most popular. A trio of Hawaiian drummers assembled and pounded buckets with sticks almost every day of court.

Others celebrated his history by performing the Samoan slap dance and the Maori warrior dance, grunting in the Hawaiian fashion. All this was unseen by Hale. He was inside. Inside was a term of art meaning in jail.

A guard opened the door. "Your lawyer."

Quinton Bell stepped in, jacket unbuttoned, legal pad tucked beneath his arm. He looked rested, composed, almost casual. Only the tightness in his jaw betrayed the calculation behind his eyes.

Hale stood.

"You see it?" Hale asked before Quinton could sit. "The Wildcatters."

"Training camp footage?"

"They're back."

The Houston Wildcatters had returned from camp, as usual, in late August. Social media was flooded with highlight clips. Receivers diving across painted turf. Linemen colliding like freight trains. Rookie interviews. Coach Brown promising a disciplined year.

And no Halestorm.

Quinton set his pad down and sat. "I saw."

Hale lowered himself back into the chair. "They've got Rios taking my reps."

"That's temporary," Quinton said evenly.

Hale gave him a look that said he knew how football worked. Temporary had a way of becoming permanent. The league did not pause for indictments and murder trials. And, he knew that if the trial started going south, the signs of support would follow.

Outside GulfTex Stadium, banners snapped in the wind. For now, a giant image of Hale still hung from a light pole, helmet tucked beneath one arm, eyes fierce beneath stadium lights. The slogan beneath him read:

UNLEASH THE STORM

It wouldn't be there for long; Rios's handsome mug would replace it soon. Talk radio dissected preseason projections. Sports anchors debated whether the Wildcatters' defense could survive without him.

None of them mentioned that he had not been convicted.

They said *accused*. They said *charged*.

"They're installing packages without me. Red zone looks. Blitz schemes. They'll build the season around whoever's there. Probably Rios."

Quinton leaned back slightly, studying his client.

Hale was built like he had been carved out of something harder than bone. Even in a jail uniform, even unshaven, even thinner than he had been in preseason photos, he looked like an NFL linebacker. But there was something else now. Not fear exactly. Displacement.

"They've denied bail again. I tried to show that we needed you out to work on your case, but the judge said we could work here."

"I knew they would. But, it's not like I'm some flight risk. I've got a contract. I've got a house. I've got..." He stopped himself.

"A life," Quinton finished.

Silence filled the room.

"You're being held because you can afford a large bail and the means to flee. They don't want their prime suspect leaving them holding their dicks in their hands."

Hale let out a breath that almost sounded like a laugh. "I stayed, even when I had time to leave."

"I know." Quinton had chosen not to share the information on the micro drive found in the lamp in Price's apartment. He had not shared it with Dart either, which caused no small amount of friction between them. He wanted deniability for all involved if he chose not to reveal it. However, a new witness made him worry about what the prosecution might have in that regard.

"There's something else."

"What now?"

Quinton folded his hands on the table. "Harris County added a financial analyst to their witness list this morning."

Hale's expression shifted. "Why?"

"They subpoenaed your bank records. Endorsements. Contract payments. Everything."

Hale stared at him. "I've got money. That's not a crime."

"No. But it can be part of the motive."

The fluorescent lights hummed overhead. Hale leaned back slowly. "You think they're going to say I killed Price over money?"

"I think they're going to show the jury exactly how much Daniel Price was making off you. And then they're going to show your texts trying to get free of him."

Hale's jaw tightened.

"You told him you were done paying through the nose. You said you could handle endorsements yourself. You said you didn't need a middleman skimming off the top."

"I was negotiating. I still need an agent. I just didn't want him as my agent. I'd still have to pay someone."

"You were threatening to cut him out."

"That's allowed. He didn't own me."

Silence settled between them.

Quinton continued, voice calm. "If they put up a chart showing Price's commissions, then your extension kicking in, then your text saying you were finished making him rich."

"They'll make it look like I decided to keep it all."

"Yes."

Hale's hands curled into fists on the table. "If that was the standard for murder, every sports figure in the known universe would have motive."

"True. But their agents are not dead."

242

By noon, Quinton was standing at a row of microphones on the courthouse steps. Cameras blinked red. Reporters angled forward. Behind him, the stone facade of the Harris County courthouse loomed with institutional indifference.

Quinton adjusted his cufflinks, waited for the noise to settle, and began.

"My client, Marcus Hale, has now been incarcerated for months without bond. I have just spoken to the judge again regarding bail and broken the news to my client. He will remain in custody over the long holiday weekend."

A murmur rippled through the press line.

"He is presumed innocent under the Constitution of the United States and the laws of Texas. He surrendered voluntarily. He has no history of flight. He has no prior criminal record. He has substantial ties to this community."

A reporter raised a hand. "Mr. Bell, he's charged with murdering his former agent."

"Accused. He is accused."

Cameras zoomed in.

"The denial of bail in this case is not about risk," Quinton continued. "It is about optics."

Quinton knew he was going to anger Judge Blaylock with his rhetoric, but he had to put something out into the public to counter the bad press his client was getting.

Another voice called out. "Are you suggesting special treatment because he's a football player?"

"I am suggesting equal treatment. He should be out awaiting trial under reasonable conditions. Maybe an ankle bracelet, maybe home detention. Instead, he sits in jail while his team returns from training camp, while his livelihood evaporates, while his reputation is tried in the court of public opinion."

He let that hang.

"Pretrial detention is not supposed to be punishment. It is meant to ensure appearance in court and protect the public. There has been no showing that Mr. Hale poses a threat to anyone or is a flight risk."

The courthouse doors opened behind him. Lawyers filtered in and out, pretending not to listen. They knew the drill. Get the jury pool on the side of your client any way possible.

"Every day he remains incarcerated without bail inflicts financial and professional damage that cannot be undone. The season is about to begin. Contracts contain performance incentives. Conditioning requirements. Sponsorship obligations. This is not a minor inconvenience. It is catastrophic harm to a man who has not been convicted of anything."

A reporter shouted, "Are you saying the district attorney is targeting him?"

"I am saying that justice should not bend to headlines."

He stepped back from the microphones.

Cameras surged forward.

"Mr. Bell, do you believe your client will be found innocent?"

"Absolutely. I believe that justice will prevail."

He turned and walked up the courthouse steps, expression controlled.

Inside, he did not slow until he reached the shade of the corridor. Cassidy caught up to him, breathless, legal pad clutched to her chest.

"That was good. Very good."

"They'll spin it."

"Of course they will."

He glanced at his watch. "Call Mo. Let her know the temperature just went up."

That evening, sports networks replayed Quinton's statement between practice footage.

The Wildcatters ran drills under stadium lights. Sweat glistened. Helmets cracked. The anchor speculated on the return of Hale.

"The owner, Jerry Cutler, and general manager, Tex Newsome, are working with Coach Zack Brown toward a successful year. Fans are optimistic that the Halestorm will be able to return prior to the first game against the Tennessee Titans scheduled for September 7."

The anchor's voice carried a note of skepticism. "Defense Attorney Quinton Bell says Hale is being unfairly detained, causing him to miss valuable training time. The district attorney's office cited the seriousness of the charges and stated they would oppose bail under any circumstances."

Onscreen, the network showed saved footage of Hale in handcuffs. Cut back to linebackers colliding on green turf. Cut to fans lining up for season tickets. Cut to protestors, wearing Wildcatters gear, holding up 'Free the Halestorm' signs.

In the jail, Hale sat and watched the segment on a mounted television in the common area. Some inmates were spellbound. Other inmates leaned against cinderblock walls, half interested. One of them nudged the inmate next to him. Starstruck.

Hale didn't show his emotions.

Onscreen, his image flashed again in his Wildcatters uniform. Halestorm. Crowd roaring.

When the chyron shifted back to *MURDER CHARGE*, Hale stood and walked back to his cell.

Hale woke in the night in a cold sweat. His cellmate was snoring lightly. Lighting from the hallway broke the darkness. He had been dreaming. In his sleepy state, he could remember most of it. Maybe.

His mother was sitting beside a river in Thailand. She was calling to him. Chaiwat. Chaiwat. He turned to look at her, and she melted away into the stream. He tried to reimagine what she looked like but could not. He wasn't even sure it was her or just an image he'd created. He turned toward the wall and choked back tears. After a moment, he gave up and let them flow into the pillow.

<h1 style="text-align:center">36</h1>

The knock came without warning. Quinton looked up from the file spread across his desk as Anna stepped into the doorway. They were both in jeans and T-shirts working over the long weekend.

"Detective Broussard is here. He apologized for not calling first."

Quinton exhaled slowly. "Of course he didn't call. Send him in."

Broussard filled the doorway a moment later, broad shoulders, rumpled sport coat, the faint scent of coffee and Cajun spice trailing behind him. He carried a thin folder under one arm and wore the look of a man who thought he was about to deliver good news.

"Counselor," Broussard stepped inside the room. "Thought you might be working this weekend. You got a minute, or you gonna bill me for the oxygen in here?"

Quinton gestured to the chair across from his desk. "Sit down, Detective. I assume you didn't come all the way up here to breathe my air conditioning."

Broussard laughed.

"What would Durant think about you having a visit with me during the trial?"

Broussard dropped into the chair with a grunt and slid the folder onto the desk. "I'm not here about that. I do have more than one case, Bell. Just like you do. We got something on that little boom boom under your fancy Range Rover."

Quinton's expression stayed neutral. "I'm listening."

The detective flipped the folder open and pushed several photographs toward him. Closeups of wiring. A metal casing. A smudge of gray residue.

"Bomb squad says it wasn't professional military grade. Homemade, but not sloppy. Whoever built it knew enough to keep it contained. Loud scare, not a kill shot."

Quinton studied the images without touching them. His pulse ticked up despite himself. "If I had been three feet closer, that might not be your report. Besides, half of Texas fits that profile."

Broussard snorted. "Yeah, well, there's more. The casing came from a marine battery housing. Real specific kind. Hard to get unless you know where to look."

Quinton felt a flicker of recognition he buried instantly.

Marine equipment. Improvised. Controlled blast radius.

He kept his expression still. Poker face.

Broussard held up one of the photos. "And there's a residue pattern. Bomb tech says whoever wired it used a trigger that looked remote, not timed. Means they were probably watching when it went off. Surveillance angle. If they wanted you dead, they'd have waited until you got in the SUV to trigger the remote."

Quinton leaned back in his chair, folding his hands together. *So, they didn't want to kill me after all.*

"Anything else?"

Broussard warmed to the reveal. "Witness over at the court-house parking lot remembers a man hangin' around earlier that week. Not local. Accent maybe Irish or British. Hard to tell. Guy kept to himself after asking a few questions. Wore a ball-cap, low."

Quinton's stomach tightened, but his voice stayed dry. "Houston has a lot of accents, Detective."

"Yeah, well, this one stood out. And one more thing. The wiring had this little flourish. Bomb squad guy says whoever built it likes to leave extra slack in the line. Habit, maybe. Signature kinda thing."

Quinton glanced down at the photos again. Extra slack in the line.

He forced himself to shrug.

"So, you've got a guy who knows enough about electronics to build a loud toy, maybe watches too many action movies, and possibly drinks imported beer."

Broussard's eyes narrowed. "You don't seem impressed."

"What do you want me to say? None of that helps me sleep better at night."

The detective leaned forward. "Look, I'm telling you this because you got a habit of knowing people before we do. Thought maybe it'd ring a bell."

Quinton met his gaze evenly. "It doesn't."

Broussard watched him for a long second, like he was trying to decide whether Quinton was lying or simply stubborn. Finally, he pushed himself up from the chair.

"Alright then. We keep digging. You try not to park anywhere stupid for a while, yeah?"

"I'll add that to my list of lifestyle changes as soon as I can get a new car."

Broussard paused at the door. "Whoever did this knows you, Counselor. That ain't random. You got enemies, maybe start thinking which one of 'em hates you enough to make fireworks."

Quinton gave a thin smile. "That list is longer than your case file."

"Yeah," Broussard muttered. "That's what worries me."

The detective left and the office fell quiet again.

Quinton sat motionless for several seconds, eyes fixed on the photographs Broussard had left behind. He waited until he was sure Anna had shown Broussard out, then pulled the folder closer.

Marine battery casing. Remote trigger. Controlled blast. Irish accent. Extra slack in the wiring.

They meant nothing to Broussard because they were technical quirks. Habits. Small things that looked like coincidence.

To Quinton, they felt like an echo. He knew a little about each of the tidbits, but not enough to be sure. It felt like Tua Dannon's guys in New York.

He stood and walked slowly to the window, staring down over the Loop while his mind worked through old memories he had spent years trying to bury.

A courtroom in New York. A man who moved like violence was second nature.

Tua Dannon? Devlin? A new Dannon soldier he'd never met?

Quinton's jaw tightened.

Devlin had never been arrested after the shoot-out in court. Just vanished into rumor and shadow. One of the few people sharp enough to notice inconsistencies in Quinton's past. One of the few who might have looked at Byron and seen through the disguise.

And Devlin loved theatrics. Controlled chaos. Messages framed as accidents.

The extra slack in the wiring. Quinton returned to his desk, opened Google, and looked around at the NY Tua Dannon postings online. He saw several clues that confirmed his suspicions that it was either Tua Dannon or one of his goons. Quinton closed his eyes briefly.

Broussard would never know that. It was the kind of detail only someone who had layers of knowledge would recognize.

Quinton re-turned to the window, then began pacing.

The surveillance angle fit Devlin. He never rushed. He studied. Watched. Waited until the moment carried the most psychological weight.

And the accent.

Broussard heard 'Irish or British.' To Quinton, it felt more specific. Memories of voices and accents from the past.

The bombing. The napkin at the courthouse. The ferry replica in his house. The man in the casino who never blinked. Each piece alone meant nothing. Together, they pointed in one direction. He stopped pacing and braced his hands on the edge of his desk.

"Devlin?" The question hung in the empty room. He was not certain. Not yet. There were gaps. Assumptions. No proof he could take to anyone else, even if he wanted to. But the pattern felt too familiar to ignore. His gut said it was Devlin.

Broussard thought he had delivered a lead. What he had really delivered was a memory.

And for the first time since the explosion, Quinton felt something colder than fear.

Recognition.

That night, Quinton stood alone in his office long after Anna had gone home.

The building had settled into its evening quiet. The hum of

the HVAC. The city beyond the glass moving in red and white ribbons along the Loop. He was in his usual position staring out the window, thinking.

Devlin.

The name did not land like a surprise. It landed like confirmation.

Of course it's him. If it was Tua Dannon, I would be dead already. But, what did Devlin want?

He felt it settle in his chest the way a trial strategy sometimes did when all the stray pieces finally snapped into place. The ferry boat model. The napkin. The explosion. The timing. The pattern of pressure that felt personal, not random.

Devlin had come to Houston. And if Devlin was back, then Quinton Bell was no longer simply a defense lawyer in the middle of a high-profile murder case. He was prey.

He lowered himself into the leather chair behind his desk but did not lean back. He stayed upright, elbows on the desk, hands clasped loosely. He had learned long ago that posture mattered. Panic crouched. Strategy sat up straight.

Do I run?

The thought came clean and sharp. He had run before. He had left New York. He had left his name. He had built Quinton Bell out of the ashes of Q. He had convinced himself that Houston was far enough, loud enough, busy enough to swallow a man whole if he needed it to.

But Devlin had found him anyway. Running had bought time. It had not bought safety.

If I run again, I confirm it.

Confirm what? That he was afraid? That he had something to hide? That Devlin was right to believe that Byron was Quinton? But, if Devlin was here, he already knew that, didn't he?

If Devlin whispered to the wrong person that Quinton Bell was really Byron? If he put that name in the wrong ear, what would happen?

Broussard.

The detective's face surfaced in his mind. Cajun drawl. Sharp eyes that missed very little. He had been dancing to and fro with Broussard for a long time. *Was this the moment when things caught up with him?*

If Quinton walked into HPD tomorrow and laid it out. Devlin is here, Devlin is targeting me, Devlin may be the one behind the bombing. Broussard would move.

But at what cost? *What if Devlin tells him?* What if Devlin, cornered, said it plainly: Ask your friend what his name used to be. Ask him about New York. Ask him about the case that put Killian Tyrone in jail and got him killed.

Broussard would not shrug that off. He would not smile and say boys will be boys. He would dig. He was a detective. He would do what detectives do.

Quinton's jaw tightened.

He could not lay low and wait. Not now. Not with Hale's trial looming. It was stay and face the music or run. He rose and crossed to the window.

If he ran, he would have to do it clean. He'd be giving up all he'd built as Quinton Bell. New name. The go bag was ready. He'd replaced most of it since the explosion.

Cash.

Passport.

Driver's license.

Prepaid phone sealed in plastic with charger.

Flash drive.

He went through it methodically in his mind.

You're planning like you've already decided.

He exhaled slowly. He wished he'd gotten a second passport, just in case. He'd had a hard enough time getting the one.

He regularly added money to his Plan B account in Europe. He had never stopped saving for a rainy day.

If he left, what about Hale? What about his other clients? They had trusted him with their stories, their money, their lives.

Marcus Hale sat in a jail cell waiting for a man who was supposed to fight for him. Hale already carried secrets heavy enough to bend his shoulders. If Quinton disappeared, Hale would drown. Mo might take over. Cassidy would try. But the prosecution would smell weakness.

Quinton returned to his desk and opened the top drawer, though he did not know why. Inside lay nothing more dangerous than pens and yellow pads. Then he saw it, the napkin he'd sealed in an envelope. Revealing. Deadly.

He fingered the scuba knife in his pocket. Always there.

Should I trust Dart?

Dart was loyal. Fiercely so. He would not flinch at the story or the consequences. He did not scare easily. But if Quinton told him now, he would be dragging him into something old and dark. Dart had pulled himself out of his old life. He had enough on his plate tracking witnesses, phone pings, and chains of evidence. He did not need Irish ghosts.

And Dart had his own past. Shady contacts. Lines he walked with ease but that could tangle fast if federal attention drifted his way.

What was Devlin waiting for. If it was Devlin?

Did he want money? If so, why hadn't he asked for it? Revenge? Did he want Quinton to be ostracized as he'd been? Was he trying to clear his own name? He could leak it back to Tua Dannon that Quinton was in Houston and was the very FBI snitch he thought he was. And once a rumor of cooperation took hold in certain circles, truth did not matter. If that was it, why hadn't he already done it?

You cannot outrun a lie once it starts moving.

What else could he do besides run? Security at the office. He could hire a guard. Quietly. But that would raise questions. Anna would ask. Clients would notice. That might not be a bad thing.

Home. He pictured the driveway. The pool and patio. The mailbox at the edge of the curb. The line of hedges along the fence. Devlin certainly was watching.

He could get more cameras. Better ones. Not the standard system. Something harder to disable. Something that stored remotely. But for what? Who would he show the footage to?

He fingered the scuba knife in his pocket again. He could change his routine. Get a secret rental car or hire a driver. Different routes to the courthouse. Different parking spots. Arrive early. Leave late. Or the opposite.

He could tell Anna to work from home for a week under the guise of trial prep.

He returned to the window again.

Back to the police. If Devlin tells Broussard I'm Byron, what then?

Quinton would have to choose between confession and denial. Confession would mean explaining everything. The case in New York. The threats. The reason he vanished. Denial would mean lying to a detective who already suspected too much. Neither option was clean.

But, he can't. He's wanted for the shootout. Devlin wouldn't dare go to Broussard.

He rested his forehead briefly against the cool glass. He had built his new life carefully. Law license. Reputation. Clients who trusted him. Anna's steady presence. Mo's sharp mind across a conference table. Dart's quiet competence. He was mentoring Cassidy and she was relying on him as well. Was he willing to torch it all again? Or was this the moment to stop running?

Devlin was not omnipotent. That much Quinton knew. Devlin feared Tua Dannon more than he feared Byron or prison. That fear made him vulnerable too.

Men who act out of fear make mistakes.

If Quinton stayed, if he tightened his circle, if he watched instead of bolting, he might draw Devlin into the open. But that meant risk. Real risk.

He straightened. No sudden moves. Not yet. First, verify.

He would increase security at the office and home using the car bombing as an excuse. He would vary his routine starting tomorrow. He would keep the new go bag ready. He would add another deposit to the foreign account.

And he would not, under any circumstances, say the name Byron Douglas out loud, not even to himself.

Quinton turned from the window, crossed the room, and shut off the lights one by one. As the office fell into shadow, a single thought followed him out the door.

If he forces my hand, I will not run this time.

But he made certain, as he locked up and headed for the elevator, that he sure as hell could.

37

Because of Labor Day weekend, the gym was nearly empty when Quinton arrived and no one was in the pool. Sound carried differently in a pool room. Every drip echoed. The faint slap of water against the lane lines sounded louder than it should have.

He stood at the edge of the water and stared down at his reflection. The events of late had shattered his sense of security, what little there was. He needed relief.

Quinton tossed his towel on a chair, adjusted his goggles, and dove in. The water swallowed him whole. For a moment there was nothing but blue and silence and the steady pull of his arms through resistance. He counted strokes. Twenty-five yards. Flip. Twenty-five back.

Devlin?

His lungs burned. His shoulders tightened. The rhythm should have calmed him. It always had before. Control. Discipline. Breath in, breath out. But his mind would not quiet. He missed a breath and swallowed water. Came up coughing.

By the time he finished forty laps, his muscles trembled. His pulse pounded in his ears. His body was exhausted. His mind was not. In the locker room he sat on a bench with a towel around his shoulders and stared at the gray tile floor.

Devlin could be outside the gym right now. He could be in his home. He could be outing him to Dannon or the police. But if he was going to do that, he would already have done it. *No, he wanted something else.*

Swimming usually sanded down the edges of his stress. Tonight it only polished them sharper. He dressed in silence and left.

The Dog Pound did not advertise. It did not need to. Quinton turned his new white Range Rover into the lot and drove up and down the aisles. Not seeing any familiar vehicles, he exited the lot and parked two streets over, just to be safe. He sat for a moment as "Desperado" by the Eagles finished on the radio. He loved that song. The new SUV had an upgraded sound system compared to his gray, demolished one. *I guess that's one good thing about a car bombing.*

He had run home after his swim and changed into one of his many disguises. Dark jeans. Faded Astros cap, pulled low. Clear glasses with dark rims. A neatly trimmed fake goatee he'd purchased on his last trip to Vegas. A cheap windbreaker instead of his tailored sport coat. He'd left his Rolex watch at home. Wore an old leather one instead.

Nothing flashy. Nothing memorable.

The alley light flickered above the dented steel door. No sign. Just a small black camera tucked under the eave. He approached casually, hands in pockets. When the slot slid open, revealing a pair of suspicious eyes, Quinton lifted his right hand chest high and made the sign. Fist turned into a peace sign.

The slot closed. A beat passed. Then the door buzzed. Inside, the smell hit him first. Wet dog, as usual. As he walked through the outer room, the scents changed. Cigars. Sweat. Old carpet. The air was thick enough to chew.

The hallway opened into a wide room lit by low-hanging industrial lamps. No one looked twice at Quinton. That was the point.

He bought in for twenty thousand. The dealer at table three barely blinked.

"Two-five no limit."

Quinton stacked his chips with careful indifference. The first orbit he folded most rounds. Watched.

A man with slicked-back hair and a heavy pinky ring played too many hands. Another, younger male, jittery, bluffed big and often. A woman in red was patient. Dangerous.

Quinton waited, playing small. Then the cards turned. Ace of spades. Ace of hearts. A small current moved through him. He almost scratched his chin but caught the tell before he showed it.

He raised modestly. Pinky Ring called. Jittery Kid re-raised.

Quinton leaned back, studied the kid's fingers. They tapped too fast against his stack.

Quinton four-bet. Pinky Ring folded with a grunt. The kid hesitated, then shoved.

Quinton did not hesitate. The flop came clean. Ragged. No help for the kid. Turn blank. River blank. Quinton won. The dealer pushed the pot toward him.

Chips sliding across felt like a promise. Something in his chest loosened. It was not the money; it was the strategy. The clarity. You played the percentages and lived with the result. No hidden discovery. No sealed indictments. No surprise witnesses.

Just odds and reading the others playing the same odds.

A few hands later he picked up pocket tens in late position. Called a raise from the woman in red. The flop came ten-high with two hearts. She bet. Calm. Controlled. Quinton raised small. She studied him. Eyes narrowing. Called.

The turn brought a third heart. She slowed. He checked, inviting. She bet big.

He let the silence stretch, then called. River paired the board. Full house. This time he led out.

She stared at him a long time. "You don't look like you got it."

Quinton did not reply. She called. When he turned over his hand, her jaw tightened. A flicker of annoyance, then respect.

To Quinton, the pot was heavy. Satisfying. The room felt warmer now. Friendlier. The hum of voices blended into a low, steady current. Chips stacked high in front of him. His pulse steadied. The sharp edge Broussard's news had carved into his evening dulled.

He played another hour. Not reckless. Not conservative. Balanced. Measured.

By the time he stood, he was up eighteen thousand. He cashed out without ceremony.

Outside, the night air felt warm, not hot, against his skin. He paused in the alley and listened. No footsteps. No engines idling. Just distant traffic and the faint scent of animals. For a moment, he felt almost normal. Almost untouchable.

He adjusted the brim of his cap and walked toward his new SUV, the rhythm of the cards still echoing in his mind.

For a few blessed hours, the odds had been in his favor.

And that was enough.

38

Devlin sat in his truck parked three blocks from Quinton's house, engine off, windows cracked. The Houston humidity pressed through the gaps, but he didn't seem to notice. His eyes stayed fixed on the rearview mirror, trained on the pale square of light that was Quinton Bell's kitchen window. He saw a shadow move to and fro, apparently preparing a meal.

He tapped his index finger against the steering wheel, slow and deliberate. "Still so cocky, Quinton," he muttered, voice low and amused. "So sure you've outrun it all."

Devlin had suspicions that Quinton Bell was Byron Douglas during the murder trial of Joanne Wyatt. He'd watched him in court most days and confirmed for himself that what Killian Tyrone had told him in New York was true. That Byron Douglas was the rat who was working with the Feds. He'd confirmed his suspicions when he and his fellow thugs had gone through the go bag that was hidden in Quinton's car. Each little clue led him to the conclusion that Quinton was indeed Byron.

Devlin had hoped to establish it with Tua Dannon when he

left Houston, but the whole plan blew up when he was caught in the crosshairs in the courtroom shootout and had to slink away and hide from the Feds. By the time he was ready to resurface, the bounty was already on his head, and he was excommunicated from the Dannons. He knew if he showed up in New York that Tua Dannon would take him out, not hear him out.

It was irrelevant that the assumption about ratting to the Feds was not true. Byron had left town and become Quinton without revealing a single confidential thing, but that didn't work for Devlin's revenge scenario. Devlin had no idea Quinton was living in his own self-created witness protection program.

Devlin reached across the passenger seat, pulled out a folded paper map of the neighborhood, and ran his finger along the highlighted perimeter. He'd walked it twice that day. All of it committed to memory. He'd also started the preparation of the evidence against Quinton. He'd put it all in an envelope waiting in the hotel room for just the right time to place it in Quinton's house. He'd prepared a copy for Tua Dannon. Ready to send when it was all over and Byron was finally dead.

"You won't even see it coming," he said to no one, then chuckled softly. "Lawyers, kill them all."

The napkin message had landed. He'd watched Quinton freeze at the windshield, that little tightening around the mouth. A twinge of the old paranoia resurfacing. Then, the bombing. Stepping up the heat. Still trying to decide his final move.

He'd decided. It was a promise Devlin made to himself and fully intended to keep. He didn't want to kill Quinton in some alley or parking lot. He wanted him to feel it beforehand. Wanted him to lose sleep, to feel every wall closing in, to know that justice hadn't saved him after all.

Devlin scratched at the stubble on his jaw and leaned back

in the seat. "You broke the family. Made me look weak. Hid behind your files and your damn logic."

Truth was, Devlin was angry and bitter because he had been unable to create a new life after he was excommunicated from the Dannon organization in New York. Although Tua Dannon was in prison, Devlin dared not contact anyone in his close group of friends. He'd defied Dannon's orders, taken matters into his own hands, and cut himself off from the Irish Mafia. He could never go back unless he did something extraordinary. He had to prove his worth again.

Devlin had no place to land. He had no skills, no contacts. He had to look at himself for the first time in his life without the protection and gravitas of the organization he once enjoyed. He was nothing, a nobody, and when he could not face that fact, he turned all his vengeance and rage on Quinton Bell. He was jealous of Quinton's ability to land on his feet, to have a beautiful woman, to start over with his fancy law firm and status. It didn't even belong to Quinton, Devlin reasoned. It belonged to Quinton Bell and Judge Bell and all the fancy lawyers around Houston who respected and supported the dead son. He was a fraud, and Devlin would make sure he was revealed as one. Or, maybe he'd just end him and feel the satisfaction of revenge.

"This house," Devlin muttered, looking toward the faint outline of the bungalow. "This life. You think it's permanent. But it's not. I'm going to blow your house down."

He put away the map, snapped the notebook shut, tucked it into his coat, and slid out into the dark. Time to get closer. Time to up the pressure. Let Quinton feel breath on the back of his neck. Let him start wondering if this time there really was no way out.

39

Prosecutor Durant called his next witness to the stand, his technology expert, Lawrence Vickers. He appeared to be a careful man wearing rimless glasses whose voice carried all the warmth of a user manual. He testified that Marcus Hale's phone had pinged in the coverage area surrounding Daniel Price's townhouse at approximately the estimated time of death.

A map was projected on the screen. Towers. Overlapping circles showing Bellaire Boulevard and adjacent streets and neighborhoods. The townhouse was marked in red.

Durant moved the expert through it briskly, wanting the point without the drag. He knew juries hated technology and tended to block them out after a short while.

"Pass the witness."

Quinton rose for cross. He buttoned his jacket and approached the lectern with the patience of a man who had been waiting for this witness.

"Mr. Vickers, you testified that Mr. Hale's phone *pinged* in the area of Mr. Price's townhouse at approximately the estimated time of death."

The expert adjusted his glasses. "That's correct."

"In the area? Not *inside* the townhouse."

"No. Cell site data cannot place a device inside a specific structure."

"It places the phone within range of a tower?"

"That is true."

Quinton took a slow step toward the jury box.

"So, this ping could just as easily place the phone driving past on a nearby street."

"It could."

"Stopped at a light."

"Yes."

"At a business in the vicinity."

"That's possible."

Quinton picked up the prosecution's exhibit, glanced at the map, then set it down.

"You also cannot tell this jury whether the phone was actively being used at that moment, can you?"

"Yes, I can."

"That isn't entirely true, is it? In fact, a ping can occur without the user being exactly as shown on this map."

"Well, things can influence the location statistics, but it's rare."

"Rare? What about automatic network maintenance? Background app refreshes? Delayed synchronization?" Quinton used the laundry list he'd been provided by Miles in their prep session.

The witness hesitated, then nodded. "Those are all possibilities, but not likely."

"Thank you, Mr. Vickers."

Durant frowned but moved on. His second witness was

supposed to be routine. Instead, Quinton stood before Durant could call him.

"The defense calls Miles Carter."

Durant bolted out of his chair. "Objection, Your Honor. The prosecution has not rested its case."

Quinton addressed the judge. "Rebuttal witness, Your Honor. With your permission, I'd like to bring this witness in now while the technical aspects of Mr. Vickers' testimony is fresh."

Durant was adamant. "Objection."

"It will save time later, Your Honor."

Judge Blaylock thought for a moment. "I'll allow it. For purposes of rebuttal only."

"Thank you, Your Honor."

Miles came through the side gate with the loose confidence of someone who knew he knew more than you did. Mid-thirties, suit that was almost a sweatsuit without the hood, no tie, easy grin. He looked more like a sports fan out for a beer than the kind of witness who could quietly dismantle a murder timeline.

After Miles was sworn, Quinton kept his tone conversational.

"Mr. Carter, tell the jury a little about what you do."

Miles smiled, warm and effortless. "I explain why computers lie."

The jury laughed.

Even Judge Blaylock's mouth threatened a smile.

Quinton kept it simple. He qualified the witness as an expert. Undergrad at MIT, grad school at Carnegie Mellon. Yankee moved to the south following a job, then went out on his own. The jury warmed to him. He was charming in a shaggy dog kind of way.

Miles leaned forward slightly, as if letting them in on a secret.

"More formally, I consult on network architecture, cellular routing, and data recovery. Companies call me when their systems fail them."

Quinton walked to the screen and brought the tower map back up.

"Miles, you've reviewed the cell data in this case?"

"I have."

"And?"

Miles glanced at the screen, then back at the jury.

"It tells us the phone touched a tower that serves this area."

Durant shifted in his chair.

Quinton let Miles have the room just as they'd rehearsed.

"Can you explain that in plain English?"

"Sure." Miles turned slightly toward the jury, charming now, like he was explaining it to his grandmother. "Phones lose signal. Reconnect. Apps wake up in the background. Old routers hold on too long before letting go."

Quinton let that sit.

"In tech terms, it's a delayed registration."

Miles smiled. "In human terms, it's an echo."

Now the jury had it. Quinton could feel the shift in the box.

"Have you seen that happen before? A delayed registration caused by a network handoff, an aging router, or a device reconnecting after dropping signal."

Miles almost laughed. "Enough to ruin people's certainty."

"And sometimes," Quinton's tone sharpening just enough, "what appears to be a real-time location event can actually be the digital equivalent of an echo, as you said."

"Yes."

"Can you give us an example?"

"For instance, there was a salon in Sharpstown where the

owner kept showing up in her own store logs at three in the morning. Security thought she was sneaking in after hours. Turned out the router was ancient. Every time her phone reconnected from the parking lot next door, it logged her inside. Ghost entries. Digital leftovers."

A juror in the front row actually smiled.

"If Marcus Hale's phone had passed that salon at some point in time, could it have created a digital leftover, as you called it?"

"Absolutely. In fact, I was able to tie the ping directly there."

Quinton moved in for the close.

"So can this ping tell the jury Marcus Hale was standing over Daniel Price?"

"No. It can tell them that at some point his phone interacted with a network serving the area. Nothing more."

Quinton turned slightly toward the jury. "So, the ping—"

"—is a reflection of a past event," Miles said. "Not proof of presence."

Quinton gave a slow nod and returned to counsel table. No theatrics. No flourish. The seed of doubt had not merely been planted now.

Miles had given it roots.

Durant stood and approached Miles. "Mr. Carter, is the fact that the ping could have bounced off the outdated router from a prior occasion proof that it did on the night of the murder?"

"No."

"So, the ping might have been an echo, as you call it, or it might have happened on the night of the murder. There's no way to be sure."

"Exactly, there's no way to be sure." Miles knew better than to hedge and lose the jury. This wasn't his first rodeo.

Quinton and Mo exchanged glances. It was probably a wash on that piece of circumstantial evidence. The jury might have been inclined to believe the prosecution's expert, but they liked Miles more.

After a short pee break, for those with tiny bladder syndrome, the judge reconvened the trial and motioned to Durant. "Call your next witness."

Durant stood as the rear door eased open without a sound. A late spectator slipped into the courtroom and stood with his back against the wooden wall.

He wore himself like an old man. Gray sport coat, wire-rimmed glasses, a veteran's cap pulled low over a thin silver wig. A white beard changed the shape of his face just enough to make him harmless. Forgettable. Except he wasn't.

He stood very still, his gaze fixed not on the judge or the jury, but on Quinton.

Watching. Studying.

Quinton never looked back. His attention stayed on the prosecutor wondering who he would call next.

The stranger's mouth moved into the faintest smile. He lowered himself into the last seat in the gallery, hands folded over the head of a cane he did not need, and sat through the testimony like a man savoring a private joke.

No one noticed him. Which was exactly how Devlin liked it.

"The prosecution calls Dr. Felix Crowe."

The fingerprint analyst took the stand, neat, precise, already holding a folder. Durant verified his credentials efficiently.

"Thank you, Dr. Crowe. Now, did you examine the town-house of Daniel Price for latent prints after his murder?"

"I did."

"And what, if anything, did you find?"

"The usual household prints in the usual places. Mostly, those of Mr. Price."

"What did you find in reference to the defendant?"

"Several usable prints belonged to Marcus Hale. On a vase in the entry. On a doorframe leading to the hallway. On a table near the living area. And in the bathroom, near the lavatory."

Durant nodded, letting it settle. "So, Mr. Hale was present in the townhouse."

"Yes."

"Did anything lead you to believe that the fingerprints were left on the night of the murder?"

"Yes, it's very unusual to find prints without overlay if someone is not frequently in the home."

"What do you mean by overlay?"

"New prints that either obliterate the older prints or that smear the print beneath."

"And, in your expert opinion, were these prints from Mr. Hale more recent, or older?"

"In my experience, they were very recent."

"No further questions."

Quinton stood slowly, buttoning his jacket as he approached.

"You found Mr. Hale's fingerprints, but you can't tell this jury when those prints were left, can you?"

"No, but as I said…"

"They could have been placed there days, even weeks before Mr. Price's death?"

"That's correct, but unlikely unless the townhouse had been empty for the days between."

Quinton turned slightly, gesturing back toward Hale. "Since Mr. Hale had been in that townhouse before. As a guest. As a client of Mr. Price, would he have left prints?"

The analyst nodded. "That would be consistent."

Quinton gave a small, almost dismissive glance toward the jury. "So, all you can really tell us is that at some unknown point in time, my client touched things in a place he was known to visit."

A beat.

"Yes."

"No further questions."

Durant stood. "Redirect, Your Honor?"

Judge Blaylock nodded. "Proceed."

"Now, you can't tell when the fingerprints were left in the townhouse, but can you tell us why you think they were left on the night of the murder or about that time?"

Quinton stood. "Objection. Calls for speculation."

Durant addressed the judge. "Expert testimony, Your Honor. He can state his opinion. He does it all the time."

"Overruled. The witness will answer."

"It is unusual for fingerprints to be in a home for a long period of time without a smudge or fingerprints layered over them from other visitors. Also, especially in the bathroom, it would be unusual for that area not to have been cleaned, removing the prints, unless they were fresh."

"Pass the witness," Durant said.

Quinton half stood in his chair. "No further questions."

Judge Blaylock said, "Let's take another break. Fifteen minutes only."

After giving instructions to Mo and Cassidy, Quinton stepped out of the courtroom and let the door ease shut behind him. He headed to the men's room thinking about the last witness. He guessed it was about a wash between prosecution and defense on the fingerprints, but he was sure he'd won the technology battle.

The hallway was bustling with people coming and going in and out of courtrooms and toward the elevators.

An old man in a well-worn gray sport coat moved past him at an unhurried pace, veteran's cap low, wire-rimmed glasses catching the fluorescent light. A neat white beard, a cane touching softly against the tile. Tap. Tap.

Quinton barely gave him a glance as he continued toward the bathroom, but something about the passing felt wrong. Tap. Tap.

Not enough to stop or turn, just a faint disturbance in the air, like walking through the edge of someone else's shadow.

Quinton kept going, yet the uneasy feeling followed him. When he turned to look, the stranger had been swallowed up in the crowd.

After the break, Prosecutor Durant called Detective Clive Broussard to the stand. Quinton and Broussard had history, bonded by fire in Joanne Wyatt's trial and again when Quinton had represented Broussard's nephew, Sonny. Neither of those cases stopped them from assuming their current roles and duking it out again.

Detective Broussard sat squarely in the witness chair, his back straight, his hands folded loosely in front of him. The jury watched him with the quiet attention reserved for cops who looked like they belonged exactly where they were. His suit was conservative. His expression was not.

Durant rose slowly and consulted his legal pad. A brief, but impressive, introduction of Broussard ensued. Years on the force, history in law enforcement, when he made detective, first in Louisiana, then his transfer Houston. After the preliminaries, Durant got down to business.

"Detective Broussard, you were the lead investigator in the murder of Daniel Price?"

"Yes, sir."

"During the course of the investigation, what steps did you take to locate a suspect?"

Broussard went through a lengthy description of all of his standard steps in his investigations, then added a few extra things he'd done in this case as clues emerged. He spoke of questioning witnesses, searching technology sites, evaluating the body in the morgue, and setting up a timeline of the movements of Marcus Hale.

"And while assembling the evidence you've referred to, part of your duties included researching the background of the defendant."

Broussard glanced toward the defense table before returning his eyes to the prosecutor. "That's correct."

"And, in your opinion, Marcus Hale is the perpetrator of the crime of murder of Mr. Price."

"Yes, our evidence points directly to him."

Quinton Bell felt the shift immediately. Not in the courtroom. In himself.

Background? Broussard was no dummy. Of course he'd done his research. It was foolish to think that he wouldn't. But, how much had he found? How for back had he gone? Does he know what I know?

The prosecutor nodded. "Tell the jury what you discovered."

"We researched the defendant's social history because of hints we found in texts on the cloud."

"From Daniel Price's missing phone?"

"Yes, the phone was not at the murder scene, so we had to subpoena the records from his phone company."

Of course, Broussard had sniffed it out. He'd read between the lines and followed the thread until he uncovered information about Hale's sexual orientation. Quinton prepared himself for the bomb about to be dropped. He had no way of preparing his client.

"What hints are you referring to?"

"Small exchanges in texts between Price and Hale. Nothing specific, but my hunch was that Price had something on Hale that he didn't want made public."

"Were you able to verify that 'hunch'?"

Broussard didn't look at the jury when he answered. He kept his eyes on Durant, steady, methodical.

"I don't work off hunches alone. I started with Mr. Hale's movements. His schedule didn't match what was being reported publicly. There were gaps. Unaccounted time between team obligations, appearances, and travel."

Durant gave a slight nod. "What did you do with that information?"

"I pulled location data tied to his phone. Compared it to access logs, hotel entries, and private club check-ins." Broussard shifted his stance. "He was frequenting certain places off record."

A faint murmur moved through the courtroom.

"Go on," Durant said.

"I obtained surveillance where available. Entrances, exits. Nothing illegal. But the pattern was consistent."

Quinton felt Hale's body tighten beside him.

Durant let that sit a moment. "At that point, did Mr. Price factor into your investigation?"

"Not initially," Broussard said. "Mr. Price came later." He clasped his hands in his lap. "Once I understood Mr. Hale's private activities, I went back through the communications between the two men. The tone made more sense in that context. The leverage, specifically."

Durant stepped closer. "Leverage?"

"Yes." Broussard's voice stayed even. "Messages from Mr. Price referencing exposure. Reputation. Career damage. Nothing explicit. But consistent with someone who knew something personal and intended to use it."

A beat passed.

"Did you verify that understanding?" Durant asked.

Broussard nodded once. "I interviewed individuals connected to those same locations. Staff. Regulars. Mr. Hale was known there. Careful, but known."

"Did you find specific evidence during those interviews?"

"Yes. I was able to obtain footage and interview witnesses from travel dates corresponding to the Wildcatters' out of town games. I discovered that Mr. Hale was involved in several homosexual relationships."

The whole room gasped. Not that being gay was that unusual but being gay and playing for the Wildcatters while keeping it a secret was astonishing.

"Are you saying Marcus Hale is gay?"

"The evidence points in that direction, or at least Mr. Price thought so."

Hale shrunk down in his seat and kept his eyes on the table. Quinton did not touch him for fear it would add to the assumption of homosexuality. Cassidy froze.

Durant continued the questioning with a bit more swagger than he had before.

"Why is that relevant to the investigation?"

He glanced briefly toward the jury. "Mr. Price's role became clear."

Durant lowered his voice. "Clear in what way, Detective?"

Broussard didn't hesitate.

"He found out, and he used it."

"How so?"

"In my opinion, Mr. Price knew of Mr. Hale's sexual orientation and he was using that to leverage him in their business dealings."

Quinton stood. "Objection. Assumes facts not in evidence."

Durant looked at the judge. "He can express his professional opinion. We've already established his credentials."

The judge looked at Broussard. "Keep your comments to facts you can actually prove, Detective."

"Yes, Your Honor."

But the damage was done. Quinton would have to wait for his chance to cross-examine Broussard, and that would have to wait until Durant was finished on direct. The judge adjourned for the weekend, giving the jury all night and two days to think about Hale's gay orientation and wondering what he would do to keep Price quiet about it.

The jail was quieter on Friday nights. Not empty. Never empty. But the noise settled into something lower, a constant hum instead of the daytime clatter. Doors still slammed. Voices still carried. But the edges were dulled.

Quinton sat at the metal table in the attorney client room, hands folded, a file open in front of him he had not looked at in several minutes. The fluorescent light above cast everything in a gray, unforgiving hue.

The door opened. A guard stepped in with Hale. He looked smaller than he had in court. Not physically smaller. The same broad shoulders, the same frame that had filled highlight reels and stadiums. But something in him had folded inward. Tightly contained.

He sat. The guard left. For a moment, neither man spoke.

Quinton studied him. "How are you holding up?"

Hale gave a faint shrug. "You heard it."

Broussard's voice still lingered in the room. Calm. Clinical. Certain. Silence stretched.

Quinton leaned forward, elbows on the table. "I'm not going to sugarcoat this. That hurt us."

Hale let out a slow breath, staring at the table between them.

"They've got motive now. They've got leverage. Control. They've given the jury a reason why you'd want Price gone."

Hale's jaw tightened, but he said nothing.

"Do you want me to contact the DA and look for a plea deal?"

Hale shook his head. "I can't do that."

Quinton held his gaze. "In that case, I think the jury needs to hear from you."

Hale didn't look up.

"They need to hear you say you didn't do this. That whatever was between you and Price, it didn't end in murder."

A long pause.

Then, quietly.

"But you know I did it, don't you?"

Quinton didn't move.

Hale lifted his eyes. There was no defiance there. No calculation. Just something worn thin.

"You've known. Since before today."

Quinton said nothing. That was answer enough.

Hale gave a small, humorless nod, like something had finally settled into place.

"The pressure was constant from Price. The walls started closing in."

His voice was steady at first. Controlled.

"Not all at once. It was slow. Like you don't notice the room getting smaller until you try to stretch out and there's nowhere left to go."

Quinton leaned back slightly, letting him talk.

"At first, it was just business. Contracts. Appearances. Where I went, who I talked to. Normal agent stuff."

A beat.

"Then it wasn't."

Hale's gaze drifted, no longer on the room.

"He wanted access. All the time. Said it was for protection. Said people were watching. He indicated I didn't understand how things worked at this level."

Quinton stayed quiet.

Hale swallowed.

"He started deciding everything. What I wore. Where I stayed. Who I saw. If I pushed back..." He shook his head faintly. "He didn't yell. He didn't have to."

A flicker of something crossed his face.

"He'd remind me."

Quinton's voice was low. "Remind you of what."

Hale didn't answer right away.

When he did, it was softer. "That I was in the closet."

Hale's fingers curled against the edge of the table.

"He said if I walked out the door without him, he'd make sure everyone knew."

Hale's voice cracked, just slightly.

"Not just about being gay. About everything."

The word hung in the air like something toxic. *Everything.*

"He said he could take it all away. Not just the money. Not just the contracts." A hollow breath. "Me. Marcus Hale."

Quinton watched him carefully.

"He said one call, one story in the right place, and I wasn't Marcus Hale anymore." Hale's eyes lost focus again. "And I believed him."

A long pause.

"I'd already lived it. I knew what it felt like."

The room seemed to shrink with the words. Hale's breathing changed. Slower. Deeper. Like he was somewhere else now.

"The final straw was the texts. That week."

His voice had gone distant.

"He wouldn't stop. Messages all day. All night. Where are you? What are you doing? Who have you talked to?"

Hale blinked, but whatever he saw wasn't the jail.

"When we met the next time, he wanted something personal. He said I was sleeping with others, so why not him? When he tried to put his hands on me, I pushed him away and told him I was done." A faint shake of his head.

"I said I was firing him. That I didn't need him anymore. I tried to distance myself."

His lips parted slightly.

"He just laughed. He said I didn't get to decide that."

Hale's hand lifted an inch off the table, then settled again.

"The next day, he told me to come over. Said we needed to talk face to face again. Said I owed him that. I knew what he had planned. He was going to trap me."

Quinton's voice cut in, quiet but firm. "Marcus?"

But Hale was already gone. Not physically. But somewhere else.

"I planned it. Left my phone at home. Found the axe from

the birthday party in the closet. I remember the drive," Hale said.

His eyes were fixed now, unblinking.

"Streetlights. One after another. Cutting through the pouring rain. I don't remember turning. I don't remember parking. Just being there."

A beat. His voice dropped.

Quinton felt it then. The shift.

Hale's fingers tightened.

"He answered the door. Like it was just another night."

Hale's breathing hitched.

"He didn't even look that surprised to see me."

A long pause stretched thin. Hale's jaw clenched. His hands trembled. His eyes flickered, tracking something only he could see.

"I don't remember pulling it out. The axe. I had it hidden under the poncho."

Quinton's body stilled.

Hale's hand lifted again, this time higher, fingers curling around something invisible.

"I remember the weight."

A pause.

"And then I remember him still talking."

Hale's face hardened, but not with anger. With something colder.

"He didn't see it. Or he didn't think I'd do it."

A beat.

"And then... one swing."

Barely a voice now.

"Danny stopped talking. I struck him again, and again."

Quinton winced.

"And then there was nothing."

Hale blinked, like he was coming up from underwater.

"I don't remember how many times. I don't remember stopping."

His hand dropped back to the table.

"I just remember being very tired. Then I could hear the storm."

The word lingered.

The room seemed to come back slowly around him.

"What did you do then?"

"I took the phone to hide our texts. I took the axe with me under the rain poncho. I got rid of them both on my way back home. The drains were rushing with water. Took the evidence right away."

The metal table. The light. Quinton sitting across from him.

Hale looked at him again.

Present now.

For a long time, neither of them moved.

40

The office sat in a renovated bungalow in the Heights just northwest of downtown Houston, the kind with wide front steps and a brass plaque beside the door that read:

Elena Marquez, PhD

Trauma and Exploitation Studies

Quinton paused before knocking. Silver Jamail had repaid the favor he'd done for her grandson by calling in a favor of her own. Dr. Marquez benefited greatly from the work that Silver, and the Judge Sirus Lamar Bell Trust, did for the charities surrounding exploitation causes. She had agreed to meet with Quinton at the odd hour because he was in trial. Anything for Silver.

Quinton went inside and down a narrow hallway lined with framed certificates and photographs of conferences in places like Washington, DC, and The Hague. On one wall hung a poster about trauma reporting. On another, statistics about domestic trafficking.

He came to a door, tapped, then opened it.

Dr. Marquez rose when he entered her office. Mid-fifties.

Dark hair streaked with gray. Intelligent eyes that had seen too much.

"Mr. Bell," she said, offering her hand. "I understand you represent a man charged with murder."

"I do."

They sat across from one another. No desk between them. Just two armchairs and a small wooden table with a box of tissues that had probably seen more use than most law books.

"He was trafficked as a child," Quinton began. "Overseas. Controlled by a group of men who treated him like property. It was alleged that he killed one of them to escape."

Dr. Marquez did not interrupt.

"One of the men who helped facilitate that control reappears years later. Powerful. Wealthy. Connected. My client believed this man could ruin him. Own him again."

Quinton had spent years dissecting motives in courtrooms. Greed. Revenge. Jealousy. Money. Those were clean motives. They fit into jury instructions. Survival was messier. It, all too often, could look like revenge.

"And then the man turns up dead. My client is charged."

She folded her hands. "I understand. What do you want to know?"

"I want to know what happens inside someone like that. Years later. When the past walks back into the room."

Dr. Marquez leaned back slightly.

"Trafficking rewires survival pathways. Particularly when it occurs in childhood. The victim learns that resistance brings punishment. Compliance brings temporary safety. Hypervigilance becomes baseline. Control becomes oxygen."

Quinton felt something tighten in his chest.

"And if the trafficker reappears?"

"The body does not care that decades have passed. The

nervous system reacts as if the threat is present and immediate. Fight, flight, freeze. In some cases, preemptive strike."

"Preemptive."

"Yes. If a survivor believes the abuser is about to reassert control, they may interpret even subtle cues as imminent danger. A threat to expose a secret. Financial leverage. Public humiliation."

Quinton thought of Hale sitting across from him. Shoulders like carved stone. Eyes that had gone distant when Daniel Price's name was mentioned.

"Would it look rational?" Quinton asked.

"From the outside?" She shook her head. "It may look disproportionate. Explosive. But internally, it feels like survival. Like a child cornered again."

She leaned forward.

"You must understand something, Mr. Bell. Survivors often say, 'I will never be owned again.' That is not metaphor. It is vow."

The words struck him hard.

"He said that," Quinton murmured.

Dr. Marquez nodded as if she had heard it a thousand times.

"If your client believed this man could strip away his autonomy, expose his sexual abuse, control his career, drag him back psychologically to that place of captivity, then even a perceived tightening of the leash could trigger drastic action."

Quinton stared at the floor for a moment.

"What if," he said slowly, "the alleged victim was also his agent? Controlled his contracts. Threatened disclosure. Implied he could destroy everything."

Dr. Marquez's expression softened.

"Then your client may not have seen a contract dispute," she said. "He may have seen a cage door closing."

"What if he tried to have sex with him?"

"Your client might see it as rape."

Silence settled in the room.

"Is that justification?" Quinton asked.

"No," she said gently. "It is context."

Traffic on I-45 crawled as Quinton drove toward the Loop. *Motive rooted in survival, not greed.*

He repeated the line in his head. *What might have made Hale snap?*

Not money or fame. Not rage for its own sake. Ownership. Exposure. The closet door kicked open by the one man who knew how to use it as a weapon.

Price had found out Hale was gay and had proof of the past. If Price threatened that he'd go public, and if he suggested he could end Hale's career with a whisper to the Houston Wildcatters, could that be enough?

Quinton did not believe that the threat of exposure was enough for Hale to kill. He had said it: The walls closing in. That was the breaking point. Ownership came to mind.

Mo was waiting in Quinton's office when he arrived. He'd asked her to join him for a midnight strategy session about the conversation with Hale. Now, he was glad he did and that she was there. It wasn't that unusual to keep late hours during trial, or even pull an all-nighter, if one had the stamina to do it. Quinton was one who needed at least two to four hours sleep in order to think straight.

"You look like you've been somewhere heavy," Mo said.

"I have."

He told her about Dr. Marquez. About trauma pathways. About preemptive survival responses. About the vows survivors make.

"I will never be owned again."

Mo's expression softened.

"Poor Hale." she murmured, thinking of the small boy. "That kind of trauma doesn't fade. It just waits."

Quinton looked at her. "I offered to try for a plea. Hale refused."

"Where do we go from here?"

"We've been dismantling the DA's timeline. Attacking the forensics. Undermining their motive theory."

"All necessary," she said.

"Yes. But we've treated motive as a hole in their case." He leaned forward. "What if motive is our case?"

Mo's eyes sharpened.

"Self-defense? We've already pled him not guilty. It's too late to plead self-defense or temporary insanity. We could ask the judge, but then we'd be revealing our hand."

"We don't have to plead it, maybe it's enough to show it."

She stood and began pacing.

"Sympathy matters," she said. "Jurors understand fear. They understand protecting yourself. Especially if we can show Price was tightening the screws."

"Exactly."

"If we pivot to that," she said, thinking aloud, going exactly where Quinton wanted her to go. "We humanize him. We stop pretending he had no reason to fear Price. We embrace the history."

"We risk opening the door with that history," Quinton said. "But what if the prosecution opens that door?"

She stopped pacing and looked at him.

"How do we get them to do that? If they knew about it, it would already be in the record. There's no discovery to that effect."

Quinton nodded. "I think I have a way."

Mo began writing.

"Survival," he said.

Mo nodded.

"Survival," she echoed.

41

Over the weekend, Quinton's office was quiet except for the low hum of the office machinery. Anna had wrapped up and left about an hour before. Early-evening light stretched across his desk, catching on the small object between his fingers.

He didn't look up when Dart walked in.

"You said it couldn't wait."

"It can't."

Dart closed the door behind him. He didn't sit. His eyes went straight to Quinton's hand.

"The card from the townhouse?"

Dart's jaw tightened.

"You can't use that. You know that. If we admit we took it, all hell will break loose."

Quinton looked up. Calm. Measured.

"I know exactly what I can't do, which is why you're going to put it back."

Dart stared at him.

"What?"

"Tomorrow morning," Quinton said. "You're going back into the townhouse."

"What? How?"

Quinton didn't react. He set the card down on the desk, sliding it forward an inch, like a dealer pushing chips into a pot.

Quinton nodded once. "The pretense is you're going back for more photos. I set it up with the DA's office."

That stopped him. Dart's eyes narrowed. "What do you mean, you've set it up?"

"You're expected. Officer Gere will meet you there. Same as last time."

Silence stretched between them.

Then Dart said, quieter, "And the card."

"I want you to put it back where we found it."

Another silence. Thicker now.

Dart looked at the card again, then back at Quinton. "Why?"

Quinton leaned back slightly in his chair, studying him.

"Because right now, it's useless."

Dart's brow furrowed.

"It's tainted. Chain of custody is broken. If I walk into court with that, Durant tears it apart in thirty seconds and the judge keeps it out."

Dart crossed his arms, but he was listening now.

"So, we fix the chain."

Dart let out a short, incredulous laugh. "By planting it."

"By letting it be found," Quinton corrected.

"That's the same thing."

"No," Quinton said evenly. "It's not. We're just putting it back right where it was. Not planting anything."

Dart's eyes searched his, looking for the angle, the trick.

"You go in. You take your pictures. Make it look routine. Then you 'notice' something out of place."

Dart didn't blink.

"You call the guard inside," Quinton went on. "Show him exactly where it is. Don't touch it. Let him see it. Let him react."

Dart's arms slowly uncrossed.

"Then what."

"Then you step back. He recovers it. Not you. He bags it. Tags it. Calls it in."

"And me."

"You stay right there. You watch. You ask questions. You make him explain what he's doing."

Dart's head tilted slightly.

"Photos. Take plenty of them. Gere picking it up. The location. The angle. Everything."

Dart's gaze drifted past Quinton for a moment, somewhere inward.

"You're making it theirs."

A faint nod.

Dart exhaled, longer this time. The resistance was still there, but it had changed shape.

"They log it," Dart said, thinking it through now. "They process it. It comes in through evidence, not through you."

"Yes."

"Son of a bitch."

The lightbulb clicked on in his mind.

Dart looked down at the card again, then reached for it, picking it up between his fingers like it might burn him.

"This is risky."

"Everything is," Quinton said.

42

———

It happened fast that night. Quinton was walking through the patio area at the back of the house. The fresh drywall was sealed tight, the smell of new lumber still lingering in the air. He saw the last of the crew pack up their tools and leave through the rear gate by the pool. The lights twinkled on the fresh water.

He sat for a while, breathing deeply, then turned, went back inside, and heard a faint footfall behind him.

He turned, instinct flaring, just as the dark figure lunged. When the weight of the intruder hit, the two crashed through a stack of paint cans, both men hitting the floor hard. Quinton got a look at him this time. Close enough to see the wild flare in his eyes, the sharp, satisfied grin.

"Devlin."

Quinton's blood ran cold.

He'd believed, or more hoped, Devlin was dead, or hidden away somewhere, afraid to be found. The idea that he could still be alive, let alone standing in Quinton's house, was surreal.

"You didn't think I'd disappear, did you?" Devlin growled,

his accent curling around the words like smoke. "You went on, built your house, your fancy life. All while I waited."

Quinton fought back hard, elbowing him off. Blood rushed to his temple, pain blooming in his ribs as they rolled across the new wood floor.

"I hoped you were dead." Quinton managed, stumbling to his feet. "Does Dannon know you're here?"

Devlin surged up and swung a hammer that had fallen from a workbench. Quinton ducked, barely. The tool slammed into the wall, shattering drywall and sending a fine mist of dust into the air.

"Are you insane? He'd have had me killed. Only I know about you and what you're doing. I know you were the informant who ratted out Dannon. I'm going to prove it."

The two men grappled, more animal than tactical now. Quinton managed to land a punch to Devlin's jaw, but Devlin came back fast, slamming Quinton into a support beam. Stars burst behind his eyes. His knees gave slightly, but he held.

"What do you want? Why now?"

Devlin grabbed him by the shirt and shoved him toward the glass doors that led to the patio. "You left me hiding in the dark. Like I was nothing. Killian Tyrone told you everything and you used it to save your skin."

"I knew nothing to tell the FBI. I wish I did. Tyrone kept as tightlipped as any client I've ever had." Quinton reached blindly, fingers scraping against a metal level on the tool cart.

"You don't get this pretty little life while I run and hide. You don't get to win."

"Win? You killed the love of my life. You took Joanne and the last of Judge Bell's sanity. You took everyone who meant something to me. How did I win?"

Devlin grabbed him around the waist. Quinton spun and

swung the level hard. It connected with Devlin's torso. Enough to break the hold. Enough to turn the tide.

They crashed through the double doors together, tumbling across the stone patio. The pool gleamed under the moonlight, calm and indifferent.

Quinton stumbled to his feet, blood on his temple, breath ragged. Devlin rose slower, the years and rage catching up.

"You did win. Look at this house. Your fancy new life. Now, I win," Devlin hissed.

Quinton stood and tried to get his balance. "I live alone in a vacuum filled with lies. I'm not me. I'm not anyone."

Devlin rushed him. They went into the water together. One final collision. They both came up spitting and coughing. The pool churned as they struggled, Devlin grabbing for Quinton's throat. But Quinton had the edge now. Position. Leverage. He was at home in the water. He pushed down hard, using the weight of his body, using the last of his strength.

Devlin thrashed. He flipped Quinton toward the side of the pool, just missing the edge with his head. Quinton pushed his feet off the tile like a swimmer's turn and plowed into Devlin, taking him down and under the water. He held him there.

Devlin flailed, then flailed one last time, then stilled.

Quinton climbed out of the pool on shaking legs, chest heaving, soaked and bleeding. He sprawled on the concrete, blinking up at the unfinished eaves of his new home.

Here he was again. The nightmare wasn't over. How would he explain this? The law would not protect him.

The body floated just beneath the surface, one arm drifting like kelp in a still tide. Quinton sat on the flagstone edge of the pool, blood dripping from his split knuckle, breath shallow and ragged. Chlorine filled his nose. His shirt clung to him like wet wool, soaked from the struggle. Devlin's eyes stared at nothing.

The adrenaline had carried him through the fight. Rage, fear, instinct, whatever it was that gave him the strength to keep Devlin's head under long enough to stop the flailing. But now it was gone, and all that remained was an unnatural stillness. The cicadas buzzed. A dog barked a few blocks over. Life resumed. Devlin didn't.

Quinton exhaled hard through his nose, dropped his face into his hands, and stayed there a long moment. "I don't know how to do this," he muttered aloud. "I don't know where to do this." He paced the length of the pool twice, then stopped, staring down at the bloated silence in the water. He pulled himself upright and staggered back inside to find his phone, dripping puddles on the newly sealed floor.

There was only one person he could call.

Dart answered on the second ring. "Yo."

"I need help," Quinton said. His voice was low, flat. He hadn't meant for it to sound so calm.

There was a beat of silence. "You a'right?"

"No," Quinton said. "Not really."

Another pause. "Where are you?"

"My house. Backyard. I can't explain it on the phone."

Dart didn't ask another question. "I'm on my way."

Quinton ended the call and looked through the French doors at the pool again. Devlin floated, limbs slack, drifting just enough to make it feel like he might suddenly move. He wouldn't.

It was self-defense, but he couldn't tell the police. The fallout would be too much to handle.

Twenty minutes passed before Dart's black F-150 rolled up the drive. He let himself through the side gate and stopped when he saw Quinton sitting in a lawn chair by the water's edge. He was bleeding and his clothes were torn. Dart's eyes followed the ripple of the pool until he saw the body. His expression didn't change.

"You wanna tell me what happened?"

Quinton spoke in a quiet voice. "He came for me. Devlin. From my past. There's a long history there."

Dart nodded once. He knew of Devlin's role in the shootout at Joanne's trial. He didn't know the rest.

Quinton looked at Dart with pleading eyes. "I don't know how to make him go away."

For a long time, Dart said nothing. Then he walked over, knelt by the pool, and studied the body like it was a piece of evidence. He'd seen worse. Quinton watched as Dart's instincts kicked in, his mind already working the angles.

Quinton nodded toward the broken glass door. "It started inside."

"You clean the house?" Dart asked.

"Not yet."

"Neighbors see anything? Hear anything?"

"Doubt it. It was fast. No one showed up."

Dart stood. "Alright. You go inside. Shower. Change. Don't touch anything else out here. I'll take care of it."

Quinton hesitated. "You sure?"

Dart gave him a look. "You called me."

Quinton nodded and turned for the house.

As he stepped inside, he heard Dart say under his breath, "Hell of a town to try and stay out of trouble."

The cicadas sang in unison in Quinton's backyard. The air came into the house through the broken door. It was the kind of night where the coolness lent relief, but Quinton didn't feel it.

Dart was at the sink, scrubbing beneath his nails with methodical care, as if this were just another job to clean up after. Quinton stood at the kitchen island mindlessly nursing a Saint Arnold brew. He'd showered. Changed into jeans and a dark polo. It felt like his skin didn't fit. He needed the drink.

Dart hadn't said much since dragging Devlin's body out of the pool and wrapping it in a couple of old tarps the painters had stashed in the garage. He'd duct taped it like a macabre Christmas parcel.

"You sure about Galveston?" Quinton asked, breaking the silence.

"Closest deep water," Dart said. "Current's right. Tides move strong. Lotta shrimp boats out there. No one notices a thing. You want clean, you get distance. Otherwise, we bury him in the nearby woods and hope some hikers don't trip over him in six months."

Quinton swallowed hard. "Galveston is the only sanity I have at times. The Bell house is my refuge. I can't go there, look out at the ocean and see a dead body in my mind's eye."

Dart looked like he didn't understand, but acquiesced. "How about Lake Houston or Lake Livingston. My brother keeps a fishing boat near Huntsville."

Quinton tried to calculate the distance. "How far is that?"

Dart rubbed his substantial chin. "Just over an hour to the boat. Then, another half hour or so to Lake Livingston."

"Let's do that."

By 9:00 p.m., the new white Range Rover was backed into the garage, trunk open, a thick black contractor's tarp stretched across the empty cargo space. They waited until the neighborhood settled. Porch lights blinked off. A baby cried two houses down and went quiet. The dog-day cicadas took over.

"You ready?" Dart asked.

"No," Quinton said, pocketing his keys. "But let's do it anyway."

They returned to the backyard and lifted the body together. Heavy, sodden, awkward, and slid it into the back of the Rover. Devlin's limbs knocked against the tailgate with a dull thud. Quinton winced. Dart didn't.

Dart pulled the hatch shut and wiped his hands on a shop towel. "We can take 59 out past Humble and Kingwood. The traffic should have died down by now. Stay under the speed limit."

Quinton nodded. His mouth felt dry. "What do we say if we're pulled over?"

"We don't get pulled over."

They drove in silence for the first thirty miles. Quinton gripped the wheel like the SUV might buck. Dart sat in the passenger seat, calm as ever, one boot up on the dash, eyes watching the side mirror every few seconds.

"Thanks," Quinton said eventually.

Dart didn't look at him. "Don't thank me."

"You didn't have to come."

"That's where you're wrong." Dart shifted in his seat, finally turning toward him. "You took a shot on me when no one else would. You saved my life, even if you never talk about it. If I'd gone to jail, I'd be dead. This? This is me breaking even."

They rode the rest of the way with headlights cutting through the dark between highway lamps. Quinton's mind circled the same questions. How would this end? Had Devlin told anyone else where he was? He said Dannon didn't know, and who else would Devlin have told? Not likely anyone who wouldn't do more harm than good to him as well.

They went through Huntsville and picked up the jon boat at Marine Storage. The rust on the lock of the unit indicated the boat hadn't been used in a while. Dart turned the boat upside down on the rack on the top of the Range Rover and strapped it on with rope and bungee cords he'd found in the storage unit. They took off again toward the water.

When they reached Lake Livingston, they turned down a gravel access road that led to a pier used mostly to launch small boats. Dart got out first and checked the perimeter with a flashlight. No fishermen were out this late.

"All clear."

They lifted the jon boat off the SUV and placed it on the unlit dock. Dart took a rope tied to the end of the boat, wrapped it around a cleat, then pushed the boat gently into the water. They moved the body from the hatch onto the end of the dock.

After Quinton moved the SUV and parked it, they dragged the body to the other end of the dock then rolled it into the boat. Dart untied the rope, then both men steadied the boat with one hand while holding onto the dock with the other. They got into it being careful not to step on the body. Dart laced two kettle bells he'd brought from Quinton's bedroom through the ends of the rope on the body, then tied several knots to hold them in place.

Quinton rowed the boat out into the more central part of the lake, then they rolled the body out of the boat and into the water. Splash! The sound was louder than Quinton expected. No ceremony. No prayers. Just effort and weight and relief at not having been stopped or seen.

Dart turned a flashlight on and watched the water until the body submerged, then turned. "We should burn your clothes when we get back. And detail the Rover."

Quinton nodded, staring at the still surface of the water. "Yeah."

By the time they returned the boat, ran through a car wash, and arrived at Quinton's house, it was after 5:00 a.m.

"I have court in a couple of hours."

Dart pulled his car keys from his pocket and got out of the SUV. "This is the second time you've asked me to cover for you. I'm happy to do it, but are you ever gonna tell me what's going on?"

Quinton's face contorted and he went silent. "If I tell you, it could hurt you."

"Fine. As far as I'm concerned, this never happened."

Quinton took a shuddering breath. "Agreed."

43

In court the next morning, Detective Broussard was back on the stand and the jury waited with bated breath for the next bomb to drop. It didn't take long, and they weren't disappointed.

With the lack of sleep, Quinton was glad that Durant was up first with his witness. The prosecutor rose slowly, a folder already in his hand, confidence measured and deliberate.

"Detective, I want to direct your attention to some new evidence. It's an item recovered from the townhouse belonging to Daniel Price. Do you recall that search?"

"I do. It was over the weekend. Something we missed during the first search."

Durant approached the witness with a small, clear evidence bag. Inside, barely visible, was the microSD card. Durant held his breath for a beat, apparently expecting Quinton to object to the late discovery. Hearing nothing, he let out his breath and continued.

"Can you identify this item?"

"Yes. That's the microSD card recovered from the townhouse."

"Who discovered it?"

"It was located by Officer Sam Gere," Broussard said. "He was called back to the scene by a private investigator working with the defense, Dione Arthur Owen, known as Dart. The investigator indicated he had noticed something that appeared out of place."

Quinton sat still, hands folded, eyes forward.

"And were you present when the item was recovered?"

"I arrived shortly after. Officer Gere secured it and waited for me to join them at the scene."

"Describe the condition in which it was found."

"It was partially concealed inside the base of a lamp. Not immediately visible."

Durant nodded, letting that settle.

"And what was done with the item once it was secured?"

"It was logged into evidence, transferred to digital forensics, and its contents were extracted and transcribed over the weekend."

Durant turned slightly toward the jury.

"Your Honor, at this time the prosecution moves to admit State's Exhibit 42."

Quinton still did not object.

A flicker of surprise crossed a few faces in the gallery. Durant noticed it too but only paused for a fraction of a second.

"Admitted," Judge Blaylock said.

Durant didn't waste the moment.

"Detective, what did the contents of that card reveal?"

Broussard reached for a second folder, thicker.

"It contained a series of files consistent with private investigative work. A man hired by Daniel Price. It contained surveillance photographs. Business records. Financial logs. Travel receipts. That type of thing."

"Surveillance of whom?"

"Marcus Hale."

The words landed heavy.

Durant began to pace.

"Tell the jury in more detail, please."

"Photographs taken over an extended period of time. Hale entering and leaving various locations. Training facilities. His residence. Hotels. Restaurants."

Durant stepped closer. "Anything else."

Broussard hesitated just long enough to draw the room tighter.

"Yes."

"What?"

"Some photographs of a more personal nature."

"Were these photographs organized in any particular way?"

"Yes. They were cataloged by date and location. Cross-referenced with what appeared to be notes. Observations."

"What kind of observations?"

"Tangible proof that Mr. Hale was or is gay."

Durant let that hang, then turned.

"Could these be used as leverage you mentioned before, Detective?"

"Yes, sir."

"Do you see it as a motive?"

"Yes, sir."

"Your Honor, the next part of the evidence on the micro card is extensive. I suggest we return to it this afternoon."

"Any objection, Mr. Bell?"

"No, Your Honor."

Durant looked at Quinton like a deer in headlights. Quinton just let him wonder why he was not objecting.

The attorney meeting room at the courthouse felt smaller at lunchtime. Not because of its size, but because of what had followed them in.

The hum of the fluorescent lights pressed down. The metal table was crowded with paper sacks, Styrofoam containers, and files that no one had the energy to open. Somewhere in the hall outside, a deputy laughed too loudly. It sounded out of place.

Hale sat at the far end of the table in a funk. He hadn't touched the sandwich in front of him.

Quinton leaned back, jacket off. Watching.

Cassidy unwrapped her food but didn't eat. Mo studied Hale for a moment, then leaned in.

"We need to talk about a plea," she said.

Hale didn't look up.

Mo continued, steady. "If we want to approach Durant, this is your last chance. He's not likely to consider a deal once we push forward."

Hale's jaw tightened. "What does it buy me?"

"Reduced charge. Still prison. Years."

Silence.

Cassidy added, softer, "But you would control the outcome."

Hale glanced at Quinton. "And if I don't take it?"

Quinton met his eyes. "Then we proceed with the trial. All the way. And if it goes bad, it goes all the way bad."

Cassidy looked as if she would cry.

Mo held Hale there. "This is the decision point. Not later."

Hale looked down at the sandwich, then finally picked it up. He didn't eat.

Hale looked at Quinton. "What would you do?"

"If it were me, I'd play it all the way to the end."

Hale sat for a long beat. "Then we play it out. All in."

Quinton knew it was only going to get worse.

———

After lunch, the air in the courtroom had shifted. The micro card had done its work. The jury had seen the photographs. Not all of them, but enough. Enough to understand that Daniel Price's PI had been watching Hale. Studying him. Building evidence that he was gay and not out of the closet. They had heard it earlier, but seeing it in vivid color was a whole new level.

Broussard returned to the stand.

Durant did not ease back in. He bulldozed ahead.

"Detective, I want to shift your attention to another set of files recovered from that same device."

Broussard nodded. "Yes, sir."

"Were there materials on that card unrelated to the surveillance of the defendant?"

"There were."

"What did they concern?"

"Records covering Mr. Price's charities. International travel. Shipping records. Financial transfers tied to operations in Southeast Asia."

Durant clicked the remote and a map of Asia appeared on the screen.

"Did you identify any specific locations?"

"Yes. Thailand. Primarily Chiang Mai, with routes extending south toward coastal ports."

Quinton's expression did not change, but his fingers tightened slightly on the edge of the table.

"And were these simply travel logs," Durant asked, "or something more?"

Broussard's voice lowered.

"Something more."

"Explain, please."

"There were cargo manifests." He swallowed. "Manifests listing human cargo."

The courtroom stilled.

Durant didn't move.

"What do you mean by that, Detective?"

Broussard opened the folder in front of him, though he didn't need to look.

"Names. Ages. Rotations. Payments. Internal tracking records. Not official documentation. Operational logs."

"Operational for what?"

Broussard met his eyes.

"Trafficking."

The word landed like a weight dropped from height.

Durant turned, slow, deliberate, giving the jury time to absorb it.

"And were any of these records connected to the deceased, Daniel Price?"

"Yes."

"How?"

"He appeared tied to a foundation operating undercover. Pretending he was funding shelters. Outreach programs. The records are extensive, covering years."

Durant's eyebrow lifted slightly. "Charity?"

"On paper," Broussard said.

A low murmur stirred again before being silenced.

Durant took a step closer.

"Did you find any connection between these records and the defendant, Marcus Hale?"

Broussard hesitated.

Quinton didn't look up.

"Yes."

Durant's voice dropped.

"What connection?"

Broussard turned a page.

"Hale appears in the logs under a different name with a notation that shows his current name as Marcos Hale."

The room seemed to shrink.

"Explain that."

"Aliases," Broussard said. "Internal identifiers. He's listed as part of the rotation."

A sharp intake of breath somewhere in the gallery.

Durant didn't press further. He didn't need to.

"No further questions."

The silence that followed wasn't empty. It was charged. Alive. And every eye in the courtroom turned toward the defense table.

Quinton did not rise immediately. He let the weight of Broussard's direct testimony settle over the room. Jurors shifting in their seats. A cough in the back. Paper sliding softly against wood.

Then he stood. Slow. Deliberate. He buttoned his jacket and walked to the lectern, eyes never leaving Broussard.

"Detective."

Broussard straightened slightly. "Mr. Bell."

"When you reviewed the evidence introduced from the micro card, and based on your experience as a homicide detective, and your prior exposure to cases involving trafficking or exploitation, you formed certain conclusions about what those records represented. Did you not?"

Broussard hesitated a fraction. "Yes."

Quinton took a step closer.

"I want to be careful here, Detective. I'm not asking you to speculate beyond your experience. I'm asking whether, within that experience, you recognized patterns."

"I did."

"What kinds of patterns?"

Durant shifted. "Objection. Calls for speculation."

Quinton didn't look at him. "I'm asking about his views based on training and experience, Your Honor. That was good enough to overrule my objections earlier."

A beat.

"What's good for the goose is good for the gander, Mr. Durant. Overruled," Judge Blaylock said. "You may answer."

Broussard exhaled slowly.

"The records, they were structured. Rotations. Names. Ages. Payments tied to time blocks. Movement between locations."

"Movement of what?" Quinton asked quietly.

Broussard's jaw tightened. "Humans."

"Children?"

A pause.

"Yes."

Quinton let that sit.

"You said ages. What age ranges did you observe?"

Durant was already on his feet. "Objection, relevance."

Quinton looked at the judge. "I'll show relevance."

"Overruled. Let's see where this goes."

Broussard swallowed once.

"Mid-teens. Many younger."

A murmur rippled through the gallery before dying under a sharp glance from the bailiff.

Quinton's voice did not change.

"These records also included photographs."

"Yes."

"Were those photographs consistent with legitimate employment records?"

"No."

"What were they consistent with?"

"Tracking the location of the children."

Quinton nodded slowly.

"Tracking for what?"

Broussard looked at him, then away.

"For use."

Silence.

Quinton let it stretch until it became uncomfortable.

"Detective, in your experience, when you see records documenting minors, their locations, time blocks, payments, photographs for identification, what is the purpose of that system?"

Durant again. "Objection. Asked and answered."

"Overruled."

Broussard's voice dropped.

"Commercial sexual exploitation."

The words landed heavy.

Quinton took another step, closing the distance.

"Let's be clear for the jury, Detective. When you say, 'commercial sexual exploitation,' what does that mean in practical terms?"

Broussard didn't answer right away.

The room felt smaller.

"It means," he said finally, "they're sold. He was laundering money by buying and selling the human cargo through the charity accounts."

Quinton did not blink.

"Sold for what purpose?"

Broussard's fingers curled against the arm of the chair.

"For sex."

No one moved.

Quinton lowered his voice even further.

"And based on the structure of those logs, the rotations, the payments, would these children have had any ability to refuse?"

Durant's objection came fast. "Speculation."

Quinton turned his head. "Experience, Your Honor."

"Overruled."

Broussard shook his head once.

"No."

"Why not?"

"Because in systems like that, the humans are treated as cattle. They are bought and sold. They would have been detained because they were valuable commodities."

Quinton let that word hang. He stepped back, giving the jury a clear view of the witness.

"In your experience, Detective, what form does that detention typically take?"

Broussard looked at the jury now, not at Quinton.

His voice was tight.

"Violence. Coercion. Drugging. Isolation."

"Physical violence?"

"Yes."

"Repeated?"

"Yes."

Quinton nodded once, almost imperceptibly.

"And the purpose of that violence?"

"To ensure compliance."

"To ensure those children continued to be what?"

"Used."

The word echoed.

"Raped?"

"Yes."

Quinton walked toward the lectern. He turned back.

"Detective, based on your review of those records, and your

experience, would a person subjected to that system as a child carry the effects of it into adulthood?"

Durant was on his feet again. "Objection."

"Overruled," Blaylock said, sharper this time.

Broussard didn't hesitate.

"Yes."

"How so?"

A long breath.

"Control issues. Trauma. Fear. Anger. Difficulties of many types."

"No further questions."

He returned to counsel table without looking at Hale, who stared straight ahead. The jury kept their eyes on Hale.

44

———————

The attorney meeting room in the courthouse always felt colder after testimony like Broussard had given. Quinton was glad for the frigidity. It helped him fight off the grogginess from lack of sleep and the soreness from the struggle with Devlin. He forced himself not to think about what had happened in his pool.

Quinton sat at the head of the table with Hale at the other end, Mo and Cassidy flanking them both. Dinner sat mostly uneaten in front of them. Turkey sandwiches wrapped in paper. Small bags of chips ripped open. Bottles of water sweating onto paper napkins to protect the legal documents.

Hale had not touched his. He sat hunched forward. His broad shoulders, the same shoulders that had once driven through offensive lines for the Houston Wildcatters, looked smaller somehow in the metal chair.

"They all know."

No one answered immediately.

Quinton leaned back in his chair, studying his client. Mo

looked at the table, legal pad open but pen idle. Cassidy sat with eyes rimmed red, jaw set tight with restrained emotion.

"They know what Broussard said," Quinton replied evenly. "They know what the prosecution chose to drag into the light. That's different than knowing you."

Hale gave a hollow laugh. "You think that jury sees a difference?"

Mo spoke gently. "Some will. Some won't. That's always true. Our job no longer is to make them believe you. It's to make them believe in you. To like you, identify with you."

Quinton nodded. "I agree. We have to put you on the stand. No one else knows what you went through."

Hale's jaw flexed. "He said it like I was some kind of commodity. Like I volunteered."

Cassidy's voice sharpened. "He had no right."

Quinton leaned forward, forearms on the table. "Listen to me carefully, Marcus. What they introduced today changes the shape of the trial. It does not change the truth."

Hale stared into space as if trying to hold onto his mind.

"Daniel Price was part of that world," Quinton continued. "He facilitated it. He profited from it. The jury heard that. They also heard that you survived it."

Hale's hands trembled slightly. He pressed them harder together to hide it.

"They know I had motive."

"Yes," Quinton answered. "They do."

Silence filled the small room.

Mo finally picked up her pen. "You do have motive, but motive is not guilt."

Hale looked up at her. "I did hate him."

"Good," Quinton said.

Cassidy blinked. "Quinton?"

"Good," he repeated, unwavering. "Because if you pretend you didn't, they'll smell it from the parking garage."

Quinton gave her a sympathetic look. It was a lot for a baby lawyer to deal with.

"You knew what Price was. You knew what he'd done in that prior life. You were a victim. He was not. That anger is reasonable. It's human."

Hale swallowed hard. Cassidy patted his hand.

Quinton kept his tone steady. "I would have to ask you on the stand if you killed Daniel Price."

Hale's head snapped up. His eyes were clear despite the moisture in them.

"They're going to look at me like I'm dirty."

Cassidy's voice broke. "You are not dirty."

Mo added, calm and firm, "You were exploited. That is not the same thing."

Quinton stood and walked the small perimeter of the room, energy tight but controlled. "The prosecution thinks they handed us motive. What they actually handed us is context."

He stopped in front of Hale.

"You were a trafficked kid. You survived. You built a life. You became Marcus Hale. Halestorm. You had every opportunity to disappear into that anger, and you didn't."

Hale's breathing was still jagged.

"When you testify," Quinton continued, "you look at the jury. And you do not look ashamed."

Hale's brow furrowed. "How?"

"Because shame belongs to the adults who sold you. Not to the kid who endured it."

Cassidy wiped at her eyes.

Quinton straightened his tie. "This is the moment, Marcus."

Mo gave him a small nod of reassurance.

Cassidy managed a tight, encouraging smile.

The deputy opened the door.

Hale stepped toward it, then paused. He turned back once more.

Quinton held his gaze.

"Go tell them."

The courtroom was silent in a way that felt unnatural. Marcus Hale sat on the witness stand, hands gripping the edge of the wood so firmly his knuckles had gone pale. Broussard's testimony still hung in the air.

Quinton let the silence sit a moment longer. For weight. Then he stepped closer, touching the Dolly Chip in his pocket for luck.

"Marcus, you heard the detective's testimony?"

Hale nodded. His throat worked before any sound came. "Yes."

"I want you to tell the jury, in your own words, about that time in your life. Where you were. What was done to you."

Durant was on his feet. "Objection, Your Honor. We are willing to stipulate that Mr. Hale was trafficked."

Quinton looked at Judge Blaylock. "They opened the door, Your Honor."

A flicker crossed Durant's face. He knew he'd been had.

"Answer the question, Mr. Hale."

"The first memory I have of being there was when I was about nine or ten."

No one moved.

"I know I had been there for some time before. Months? Years? All that is lost to me. I just can't remember it." He swallowed.

Quinton didn't interrupt.

"They moved us around. Chiang Mai first. Then farther south. Near the ports. Different houses. Different rooms. Always different men." His grip tightened on the stand. "You weren't called by a name. There were numbers on the doors or above the curtains on the rooms."

A juror shifted in her seat. Another looked down.

Cassidy sat motionless at counsel table, eyes locked on him. Fighting back tears.

"They drugged us daily to keep us in line. They told us nobody would come for us. That nobody wanted kids like us back. That we were already ruined." A faint shake of his head. "After a while, you start to believe that. You start to think this is just what you are now."

The courtroom air felt thinner.

"How long were you there?" Quinton asked.

"I don't know. Years," Hale said. "I stopped counting."

"Marcus," he said, softer now, "did you know Daniel Price at that time?"

Hale's eyes flicked toward the jury, then back to Quinton. "Not like I know him now."

"When did you first meet him?"

"Hawaii," Hale said. "It was later. I was older. Playing football. Trying to build something normal. I was still struggling but making progress." His jaw tightened.

Quinton waited. Nothing came.

"Marcus," he said quietly, "what happened in Hawaii?"

Hale nodded slowly.

"That's where Price found me. I was playing ball there. Smaller league. Not the NFL. Just trying to get noticed."

Hale rubbed a hand across his jaw.

"Price showed up after one of the games. Said he represented athletes looking to move up. Said he had contacts with teams on the mainland. He approached me like a savior. Said he might get me an NFL deal."

"You believed him."

Hale nodded once.

"He knew the business. Contracts. Agents. Endorsements. Everything I didn't."

Hale's eyes dropped.

"He said he could get me to Houston. Sort of a tryout."

Quinton leaned back slightly.

"And he did?"

"Yes."

Hale exhaled.

"I came to Houston as his client."

Silence filled the room for a moment.

"It was business. When I made the team, he negotiated my contracts. Introduced me to people. Sponsors. Product promotions. Team executives."

Quinton nodded.

"You trusted him."

"I thought he was helping me."

Hale paused.

"When did he reveal that he knew you were gay?"

"A few months before he died. It was during the time I was trying to negotiate with him. I didn't think he would out me because it would cost him money, too."

"At some point, did you learn something new about Mr. Price? Something about those operations in Asia?"

Hale's fingers tightened again, whitening.

"Yes."

"When?"

"The week before he died."

"What did you learn?"

Hale closed his eyes briefly, as if bracing against the

memory.

"He told me. Not all at once. He liked to drip things out." His voice hardened. "He said he knew about my history in Asia, before Hawaii. He had records and he could prove that I was owned, bought and sold."

A murmur rippled through the gallery before Judge Blaylock's gavel brought it down.

"Order."

Quinton didn't look away from Hale.

"What was your reaction when he told you that?"

"I told him I was done. I was finished."

"And did he accept that?"

Hale let out a hollow laugh.

"No."

"What did he say?"

Hale's eyes puddled, then tears streamed down his face.

"He said I didn't get to walk away. That everything I had could disappear overnight." His voice tightened. "He said he could tell people what I was. Where I came from. What I'd done to survive. That I was a child prostitute."

A juror flinched.

"He used that phrase," Hale went on, quieter now. "Child prostitute. Said it like it was nothing. Like it was a brand he could slap on me whenever he wanted."

Quinton let the words sit there, raw and unsoftened.

"Did you believe him?"

"Yes."

"Why?"

"Because he knew things. Details I never told anyone. Places. Names. Things you don't just guess." His voice dropped to a near whisper. "He finally told me he'd been there. In it. The whole time. Almost like he was bragging."

The courtroom had gone completely still.

"What did you do after that conversation?"

Hale stared at the grain in the wood of the witness stand, as if the answer might be written there.

"I tried to get away. I stopped answering calls. Stayed at the house. Told myself I could just wait him out." He shook his head faintly. "But he didn't stop. Messages. Threats. Showing up at places he wasn't supposed to be."

Hale's hands gripped the edge of the wood so tightly his knuckles had gone pale.

"Marcus, can you tell us how you managed to leave the situation in Asia and wind up in Hawaii?"

Hale's world turned milky-white. He did not remember raising his right hand or swearing to tell the truth. He did not remember taking the stand or Quinton's questions.

One moment he was sitting down facing Quinton, the next, he was somewhere in the past. The world did not feel new. It felt ancient. Buried deep in bone.

The noise of the courtroom receded. The hum of the fluorescent lights thinned into another sound. Water slapping against wood. Wind pressing through warped boards. Heat so thick it coated the back of his throat.

He closed his eyes and was back in Thailand. The shanty stood on splintered stilts above black water. Boards eaten pale by salt and sun. At night, lantern light bled through the cracks, turning the air the color of rust. The smell never changed. Fish. Sweat. Stagnant tide. Fear.

He had not planned to escape that day. He had not hidden tools. He had not counted guards or mapped routes. He had learned to avoid the drugs that were administered to him by hiding most of them and faking sleep. His mind started to work again. He had been getting stronger and suddenly he was ready without realizing it. He had endured. Until that night.

He began to speak.

"They sent in one of my regulars. A big man. Thick wrists. Heavy breath. A grin that was not a grin but a leer. The door shut behind him with a final sound I had heard too many times."

Seeing Marcus in this fragile state, Quinton started to interrupt, but his gut told him to hold back.

"There was only a lantern lighting the room. The man stepped forward and I could smell the liquor on his breath. Something inside me recoiled. Not fear. Revulsion."

He could see in his mind's eye what was happening in the room as if floating near the ceiling. He saw it as if he was watching a movie.

The man's hand closed around his waist and the boy felt it all at once. Every prior night. Every forced stillness. Every swallowed scream. It rose up in him like bile.

In that instant, he did not calculate or strategize. He did not care if he lived or died. He only knew one thing with a clarity that split him open. This would be the last time.

The man shoved him around. A familiar position. A familiar helplessness. Not anymore. Not this time.

The boy turned back around and drove his forehead forward with all the force in his neck and shoulders. Cartilage crunched. The big man staggered, shocked. The boy followed without thinking. He slammed his palm into the man's throat. Felt the resistance. Felt it give.

A fist caught the boy across the ribs. Pain flared white. He did not retreat. He lunged. The two crashed into the table. The lantern teetered. Oil sloshed.

The man grabbed for his hair and the boy bit down on the hand near his face, tasted blood that was not his. The man roared and swung again. The boy ducked and drove his shoulder into the man's midsection, pushing with everything he had. The man went down and the dripping oil from the lamp splashed over him.

The boy did not think about consequences. He did not think about being caught. He did not think about tomorrow. His hand pried a loose board from the floor. He did not remember grabbing it. Only the weight of it in his palm.

He swung. Once. The sound was thick. Final.

The man staggered but did not fall. The boy swung again. Harder. The man hit the floor, woozy, and pulled on the table to help himself up. The lantern toppled and sputtered. The boy picked up the lamp and threw the flame into the spilled oil.

The fire not only caught on the big man's clothes, but it also caught on the boy's ragged T-shirt. He jerked it over his head and threw it into the flames that were engulfing the burning man.

The boy watched him, chest heaving, vision narrowed. He could hear voices in the other rooms. He did not wait to find out who was coming. He ran.

Naked. Barefoot. Blood on his face. Skin torn along his shoulder. The night air hit him like cold water despite the heat. He burst through the door and onto the dock, splinters driving into the soles of his feet.

Shouting erupted behind him. Another door slammed open. Voices barked orders. He did not look back.

He ran past crates and coils of rope, past nets heavy with the stink of old fish. The port lights flickered over black water. Boats knocked against their moorings like teeth chattering. Pain registered somewhere distant. His ribs throbbed. His jaw pulsed. His feet left faint smears on the wood.

Inside him there was something else. A hard, unbreakable line. Never again. If the men from the brothel drew near, he'd fling himself into the water and drown. He'd rather be dead than owned any longer.

The boy reached the cargo ships that towered over the smaller vessels, metal hulls dark against the sky. A crane groaned overhead. Men shouted near a ramp on the far side. No one looked down at the shadow pressed flat against the steel.

He found a ladder slick with salt and climbed. His muscles shook. His hands slipped. He did not stop until he dropped into a hold. Inside, it was black and close, thick with the smell of rope and oil. He crawled behind stacked nets and curled himself into a hollow space, heart hammering against metal.

Footsteps rang above him. Voices drifted down. Once, a beam of light cut through the darkness and he pressed his body flat. Then the engine roared.

The vibration shuddered through the ship and into his bones. The dock sounds shifted. Chains rattled. Water churned. Movement. He felt it before he trusted it. The subtle pull away from land. The widening gap between hull and shore.

He lay there naked and shaking and understood. He had not planned an escape. Freedom did not arrive with celebration. It arrived with space. With air that did not belong to someone else. With the absence of hands.

He had drawn the line that night in Thailand.

Back in the courtroom, Hale opened his wet eyes. Marble replaced wood. The fluorescent hum replaced the churn of engines.

"I was able to free myself that evening when I was older. I had reached a breaking point, and it took all I had to escape. I stowed away on the ship out of Thailand. I went through several ships and islands and finally wound up in Hawaii."

Two of the women on the jury were sobbing. Several of the men were shedding fought back tears. The press controlled their emotions and scripted stories.

Quinton took a step toward Marcus. "Did you start your life over there? In Hawaii?"

"Yes, I found help, improved my English, and pulled myself away from my past."

"Thank you, Marcus. Thank you for your bravery. Nothing further, Your Honor."

The prosecution approached the witness for cross-examination and blocked Hale's view of his defense team by positioning his body between them.

"Now, Mr. Hale. Did you know of Mr. Price at the time you were in Thailand? Did you know him and know that he was part of the group that held you captive?"

"No. No. I didn't know him. I found out after I got to Houston."

"How about the man you escaped from at the brothel? What did you do to him?"

"I was so upset. I was just looking for any way out."

"I can tell you that if someone had done that to me, I would scratch his eyes out. I'd hit him with a board until he was dead and leave him to burn."

"I didn't plan it. It just happened."

"And later, if I found the man who'd repeatedly bought and sold me, I'd confront him and slice him until he bled to death."

Hale crumbled into a mass of humanity without speaking.

"Did you do that to Daniel Price? Did you kill the victim?"

"Victim? Victim?" Hale gagged and anger brought him back to life. "He was no victim. He was a child-trafficking asshole with evil through his heart. He was trying to buy and sell me, again. He tried to rape me. He was going to tell everyone."

Durant moved toward the witness stand. "Tell everyone what?"

"That I'm gay. That I was used. Owned. That I'm not the hero they all think I am."

"So, you took an axe and gave him justice. Didn't you?"

Hale's eyes glazed over and he was once again out of his body and back to the night he went to Price's house. He remembered the pouring rain, the hatred and fear he felt. The deep need to protect himself one more time.

Quinton rose to his feet but didn't object.

Durant was yelling. "You killed him. Didn't you? Didn't you? You cut him up and left him bleeding on the floor."

Hale yelled back. "Yes. Yes, I killed him. I had to." He confessed. Not an accident. Not a misunderstanding. Not a convenient alternative theory. Killed.

A murmur rippled through the gallery before the judge called for order. Jurors stared at Hale as if seeing him for the first time. Not Halestorm. Not the disciplined linebacker. A man who had taken another man's life. Two men.

At counsel table, Quinton did not speak for a full second.

"Your Honor, may we approach?"

The judge, already ahead of him, nodded.

Quinton, Mo, Cassidy, and Durant stood before the riser and spoke to the judge in low voices that the jury could not hear. Hale remained seated on the witness stand. He lowered his head to his arms and began to babble.

Before Quinton could speak, Judge Blaylock looked at the DA. "Sawyer, if you have no objection, I'd like to dismiss the jury and rule on this from the bench. We can meet in my chambers and decide on the best course of action. A plea."

Durant looked relieved. "No objection, Your Honor."

Judge Blaylock looked at Quinton.

"Please. I'm sure my client would be very grateful, Your Honor."

"Take your seats."

Judge Blaylock looked at the jury. "Ladies and gentlemen. In light of the occurrences here today, I'm going to take this case under advisement and thank you for your service. You have been a remarkable jury and a fine example of citizenry. Thank you. Bailiff, please clear the courtroom."

The gavel fell.

Quinton approached Hale, still in the witness chair, and tried to lift his head.

Cassidy rushed up beside them, pushed Hale's head to the side, and said, "I think we need an ambulance."

45

____

By the time they gathered in his office, night had settled over Houston. The city lights pressed against the windows, distant and indifferent. Inside, the room carried the stale weight of too many long days stacked on top of each other.

Cassidy sat first, dropping into the chair without ceremony. Mo followed, shrugging out of her jacket and tossing it over the back of a chair. Dart leaned against the wall near the door, arms folded, saying nothing.

Quinton stood at his desk for a moment before speaking. Not sitting. Not yet.

"Hale is in the hospital, but he's going to be okay. Physically, at least. He's sedated. Cassidy, would you check on him in the morning?"

"Of course."

"Durant and I met with Judge Blaylock in his chambers. He took it from the jury and made a ruling from the bench."

That got their attention, even though they already knew. It still sounded different out loud. Final.

Mo exhaled slowly. "I've never seen Blaylock do that."

"He doesn't," Quinton said. "Not unless he thinks the verdict would be wrong or incomplete."

Mo rubbed her face with both hands. "There was nothing the jury could do that would be right. Not fair to put it on them."

Cassidy nodded. "So, what happens to Marcus?"

Quinton rested his palms on the edge of the desk. "Blaylock changed the plea to involuntary manslaughter. I agreed, pending a conversation with Hale. I'm sure he'll take it. He won't go to prison. Not now. He's ordered him into a secure criminal rehabilitation facility. One year minimum."

Cassidy straightened slightly. "Mandatory?"

"Yes. After that, Blaylock will review reports from the doctors. Psychological evaluations. Progress. Risk assessment. He'll decide what comes next based on that."

Silence settled over the room.

Not the heavy, suffocating kind they'd been living in for weeks. Something quieter. Looser around the edges.

Cassidy let out a long breath. "So, not a cage."

"No," Quinton said. "Not a cage."

Dart shifted against the wall. "He'll live through it. He's been through worse."

Quinton glanced at him. Dart didn't say things like that unless he meant them.

Cassidy's voice was softer. "He told the truth."

"Yes," Mo confirmed. "And it mattered."

Quinton didn't answer right away. He thought of Hale on the stand, hands white against the wood, voice breaking and then steadying, the room hanging on every word whether they wanted to or not.

"It mattered," he said finally.

Dart leaned back, closing his eyes for a second. "Hell of a way to end a case."

"It's not an ending," Quinton said. "It's a fresh start."

Cassidy gave a faint, tired smile. "That's optimistic."

"It's accurate."

Another quiet stretch. Quinton looked at Dart, knowing the secret they shared about hiding Devlin's body. Quinton, too, had been given a fresh start with Devlin's death. The death of one man gave a new beginning to another for both himself and Hale.

The adrenaline that had carried the team for days was gone now, leaving something heavier in its place. Fatigue settled into bones, into posture, into the way no one quite knew what to do with their hands.

Quinton stepped away from the desk at last.

"We'll celebrate, but not tonight."

Mo huffed a soft laugh. "Good. I don't think I could lift a glass if you put it in my hand."

Cassidy nodded. "I need sleep more than anything."

Dart pushed off the wall. "Same."

He and Quinton both had less than four hours' sleep in two days.

Quinton looked at each of them in turn. This team. Worn down, stretched thin, but hanging on.

"Go home. Get some rest. We did our best."

Mo grabbed her jacket. Cassidy stood a little slower, rolling tension out of her shoulders. Dart was already at the door, holding it open without looking back.

One by one, they filtered out. The office grew quiet again.

Quinton remained where he was for a moment longer, listening to the distant hum of the city, the echo of a case that refused to tie itself neatly into anything resembling justice.

Then he reached for the light and turned it off. Tomorrow would come.

The facility sat back from the road behind a stand of live oaks, the kind of place designed to look like nothing had ever gone wrong there. Low buildings. Clean lines. Quiet.

Quinton signed in, accepted the visitor badge, and followed a staff member down a long hallway that smelled faintly of citrus cleaner and something medicinal beneath it. Doors were closed. Voices low. Controlled.

Marcus Hale was already in the recreation room when Quinton stepped inside. A couple of men played ping pong across the way and several others sat in chairs, reading in a library corner.

Hale looked different.

Not smaller. Not weaker. But settled in a way Quinton hadn't seen before. The edge that had lived in his shoulders, in his eyes, had eased. Not gone. Just no longer driving him. No longer Halestorm.

Hale stood.

"Counselor," he said, a faint smile pulling at one corner of his mouth.

Quinton shook his hand. "Marcus."

They sat across from each other at a small table bolted to the floor. No restraints. No guards in the room. Just a camera in the corner, quietly watching.

"How are they treating you?"

Hale leaned back, considering the question like it deserved a real answer.

"Like I'm worth fixing," he said finally. "Took me a minute to get used to that."

Quinton gave a small nod.

"What kind of work are you doing?"

Hale exhaled slowly. "At first, a lot of it was unpacking. They don't let you skip parts." He tapped a finger lightly against his temple. "Memories. Patterns. The way you learn to survive something like that and then carry it into everything else."

He glanced down, then back up.

"Now, they've got me in group sessions, too. Didn't think I'd say this, but hearing other people say things I thought were just me." He shook his head. "That helps."

"You look better," Quinton said.

"I feel better," Hale replied. "Stronger in a different way. Every day, a little more."

A beat passed.

Hale's expression shifted, something more personal edging in.

"Doesn't mean it's easy," he added. "All of it being out there now. The trial. What Broussard said. What I said." He let out a breath. "I would've liked to come out on my own terms. Being gay. That part. Not dragged into the light like that."

Quinton didn't interrupt.

Hale's shoulders lifted slightly, then settled.

"I hate to bring bad news, but the Wildcatters, they've terminated your contract."

Hale didn't look up right away. His eyes stayed on his hands, resting loose now instead of clenched.

"Yeah. Figured that was coming."

Quinton leaned back slightly. "Morality clause. Personal conduct. They don't even have to wait for a conviction. Anything that brings disrepute to the organization, they can cut ties. Void guarantees."

Hale gave a small nod, like he was checking a box.

"All that language they rush you through on signing day. Agent tells you it's standard. Don't worry about it."

"It is standard," Quinton said. "And it's enforceable."

A faint smile touched Hale's mouth, gone almost as soon as it appeared.

"They're not wrong. I brought it on them. Cameras. Headlines. Their linebacker on trial for murder." He exhaled. "Hard to sell jerseys with that."

Quinton studied him. "You're getting it better than most. No negative press releases, just words like moving forward and wishing you a speedy recovery. No request for mitigation of damages."

Hale finally looked up. There was no anger there.

"Football was always going to end one day," Hale said. "Just thought I'd get to choose when." A pause. "Guess I lost that too."

Quinton nodded once. "Maybe. Maybe you eventually go somewhere else. We'll deal with the fallout later. Right now, we focus on keeping you from losing anything else while you're healing."

Hale held his gaze.

"Well, it's done now. And I'm still here." A faint, steadier smile. "And when I get out, I don't have to hide anymore. Not any of it."

"That's worth something," Quinton said.

"Yeah," Hale agreed. "A lot."

He leaned forward then, resting his forearms on the table.

"That's actually why I asked you to come."

Quinton waited.

"I've been contacted by a publisher. Hardy Books."

Quinton's expression didn't change, but his attention sharpened.

"They want me to write about everything. My life. The trial. What happened over there. What happened here." He gave a short breath. "Said there's already interest in a film. People circling."

"They will if they smell a buck," Quinton said evenly.

Hale nodded. "Yeah. That's what they told me here, too. That once it starts, it doesn't stop."

He looked directly at Quinton now.

"I don't want that happening to me again," he said. "People making deals off me. Using my story. Taking their cut while I'm just along for the ride."

Quinton said nothing.

"I've spent my whole life being owned by somebody," Hale went on. "One way or another." His voice stayed steady, but the weight behind it didn't. "I'm not doing that again."

A quiet settled between them.

"I want you to represent me," Hale said. "On all of it. The book. The film. Whatever comes next."

Quinton leaned back slightly, studying him.

"Why me?" he asked.

Hale didn't hesitate.

"Because you never treated me like a product," he said. "Not in that courtroom. Not when it would've been easier. And because you see angles other people don't. You know when something's not right before it goes bad."

Quinton considered that.

"This won't be simple. Once it's out there, you don't get to pull it back."

Hale nodded. "I know. But the worst of it is out."

Another pause. "True."

"I still want to do it," Hale said. "But I want to do it right."

Quinton held his gaze a moment longer, then gave a small nod.

"I'd be honored," he said.

Something in Hale's expression eased further at that. Not relief exactly. Something steadier than that.

"Thank you," he said.

Quinton thought for a moment.

"Alright. Then we start by slowing everything down. Nobody signs anything. Nobody agrees to anything. Not yet."

Hale gave a faint, almost amused breath. "That already sounds better than what they were telling me."

"First thing we do is get eyes on whatever Hardy Books sends you. Then we control the narrative before anyone else does."

Hale nodded, more certain now.

"For the first time," he said, "it feels like I might actually get to tell my own story."

Quinton smiled. "That's the only version that matters."

46

———————

The heavy wooden doors closed behind them and the tension of the courthouse finally fell away.

Inside Vic & Anthony's Steakhouse the atmosphere was rich and deliberate. Dark wood paneling absorbed the noise of the room into a low civilized murmur. Candlelight flickered against polished glass. The scent of seared beef, garlic, browned butter, and oak-aged wine lingered in the air, layered and warm.

Quinton had reserved a table toward the back, removed from the bar traffic but still close enough to feel the hum of celebration around them. This dinner was not for headlines. It was not for clients. It was not for show. It was for the team.

Mo took the seat to his right. Cassidy settled across from him. Dart chose the chair with a clear view of the entrance, habit ingrained from years of watching doors. Anna slid into the remaining seat, smoothing her napkin into her lap with visible excitement.

She looked around the room. "This is..." she began, then stopped. "This is not the courthouse cafeteria."

Laughter circled the table.

"You earned it," Quinton said simply. He was already starting to easily smile again.

Menus opened, though most of them had already decided. The server moved with quiet precision, describing cuts of beef aged for weeks, the marbling of a ribeye, the tenderness of a filet. Wine was poured. Deep red, fragrant with blackberry and cedar.

The first course arrived in elegant procession. Shrimp cocktail resting on crushed ice. A wedge salad draped in blue cheese and thick-cut bacon. Bread still warm from the oven, steam rising as butter melted into its surface.

Anna inhaled deeply. "I think this is what victory smells like."

"It smells like garlic and money," Dart replied and laughed.

When the steaks arrived, the table fell into appreciative silence. Ribeye glistened beneath a crust of pepper and salt. Filets sat tall and perfect, their centers warm and pink. A New York strip exhaled a fragrant plume of thyme and butter as it was set down before Mo.

Sides followed. Lobster mac and cheese bubbling at the edges. Creamed spinach bright and silky. Truffle fries dusted lightly with sea salt.

For several minutes there was only the sound of knives cutting and the soft murmur of approval.

Quinton placed his fork down and stood.

He did not command the room. He did not need to. His team quieted immediately.

"There is language we use in a courtroom. Burden of proof. Presumption of innocence. Evidentiary sufficiency. Justification. Reasonable doubt."

He let the words rest between them.

"Those phrases are sterile. Clinical. But what gives them power is preparation. Discipline. Relentless attention to detail."

He turned first to Anna.

"You tracked every exhibit. You flagged every inconsistency. You kept us all on time and on track."

Anna blinked, surprised. "That was just organization."

"That was trial support," Quinton corrected gently. "And it mattered."

He looked to Cassidy.

"You carried the emotional weight of this case. You sat with our client when the press vilified him. You kept the narrative anchored when it would have been easier to panic."

Cassidy laughed. "I had some growing up to do."

"And, you were a good sport about it all," Quinton said.

He turned to Mo.

"You sang the song of strategy. You made sure we had impeachment material ready before I even asked for it. When the prosecution attempted to introduce evidence outside the scope of discovery, you were the one who caught it."

Mo's lips curved faintly. "We were not leaving that to chance."

"No," Quinton agreed. "We were not."

His gaze settled on Dart.

"You found the facts beneath the narrative. You uncovered motive that led to a new path. You reminded us that evidence wins trials, not outrage."

Dart lifted his glass. "Facts are stubborn."

"Yes." Quinton lifted his own glass now. "They are. This dinner is not about the verdict alone. It is about the way you conducted yourselves. Professional. Ethical. Precise. The system worked because we respected it. And because you trusted me."

The room felt warmer then, the candlelight softer.

"To the team."

Glasses rose.

"To the team."

Crystal met crystal with a clean, bright sound. Quinton was not alone. He didn't know how long it would last, or how much he would allow them in, but for now, he felt a part of something.

Around them, the restaurant continued its low elegant hum. Outside, H-Town moved on to its next headline.

Inside, there was no mention of clients, indictments, cross-examination or jury instructions. Only gratitude.

Quinton sat back down and allowed himself something rare.

Peace.

The night air outside Vic & Anthony's was cool and easy, fall had come to Houston and grabbed hold, leaving the summer heat for the next year.

Quinton stood near the valet stand, jacket unbuttoned, tie loosened for the first time in weeks. He breathed deeply. Behind him, laughter drifted through the heavy doors as Mo and Cassidy finished saying goodnight to Anna and Dart inside.

He felt light. Not triumphant. Not arrogant. Just unburdened.

One of the valets jogged past with a keyring swinging from his finger. "Mr. Bell, we will have your Range Rover up in just a minute."

"No rush," Quinton replied easily.

Another valet chimed in. "Congratulations on saving Halestorm. We saw it on the news."

Quinton lifted a hand modestly. "Justice was served."

He meant it. The system had functioned. The judge had done the right thing. For the first time in months, his shoulders were not braced for impact.

His phone vibrated in his hand. He glanced down casually, expecting nothing in particular.

The screen displayed a system notification.

Odd.

Two Factor Authentication Request. Approve login for: **Byron Douglas.**

The smile faded from his face.

The noise of downtown Houston seemed to drop away, as if someone had turned down the volume on the world.

He stared at the name. Byron Douglas.

A second line populated beneath it.

Location: Unknown. IP Masked Through International Relay Authentication Token Attempted.

His skin went cold.

The deprecated key reference was precise. Technical. Deliberate. Whoever initiated the request had not stumbled into the system. Someone had attempted to access it through an older pathway, one that should have been sealed.

The valet pulled up in his white Range Rover, headlights washing across the pavement.

"Right here, Mr. Bell."

Quinton did not respond.

Another notification appeared: Secondary Challenge Initiated. Approve login for Byron Douglas?

Thirty seconds to respond.

The cheerful ease that had buoyed him moments before drained from his face. The valet hesitated, keys in hand.

"You okay, sir?"

Quinton forced his eyes up, but the color had already left them.

"I am fine," he said automatically.

His thumb hovered over the screen.

Another line flashed: Device Alias: StatenFerry-1917.

His breath stalled.

Staten Island Ferry.

A name that did not belong in Houston.

The timer ticked down.

Twenty seconds.

The valet shifted uneasily, unsure whether to interrupt.

Ten seconds. Quinton let the clock run.

Five.

Four.

Three.

The notification disappeared: Authentication Failed. Access Denied.

For half a heartbeat, relief tried to surface. The screen went dark.

The Range Rover idled at the curb.

The valet extended the keys again, more cautiously this time.

"Sir?"

Quinton took the keys.

"Thank you," he said quietly and handed him a tip.

Quinton slid behind the wheel and closed the door.

The celebration inside the restaurant felt strangely distant, almost irrelevant.

Someone, somewhere, had just tried to log into a life he had buried.

And they knew exactly what name to use.

THE END

Can Quinton continue to hide in plain sight? Find out in the next page-turner here: Proxy Legal Thriller Series

Sign up for Manning Wolfe's FREE newsletter and get a FREE book. Claim your copy: www.manningwolfe.com/giveaway

PLEASE LEAVE A REVIEW!
Thank you for reading **Alive By Proxy**. Help future readers find their way to this series.
Click here, or go to Amazon and Goodreads. Thank you.

ALSO BY MANNING WOLFE

Merit Bridges Legal Thrillers

Proxy Legal Thriller Series

Bullet Books Speed Reads

MANNING WOLFE, an award-winning author and attorney, writes cinematic-style, smart, fast-paced thrillers and crime fiction. Manning was recently featured on Oxygen TV's: Accident, Suicide, or Murder, and has spoken at major book festivals around the world.

* Manning's Merit Bridges Legal Thrillers features Austin attorney Merit Bridges, including Dollar Signs, Music Notes, Green Fees, and Chinese Wall.
* Manning's new Proxy Legal Thrillers Series features Houston attorney Quinton Bell, including Dead By Proxy, Hunted By Proxy, and Alive By Proxy.
* Manning is co-author of Killer Set: Drop the Mic, and twelve additional Bullet Books Speed Reads.

As a graduate of Rice University and the University of Texas School of Law, Manning's experience has given her a voyeur's peek into some shady characters' lives and a front-row seat to watch the good people who stand against them.

www.manningwolfe.com

Visit Manning Wolfe's website:
www.manningwolfe.com

Follow Manning Wolfe on Social Media:
www.facebook.com/manning.wolfe
www.twitter.com/ManningWolfe
www.instagram.com/manningwolfe/
www.tiktok.com/@manningwolfe

Sign up for Manning Wolfe's FREE newsletter and get a FREE book.
www.manningwolfe.com/giveaway